When
the Last Teardrop
Falls

When the Last Teardrop Falls

The Memoir of John Jones

John H. Cunningham

To order additional copies of this book, contact:
Xlibris Corporation
1-888-795-4274
www.Xlibris.com
Orders@Xlibris.com
18360

Acknowledgements

It is a pleasure to acknowledge my wife's help. Rose has been a source of inspiration for my writing.

It is also a pleasure to acknowledge the help from members of my Crit Group of the Village Writers in Decatur,Georgia. Their help has been valuable in my efforts to get it right. Their names are: June McNaughton, Dudley Hinds, Kip Kimbrough, Barbara Lucas, Larry Smith, Bob Hamilton, Saribenne Evesong, Tony Miller and Jay Clark.

CHAPTER ONE

"Three months of freedom! Wow! Won't that be great?" I yelled and looked at Carl Wilson, my roommate, across the room, lying on his bunk.

"The summer of 1941 is almost here. We'll be out of school for three months. Boy, oh boy! It'll be great. All that hard work and the full schedule may have been good for me, but I want a change of pace and look forward to three months of relaxed living. Just what I need."

I turned to Carl, sitting on his bunk across our dormitory room at the boarding boy's high school we attended and asked, "Carl, what'll you do this summer?"

He stretched his tall, well-muscled body and made himself comfortable. Carl was fun to be around. We had been roommates since we were freshmen.

"Hope I can get a job and make a little spending money. It's hell to be poor," Carl said in his well-modulated voice. Singing baritone in the school quartet had improved the tone quality of his speech.

He continued, "My mom just moved to Fairhope, Alabama, and is taking care of an old lady there. About twenty miles away the government is building liberty ships in Mobile. Jobs should be easy to find. How about you?"

"Work somewhere, I guess. But I don't want to go home."

"Why?" Carl asked.

"Oh, don't get along with my dad. He believes too much in ass kicking. That's the reason I'm here and not in a public school," I said as I sat up and leaned against the wall. "The last time we had it out was too much. I swore I would never stand still and take another beating. If he ever had any feeling for me, he never let on. My brother's sisters and I were also treated like second-class citizens. He never touched any of us except to punish. I learned to live with his mean disposition and take the punishment."

"Damn! You had it rough. You didn't tell me this before," Carl said.

"Didn't want to bore you. The last beating is still fresh in my memory as if it happened yesterday. His inflexible nature makes him difficult to approach. If I didn't follow his instructions to the letter, he considered that an assault on his authority. He couldn't handle that. At home on the farm when I was thirteen, he yelled, 'You'll never be worth a damn for anything. Take that plow over to Shelton Dillard in the back field, so he don't have to waste time coming over here to get it. Now git or I'll whip your ass again.'

"The big welts on my arms, legs and back made by the cane stood out against my white skin. The marks were red, ugly and burned like a branding iron."

"Wow! That is rough living," Carl exclaimed.

"Yeah, but what are you gonna do? That's my dad. My thirteen-year-old body wanted to scream, but I was determined not to give him the satisfaction of knowing that he had really hurt me. Looking up in defiance with all the hatred I could muster, I swore under my breath never to allow this big bully to punish me again.

"As far back as I can remember, my legs and back always carried fresh marks from this mean-tempered man. Looking at him the wrong way could trigger a thrashing. He mistreated me, tried to break my spirit and told me I was no damn good and couldn't do anything right. To get away from him was my greatest wish. So here I am."

"That's a good enough reason for not wanting to go back home," Carl said. "I can't blame you for getting out of that situation.

"My situation is different. My dad died," Carl said. "My

three older sisters left home to take jobs. Mom was living with a family, taking care of a rich old lady and couldn't keep me there. There was no room for me anywhere. She found this school and made application. Now she's bought a house in Fairhope. How did you find this school?"

"I worked one summer as a tile setter's helper with my second cousin, Larson Key," I said. "Together we did the tile work in the pool of the gym here on campus. The boys in school working their way were building other parts of the buildings. They talked me into making application. This was a wonderful opportunity to get away from home and my dad. I was pleased when the administration accepted my application, and the school assigned me to work on the brick crew.

"My mom cried when I left," I continued. "She is a strong person, kind and patient. Maybe because Dad was so severe, she dedicated her life to her children to see them develop to their full potential. She neglected her own looks and health, so we could be better dressed and healthy. My mom acted out of love. She inspired me to work harder and set goals for myself.

"I want to amount to something just to prove my dad wrong and my mom right."

"You seem to have stood up well for your sixteen years," Carl said. "You look okay, well built with no real hang-ups.

"Boy, you did have it tough," Carl said. "I didn't get much punishment. Don't remember ever getting a paddling.

"I would have thought the death of your sister would have softened your dad some," Carl said as he rearranged the pillow under his head.

"No, the experience seemed to make him worse. It was the only time I ever saw him cry."

"John, you have been tight-lipped about your family until now. I knew you lost your sister, but I didn't know how. Want to talk about it?" Carl asked.

"No. The story is painful and makes me want to cry. It's extremely difficult to think about. Bringing up my sister's death opens up old wounds. Just to talk about her murder requires reliving the event, which hurts. This disaster could have been avoided if we had thought about it and prepared ourselves. No one in our family every dreamed my sister would get killed."

I moved to my chair directly across from Carl and leaned back.

"John, I didn't have a clue that all this had happened to you. You never talked about it," Carl said.

"Maybe I should have. Most people are not interested in other people's problems. This experience changed my life and the way I react to the world," I continued. "The shock passed, but the mental scar will never go away. It will be there for the remainder of my life.

"A shrink told me if a person can talk about his problem and accept the situation as it is, that person can overcome the effects of almost any disaster. Perhaps that is the reason I am not a basket case today."

"You seem all right now," Carl said.

"Yeah, I'm okay. Mom helped me through the worst."

"You say your dad was changed for the worse by your sister's death. Did your sister know the man who killed her?" Carl asked.

"Yes."

"What was your sister like?"

"Carl, I had rather not talk about her."

"I don't want to upset you," Carl said. "Did she know him?"

"Yes. She was married to him. Edna had just turned sixteen. She was bright and a good mixer with a zest for life which made her a leader in school and church. She was also pretty with a glow of health and vitality. I looked up to her. I was proud of her good looks and leadership qualities," I said with a catch in my voice.

"A death in the family must have been hard to take," Carl said in sympathy. "Your sister sounds special."

"Tall for a girl, Edna was slender and well built," I said. "Her face and body seemed naturally good looking. Attractive with light brown hair, she turned some heads.

"One of the heads belonged to a neighbor's son, Hobart

Randolph, who noticed her developing feminine charms and asked her out.

"Hobart was employed by Dad on the farm part-time. None of our family liked Hobart and said so. My mother said 'no' when Edna asked if she could go out with Hobart. Edna persisted. You know how young girls are.

"Edna was bored and wanted to see something other than our farm. My mother reluctantly agreed. Hobart and Edna dated several times, which was a big mistake. The year was 1937. Carl, do you remember when 'Maple on the Hill' was popular? The record was in all the jukeboxes that year."

"Yeah, I remember that. It wasn't too popular in Hazleton, Pennsylvania, where I lived."

"My dad was lucky to have a job with Georgia Power Company. This part of the country was in a depression," I said as I stood up and walked back and forth down the middle of the room between the two bunks and two tables.

"Hobart didn't have a car, so he borrowed his dad's and took her to a movie in nearby Conyers, Georgia. On one of these dates, Edna did not come in at the right time of ten thirty in the evening. She returned at twelve thirty in the morning. She ran into the house to my mother and said, 'Mama, Hobart and I are married.' Mom became hysterical."

"Gosh, that was a shock. Your sister was married at sixteen?"

"Yes and all hell broke loose. My mom screamed, 'Oh no! God, it didn't happen. Edna, how could you? Why didn't you come home and talk with your dad and me? I am so disappointed.' Tears ran down my mother's face as she tried to control herself.

"After a tearful good-bye, Hobart and Edna left to spend the night with his mother and father.

"After Edna was gone, Mom said, 'Where did I go wrong? She had a bright future and good prospects. Edna is throwing her life away on an early marriage. Hobart is inferior to Edna in brains. He's a country bumpkin. This marriage is stupid and makes me sad.'

"My mother cried. We all cried. My father was at work. He would have to be told. He would be tremendously upset.

"Until now, our family had lived a fairly uneventful life with no great highs or lows. We lived in a rambling farmhouse near Conyers. Painted white, the house had a large front porch, a smaller side porch and was comfortable. There was no inside plumbing or central heat. Light at night was from kerosene lamps.

"After my dad returned at one thirty in the morning, Mom, Dad and I sat in the living room. Mom and Dad took the matching chairs. I sat on the sofa and looked at them and at the dark walls and ceiling. The wall finish soaked up most of the light from the one lamp and made the room and furniture dark. It was painful for me to see my father and mother suffer because of Edna's decision to marry so early and to someone whom I considered a no-good bastard."

"Your family tried to help," Carl said.

"My family tried to make the marriage work. Dad helped Hobart get a job and repaired the second house on the farm for them.

"This boy Edna married never graduated from high school. He flunked out. He didn't have any particular skills. In a physical way, he was not bad looking. His youth and muscular body gave him a sort of redneck look. He was without ambition and operated at a seventh-grade level mentally.

"No one expected him to be a member of the family and laughed at him when he did strange things. From somewhere he bought and drank raw ox blood. This convinced me that he was completely off his rocker. He did have an ambition to be a prizefighter."

"Yuck. Did he really drink raw beef blood?"

"Yeah, and he practiced punching the bag and running long distances. To my knowledge, he never fought anyone except for a little sparring with his brother.

"Instead of settling down as a loving couple ordinarily do, Hobart and Edna fought. He beat Edna with his fist. She returned home with her eye and cheek bruised by this mean bastard. Edna decided to give up on the marriage and have it annulled. My parents took the steps necessary for the annulment."

"He was a sorry bastard," Carl said.

"The more we found out about Hobart, the more my family was determined to protect Edna from any future contact with him. We were successful until that night of horror.

"On the evening of September 8, 1937, my mom, Edna and I were in the kitchen. The kitchen was large with space enough for a dining table. There was no electricity in our part of the county. The kitchen was lit with two kerosene lamps. The light level in the room was low.

"You didn't have electric power in your house in 1937?" Carl asked.

"No one in our area had it. A fire was burning in the wood stove. Edna was making some chocolate candy. A dining room table was in one corner of the room. The wood stove was located in an adjacent corner. Another corner contained kitchen cabinets for storage of dry goods and tableware. Edna's back was to the window between the kitchen table and the stove. She was busy picking the meat from a bowl of cracked black walnuts for the candy. Very absorbed in her work, she was in a rush to finish the candy.

"'Edna, I cleaned the three doves I shot this afternoon, and they are ready to place in the kerosene refrigerator. How was your day?' I asked.

"'I love being back in school,' Edna said as she looked up from her bowl of walnuts.

"'This is your last year of high school. How do you like your teacher?' I asked.

"'Don't really know,' she said. 'I've only attended a few classes. Haven't seen enough of him to make up my mind. Being married makes me feel older. The other kids look at me differently and consider me an older woman. I don't like that.'

"Suddenly, there was an explosion, a loud bang! Something blew up in the room. The glass in the window blew all over the room. One lamp went out. I heard my sister moan and saw her slump forward to the floor. My mother rushed to my sister. A second explosion shattered the remaining glass in the window.

"My mother screamed, 'Edna has been shot!' In her concern for Edna, she did not notice that she herself had also been shot in the left leg. Blood and glass were everywhere. Edna was lying on the floor crumpled up. My mother was screaming. Hearing my mother scream totally immobilized me. I was unable to move or speak. I stood in the middle of the room and looked at my bloody mother and sister. This could not be happening. My mom was throwing up her hands and screaming, 'Oh, my God. Edna is dead. Edna is dead. What're we gonna do?'

"The smaller children had been in another room, and now they too were in the kitchen, screaming and holding onto Mom. Only one lamp was lit in the dark kitchen.

"Mother turned to me and said, 'You're the oldest. You must go for help.'

"Together, we laid Edna on the kitchen floor on her back, the sweet smell of her blood and her lifeless face destroyed my will. I could see she was dead.

"My mother, now more in control, said, 'Go to the nearest telephone—that would be Smith's Service Station—and call the doctor and the sheriff.'

"It was three miles to the service station and a telephone. I ran all the way. We lived on an unpaved road that meandered over the countryside following the contours around the hills and the hollows. There was one hollow that was dark and forbidding. To walk through this area by myself frightened me even during the day. After the horror of the past few minutes, I was traumatized. I felt no fear, no fatigue and ran as if my feet did not touch the ground. When I reached the service station, the words came out but made no sound. Out of breath, I couldn't bear to hear the words that I must speak. Crying but trying to control myself, I screamed, 'My sister's been shot. Please call the doctor and the sheriff.'"

"Gee, you must have really been upset," Carl said as he sat up in his bunk and looked at me intently.

"The Smith family, who operated the service station, tried to calm me and get the whole story of what happened. There was little that I could tell them. They took me home in their car. When we arrived, my mother was still holding Edna in her arms and crying."

"John, how could you stand the horror?" Carl asked.

"I really don't know. The Smiths took my mother into a bedroom and had her lie down. She was still bleeding from her left leg. Other people began to arrive. Soon our yard was full of people, milling around and talking in low voices in small groups.

"The night was warm. Some came into the house to look around. These people were poor farmers. They couldn't understand why this happened to such a pretty girl. Gradually their pity turned to anger. This group was ready to lynch the person who did this cowardly deed.

"The doctor and the sheriff arrived at the same time, shortly after my return. Then people came from the local newspaper. They took pictures of my family and me. They pushed their way into my mother's bedroom and photographed her. They even photographed my dead sister on the floor in the kitchen."

"Why didn't someone stop them?" Carl asked.

"Dad wasn't there, and no one was in control. Things just happened. Somebody called my daddy, and he was on the way home. The house was a wreck. Everything was disorganized. The doctor was now with my mother, tending her wounds. A neighbor in another bedroom was caring for the small children.

"With all the activity, I felt crowded and oppressed. I walked out of the house, down the road toward the tenant house. In the dark, I stumbled over an object in the road and picked it up. It was a double-barreled shotgun. I cracked the breach. There were two empty shells in the gun. Somebody had shot my sister and mother with a double-barreled shotgun and dropped the gun in the road."

Carl saw how upset I was and said, "Damn! When I asked about your sister, I didn't know it would upset you so. God, I'm sorry I insisted."

"That's okay. I felt numb. This was just another hammer blow to beat down my spirit. I cried as I closed the breach and took the gun back to the sheriff, who was now interviewing my mother.

"Then the ambulance came, backed up to our front door and took away my sister's body. As the dead girl was being rolled out the door, my mother was up again and so distressed to see the lifeless body of her child being taken away. Once more she threw her arms around Edna and sobbed her heart out. The attendants slid the stretcher into the ambulance and closed and locked the doors.

"With the help of the doctor, we got Mom back in bed, and the doctor gave her a stronger sedative. My concern for my mother had momentarily diverted my attention from my younger brothers and sisters. I took them back to their bedroom and held them in my arms.

"The sheriff called for the bloodhounds. He and his men and the dogs disappeared into the night in the direction I found the shotgun.

"Then my daddy came home. I was totally unprepared for his reaction. He was a large, healthy, robust man, and no one in the family had ever seen him cry. His world, too, was destroyed by the two shotgun blasts, which ended the life of his daughter. His crying revealed his hurt and loss. His heart-breaking and uncontrolled combination of sobbing and crying undid me. Inconsolable, his body moved with the rhythm of his sobs. Unable to control himself, his sobbing increased my sorrow. I wanted him to be a father who was capable and could handle the situation. However he could do nothing but sob his heart out. I watched him in awe and cried with him. The doctor was still there and gave him a sedative. My mother had already been treated for shock and resting quietly in her bedroom. The small children were with a neighbor in another bedroom.

"Some of our neighbors mercifully mopped the blood from the kitchen floor and swept up the glass. Edna's candy was still on the stove. The fire was out, and the candy was overcooked."

"John, I don't see how you stood it, the suffering," Carl said. "Now that you've told me part of the story, I know why you didn't want to talk about it."

"About two o'clock in the morning everyone left. I thought it bad when everyone was there, milling around and talking in small groups. They were in the way, looking into everything, invading our privacy and witnessing our hurt. When they left, the house was empty. The quiet and darkness distressed me. I felt empty and alone and didn't want to be. For a while I held my mother's hand, as she lay sedated in bed. She had changed into a nightgown and was covered with a sheet.

"'John, go to bed. Try to get some sleep,' she said."

"How could you even think about sleep?" Carl asked.

"Totally exhausted after seven hours of horror, I needed some rest.

"People were interested when there was a dead girl lying in her own blood on the kitchen floor. Now she was gone. The crowd had satisfied their own curiosity and left. The family was painfully alone with our memory of this cold-blooded murder. We could do very little to comfort each other because of the shock.

"None of us wanted to sleep even though we were all exhausted. We derived some comfort in being together. My daddy placed a mattress on the floor in his room, and the smaller children slept on that mattress.

"Next day, the sheriff brought us photographs of my sister from the undertaker. One load had hit her back on the left side of the spine at the level of her heart. She died instantly. The next shot ripped away her right arm. The stray shot from the second load hit my mother.

"The killer had laid the barrel of the shotgun on the window sill and shot through the sash. The kick from the gun knocked him back so that his second shot blew the remainder of the glass out of the window.

"As the bloodhounds were closing in, the murderer received word that the sheriff would pick him up shortly. His brother and father put him in their car and drove him to the county seat where he confessed. Hobart Randolph, my sister's husband, was her killer."

Tears were running down my cheeks, and I sniffed as I remembered the unhappy event.

Carl said softly, "That experience must have been terrible for you."

"It practically destroyed my way of thinking. Everything seemed so useless and without purpose.

"We rode home from the funeral in the limousine just back of the hearse. Crushed over Edna's death, the motion of the car seemed to blend with my inner feelings. There was comfort in doing nothing except watch the roadside slip by. I had no interest in going home, no interest in food, and no interest in doing anything. It was as though my spirit had been crushed."

"John, you look so normal now. I just don't see how you stood it. That experience would have finished me."

"My mind could not understand or accept the loss. One minute there was vibrant life, the next minute death. At my age, it disturbed me to find and acknowledge a fine line between living and dying.

"We were constantly reminded of my sister's death, and we could not live in the house. My father sold the farm. We moved to another county. There my dad changed from strict to a tyrant.

"I said I didn't want to talk about it, and now you have had to sit through the whole story. I'm sorry," I said, wiping away the tears from my face.

"That's okay. Maybe it will help you to talk about it. I hope as you grow older, you will be able to forget," Carl said.

"Forget? Never," I said. "That night is so burned in my memory it will never be forgotten. However, life isn't easy. 'Growing up is never easy,' my mom said. 'It is remarkable that the majority of the human race turns out as well as they do.'

"The economic depression and living with my dad's mean disposition required a tremendous effort and personal sacrifice from my mom and me."

"You have my respect, John," Carl said. "You've been through some bad times. You have remained a pretty levelheaded guy. You look relaxed and normal."

"Since everything I did was a disappointment to my dad, I have since tried to stay out of trouble."

"You haven't been in any trouble here at school. You only had trouble when those boys tried to cut off your mustache. You won that fight. They didn't shave your upper lip."

"Yeah. I've always tried to avoid a fight. Having my teeth and face busted up is not part of my plan for the future. My few positive physical attributes such as good skin, regular features, brown eyes and good teeth will be helpful in making a go of anything.

"Opportunity for success is all around us. I need to think about what to do for the future. I want to be a successful architect. To be ready to step in the right slot requires preparation. Success requires hard work and perseverance. It is difficult for me to stay focused on my goals because so many things compete for my attention."

"You'll do well," Carl said. "Together we'll make a fortune."

"I'll be happy to get a job for the summer," I said.

I did get a job and lived in a boarding house with a lot of older girls. The summer was very educational.

CHAPTER TWO

Hating my dad gave purpose to my life. The hatred was difficult to maintain. I missed it. This grudge which fueled my ambition to excel slipped into my subconscious. Dad was not around to keep it alive.

"Carl, so many things are happening in the world and in my life that distract me," I said as we walked up the stone walk to the Hill Dining Hall to breakfast. "When I lose some of the contempt for my dad, my motivation suffers. The girls and the exciting events here at school compete for attention and make me forget."

"Just relax and do what comes naturally," Carl said, "It won't hurt to date girls. I love to be with them too. You're gonna make it. Just don't get up tight about success.

"The war is heating up in Europe. Many boys who have just turned eighteen are being drafted into the army," Carl said. "I hoped this lack of competition would make it easier to find a job."

"I'm sure it will," I said.

"This is the summer before our last year of high school," I continued. "To work in Atlanta and save some money for college is important to me. A job will provide money for clothes and books. You are in the same boat. I wish you the best and hope you get a good job. Drop me a line and tell me how you are doing."

"I will. I hope you enjoy the summer," Carl said.

Later that day, Carl walked off with his bag to catch the bus to Rome. I shouted, "See you again here at school in the fall. Bye."

After several days of looking, my sincerity and apparent honesty landed me a job at the Southern Dairy Milk Processing Plant on Glen Iris Drive. It helped that I attended a school with a work ethic.

The work was not easy, I discovered. In the mornings, milk came in a covered truck, iced down in ten-gallon cans. Before pouring up the milk and weighing it, I taste-tested the milk in each can for "bitter weed" and "wild onions." Yuck! I still have that bitter-weed taste in my mouth when I think about it. From the weighing machine, the milk was pumped up to a 1,700-gallon refrigerated tank located on the second floor for processing. In the afternoon, I made cottage cheese and buttermilk and washed the vats which were used to pasteurize the milk.

Ten girls worked at processing ice cream and packaging cottage cheese. They were not very pretty but a couple looked good enough for dating.

The pasteurizing vats, ice cream, cottage cheese and the buttermilk operation were on the second floor. The stainless steel tanks and vats filled the processing room. The first floor contained intake, the cream separator, homogenizer, bottling, bottle washing and freezer and cold storage.

Amazed at the volume of good-tasting milk and ice cream processed in that facility, I knew why it required so much work. The company did give us the half-filled ice cream containers, and I took home a lot of black raspberry, my favorite ice cream flavor.

One of my jobs was to wash the 1,700-gallon milk tank when it became empty. To facilitate the cleaning, the cleaning person crawled through a round sixteen-inch hole into the inside lit by a watertight light at the top. To some people, being inside the enclosed tank was frightening. I placed the hose through the small opening. When the water was six inches deep, I cut off the water and dumped in some soap powder and pulled my body through the opening into the tank. With the water six inches on my rubber boots, I scrubbed the tank with the fiber brush.

Busy washing down the inside, I was startled when the light went out. The escape hole closed and latched. The unmistakable smell of BK water came through a vent. (BK water is a toxic mixture of water and chlorine used as a disinfectant for the vats. Chlorine was used as a battlefield poison gas during World War I.) I beat the inside of the stainless steel tank with my two-foot-long, wood-handled brush. Greater on the inside than on the outside, the sound became a problem, but I beat the tank anyway.

After five minutes, my fellow workers decided I had had enough and opened the door. After finishing my scrubbing, I pulled my body through the small opening and hosed the inside down with hot water.

Jim Wright, the operations boss, said, as he scrubbed a cottage cheese vat nearby, "This is a standing trick we play on all new people You took it very well. Being locked in a dark tank is a real trauma for some people. Those with a touch of claustrophobia climb the wall."

He laughed, and I said, "Sure, if you will tell me who locked me in the tank, I will play the customary trick on him by knocking out his front teeth."

No one came forward. The other workers laughed a lot.

My parents lived in Tucker, Georgia, about twenty miles from my job. There was no convenient bus transportation from Atlanta to Tucker. A boarding house nearby on Ponce de Leon Avenue was my best option for living space. The rent was cheap, and the house provided two meals a day, breakfast and dinner.

"Glad to have you as a roommate," Gene Hampton said as I looked around the small room with two beds, a dresser and one window.

He was around five feet nine inches tall, strong and well built, and his face had a look of relaxed gentleness. His soft voice was made for singing. He was sitting in a chair near the window and playing a guitar.

"Thanks. What do you do, Gene?"

"I am a truck driver. I was a staff sergeant in the army. One day, I stopped at a service station. The guy there called me a dogface, and the bastard made me mad as hell. I lost my cool and took my service revolver and shot up the place. The police arrived and arrested me, and the army promptly court-martialed and drummed me out of the service with a dishonorable discharge and loss of citizenship."

"Gene, you play that guitar well. Did you take lessons?" I asked.

In a mild-mannered husky voice, Gene said, "No. Just picked it up. Playing a guitar is easy. If you memorize a few chords and strum a little, you will be on your way to the mastery of this stringed instrument."

"Gene, you are lucky you got a job as a truck driver. I would like that. Have you had any accidents or close calls?"

"Not really," Gene responded, "but a driver cut sharply in front of my truck. I chased the bastard down, forced him off the road and out of his car and beat the hell out of him with my fists. I knocked him down a twenty-foot bank."

"Gene, I promise I will never cut in front of you," I said.

He laughed and said, "You don't have anything to worry about."

The boarding house was ruled and run by an overweight woman of forty named Mrs. Sand. Her boarders were not allowed to entertain the opposite sex in their rooms. Rent had to be paid on time. Loud conversation and radios were not allowed. Lights went out promptly at 10:00 P.M.

These rules were for everyone except the landlady. Her truck-driver boyfriend would stay over a couple of nights a week. When in town, his truck was parked in the lot down the street.

My mom sent Dad to check on me and make sure I was not in trouble. "Son, are you living in sin?" he asked.

My first inclination was to tell him, "Yes, every chance." Instead I said, "Dad, I'm doing okay." Because of our past conflict, I wanted nothing to do with him. I didn't like it because he pretended to be interested in my welfare.

"Gene, did you notice that three good-looking girls live in our boarding house? There are more who are not bad looking." I asked from my seat on the bed.

"I noticed that also. Two and sometimes three girls occupy a room," Gene said. "A total of sixteen people live in this boarding house, counting both boys and girls. Most boys and girls spend their free time in their rooms. The house has a living room, but it's staked out and occupied by the landlady. Not many boarders enjoy the company of Mrs. Sand."

"I've met several girls, but I like Polly the best," I said as I relaxed on my bed. "She's not beautiful, and she's five years older than me. Her captivating personality is dominant, and one doesn't notice that she is a little short and plain. Her enthusiasm and zest for life make me look past the physical to the real Polly. She is always thinking up tricks to play on her fellow boarders. Has she played a trick on you?"

"Stay clear of Polly. She will get you in trouble," Gene advised.

"Polly is fun, and she makes me laugh," I insisted.

"Remember what I told you. That girl will get you into trouble."

"Why are you working at the five-and-ten-cent store for twenty-five cents an hour?" I asked Polly one evening while we were walking up to the drugstore for a Coke. "Why don't you do something different?"

"Because I want to eat," she said with candor. "Please allow me to treat you to a history lesson. You just haven't been aware of what is happening in this country. The stock market crashed in 1929, the Depression lasted through 1932 and another depression occurred in 1936 and 1937 and lowered my expectations for 1941. A whole hell of a lot would have to happen to improve my lot. There is nothing for a girl to do on our farm. Girls like me come to the metro areas like Atlanta by the thousands. They work in ten-cent stores, dairies, laundries and anywhere they can for twenty-five cents per hour. Room and board is only five dollars a week. By the time we see a movie, buy a few things to wear, we are broke. We are bored. The whole country is stagnant both economically and spiritually.

"Cheer me up, John. Tell me I'm going to be rich and marry a good-looking man. I did graduate from high school, but I don't have any special skills that would land me a good job. I'm taking typing at night. That might help."

"What happens to these girls who come to Atlanta to work? Do they get married?" I asked as we sipped our Cokes at a corner table in the drugstore.

"Some marry and go back to the farm. Some work in dead-end jobs and never get a chance at life," Polly answered. "If they get into trouble or become pregnant, they are not accepted at home. Their families don't want them or the disgrace. They know they cannot raise a child on the small amount of money they make. As a result, most girls are careful about petting. However, they are bored and lonesome."

One night, one of the older girls had gone to bed early and her roommate was out of town. Mrs. Sand, the landlady, was also out of town for the weekend. Polly came to my room with two other girls and said, "John, I want you to get into bed with Ruth."

"I wouldn't be caught dead in the bed with Ruth," I said.

"She will think you are her roommate. You will be okay. When she discovers it's you, she will jump out of bed and cut on the light and scream. We will come in and accuse her of having an affair with you."

My time in the Christian Boys' School had not prepared me for Polly. It was wrong and could get me into real trouble, but I agreed to do it.

Ruth was not very good looking but a nice person. She was a dishwater blonde, around twenty-eight. She had the washed-out look of someone who had lost some of her body juices. Of medium height, her body from the side took on the shape of a segment of a circle.

"Remember to make this a good joke," Polly said. "You must pull off your shoes, your pants, and shirt."

"You don't expect me to strip down to my shorts, do you?" I asked.

Polly moved her head up and down indicating that was what she expected.

"Okay. I'll do it, but it's not right. This may get me in trouble. When you hear the scream you will come in quickly."

Polly moved her head up and down, indicating she agreed.

The head of the bed was against a wall with space on both sides. There was a dresser and closet on the wall at the end of the bed. The door opened between the dresser and the foot of the bed on the left. A window was in the wall opposite the door.

I opened Ruth's door and looked in. The light from the street showed she was on the left side of the double bed, breathing easily in a light slumber. Sitting down on the right side of the bed, I pulled off my shoes and pants and then my shirt. Ruth didn't wake up. This little joke could last all night. To speed up the process, I slipped my hands under the cover and touched her on the softer parts of her body. She smiled in her sleep and reached for me. Suddenly, she realized something strange was happening. She screamed, jumped out of bed and turned on the light. I was unprepared for the volume and the intensity of her scream. The hair on the back of my neck stood straight out. All my instincts said, "Run like hell." It was difficult to sit still.

Ruth was in her nightgown with her hair in rollers. When she recognized me, her fright turned to anger.

"You sex pervert!" she yelled. "You have some nerve getting in my bed! I ought to call the police. You've made a mockery of my privacy and my personal life. Everybody in this boarding house will know about this."

"Hold on, Ruth," I said. "This is a joke. Polly put me up to it. In just one minute Polly and the other girls will be coming through that door."

They didn't come. I continued to wait, and Ruth continued to tell me how wrong it was to get into bed with an unmarried girl, and how religious she was.

"The minute Mrs. Sand gets back in town, she will know about this," Ruth replied. "I thought you were a nice Christian boy. As far as I'm concerned, you are a corrupt person. I will have you thrown out of your room. Now get out of here and don't ever speak to me again."

Dressed only in my shorts, I tried to reassure Ruth in my most convincing voice that I was not a pervert and this occasion was a joke dreamed up by Polly. Ruth felt used and hurt. She was not ready to give up her assault on me.

"Polly made a fool of you," Ruth said.

"No woman has ever made a fool of me."

"Who did then?"

At that moment, Polly burst through the door with three other girls, her eyes wide at the shock of seeing Ruth and me in a compromising position.

"What is all the screaming about? We thought you were nice people." Polly said with a holier-than-you smirk on her face. "How long has this been going on? John, what are you doing here in your shorts? Ruth, it is shocking to see you in your nightgown with a man present. We plan to report this to Mrs. Sand when she returns to town. How can anyone sleep with all this screaming?"

Polly continued, "I am also surprised at the morals of some people. Some folks will sin at any opportunity. You two have just been waiting for the proper time when Mrs. Sand is out of town. I'm not sure I want to live in the same house with your kind of people."

Ruth got back into bed, pulled up the covers and said, "All of you get out."

"Polly, next time just take me to the zoo," I said.

"Nothing doing," she said. "If they want you they will have to come get you."

Picking up my shoes, pants, and shirt, I walked to my room and got dressed. Polly's humor was bad for my masculine image. There would be no next time for me. Ruth didn't report the incident. Polly made sure everyone in the boarding house knew about the silly prank.

The boarding house was not usually a lively place, but on Sunday afternoons it was quiet as a tomb. Back from a visit to my parents, I returned a little after noon. The weather was hot and there was no air-conditioning. Turning on a fan and reading the paper until about 2:00 P.M. was a diversion. Then I looked for something to do. No one was around. Even the landlady had not returned from the weekend. I decided to walk up to the corner drugstore and have an ice cream cone. Someone should be around by the time I returned.

Vera saw me pass in the hall and yelled, "John, come in and talk to me. This is a boring afternoon."

Vera wasn't one of my favorite girls. At thirty, she was too old for me, but she did have an earthy look about her that was appealing. Her five-foot-six-inch body was well formed, her blonde hair was down to her shoulders, and her white, irregular teeth gave her a wholesome look. The quality that made Vera stand out was her ample and well-formed breasts. Her smile was a plus. It lit up her face like a June sunrise.

I walked into the small room with one window and a private bath. One double bed and a dresser almost filled the room.

Vera was lying on the bed, dressed in a simple, cotton, print dress.

I sat down on the bed and asked, "What do you want to talk about? I am prepared to talk about any subject of national interest or anyone in the boarding house."

"Talk about anything," she said. "I'm so bored not having anything to do."

We started to talk. Before I knew what was happening, I was telling this older woman all about myself, about my summers in

Alabama with my grandparents, uncles and aunts. Vera lay back and relaxed. Her foot was touching my leg. I reached out and stroked her foot. She indicated she liked this by moving her foot closer for my convenience. As I talked, I ran my hand up her leg a short distance. When my hand reached above her knee, she purred like a kitten. I was also stimulated by the contact.

Then I ran my hand up her dress and massaged her panties between her legs. As I worked my fingers back and forth, her response was pleasing. Her body was moving up and down. Moisture seeped through her panties. My heart was pounding. Stopping the conversation might break the spell, so I continued to talk.

Slowly my fingers slid under her panties. She jumped as if she had just realized what was taking place and started to crawl away. I caught her, turned her over and started to kiss her lips, face and neck. With my free right hand, I slipped off her panties. I had already kicked off my shoes. Unzipping my fly, I was over her, separating her thighs with my right knee. Vera helped me.

Her body arched against mine as she contributed to the lovemaking. The bed creaked. We didn't care. The door was not even locked. The most important thing in our lives was to continue, with all our energy and enthusiasm, this act of nature. I kissed her mouth, her neck, her eyes. Finally, we lay exhausted, locked in each other's arms. We had not even taken off our clothes.

Suddenly, Vera said, "Did you?"

My normal thinking was a little disoriented. I said, "Did what?"

She said, "Come inside me?"

In my enthusiasm for the conquest, I forgot our activity creates babies. Vera didn't want to have one, not with me anyway.

Sheepishly, I said, "Yes."

She ran into her private bathroom. I heard water running and the toilet flush. After a while, Vera came out with fresh makeup and her hair combed. She was alive with vitality, and with the pink in her cheeks this girl looked beautiful. She said, "Why didn't you tell me you were going to do that?"

"I didn't know," I said. "At any rate, you are not bored anymore, are you?"

She kissed me on the lips and said, "John, you are a good boy. There just isn't any demand for good boys. You said you didn't fool around with women."

"That's not what I said. When it comes to women, I don't fool around."

"I can believe that," she said.

I wanted to tell her that this type of thing was not a common occurrence in my life. She had been helpful in overcoming my shyness, and I was grateful. Grateful! It was lovemaking I would remember forever.

"How about an ice cream cone?" I asked. "My treat."

She accepted, and we walked to the drugstore together.

Later that evening, my roommate, the truck driver, said, "Look at this. Thirty thousand Georgians have been rejected by the army because they were illiterate."

At school I learned the importance of discipline and telling the truth in a school encounter.

CHAPTER THREE

In the fall before returning to school, my mom and dad drove me to Sears to buy a new suit with the money I had saved. I had only one dress shirt for church and now it was too small and worn around the cuffs. I also bought shirts.

My school had a loose requirement that everyone wear a blue serge suit for Sunday services.

"They wear like iron and hold a crease," Dad said. "The blue serge is your best suit for the money."

"Sure, Dad. I'm looking for something that will look good on me," I said. "This double-breasted brown suit looks very sporty. Mom, what do you think?"

"You're right. It does look better. Will they let you wear it at school?"

"Yeah, I guess so."

I paid for the suit and later returned to school near Rome, Georgia.

When I arrived at school, Carl was already there. We were assigned to the same room as last year in Friendship Hall.

"How did your summer go?" I asked Carl when I saw the glum look on his face.

"Terrible," he said. "Couldn't get anything to do except this job of 'loading and hauling half-rotten cow hides.' It was the dirtiest, stinking thing I've ever done." He plopped down on his bed. "How was your summer?"

"Great!" I said. "Wish you had been with me. You should have seen all those girls in my boarding house. Maybe we can be together next summer before college, the summer of 1942."

"Don't know about that. This war in Europe has got me worried. We may have to fight."

"The war continues to rage in Europe," I said. "The British Army backed itself into a corner called Dunkirk in 1940 and has had to be taken out in small pleasure craft. It will take a major effort to put them back. Hey! All that is across the Atlantic. Why should we be interested in a war in Europe? Great Britain is a long way off. Involvement in a war is not part of my plans. I have many things to do before I can call myself an architect. How can I ever do all those things required to make progress unless I get started?"

"The war is something we'll be forced to think about," Carl said.

The summer of 1941 had passed, and now we were back at the boys' school, working hard and trying to keep up our grades to ensure our acceptance in college. My classes and part-time work made the fall semester appear routine, but the times were exciting. Great changes were occurring. Soon I would graduate and hopefully be caught up in events that dominated the news.

At a social on the girls' campus I met Mandy. She was a college freshman, class president and worked at being a good student. Not only did she have good looks but brains as well. These talents in combination impressed me.

I asked Mandy to dance and was pleased she danced well. Mother Nature blessed her with those physical attributes that made women attractive to men—nice figure, good even teeth, beautiful, dark, curly hair and a bright smile. These outstanding assets caused Mandy to be popular with both boys and girls.

As we danced, I said, "Where have you been all my life?"

"This may surprise you, but that's not an original line," she said as she looked up and smiled at me. "To be truthful, I've been right here for the past four years. It's been fun. The time did pass quickly."

"Why haven't I noticed you before?" I asked, pretending surprise.

"Perhaps you didn't look in the right direction. Or perhaps you were looking in a different direction. I've seen you with other girls."

"My eyes are strongly attracted to someone with good looks. Surely you have been hiding under a bushel."

"Perhaps you've been too busy telling the other girls what a good-looking guy you are."

"With my looks I have to point out my good features or no one will notice. Tooting my own horn has been a help."

"Are you sure? Perhaps you are too forward. If you gave people a chance to look you over well, they might decide to give you the benefit of any doubt."

"You've put your finger on my shortcoming. Doubt. Mother Nature shortchanged me. Self-assurance is not my long suit. How about a date for this Sunday afternoon at the girls' school?"

"It is against my better judgment," she said. "I'll accept on the condition that there is no test in any of my classes the following Monday."

"This is the first time I've played second fiddle to a freshman college course."

"Those are the conditions. I'll drop you a note and let you know if a test has been scheduled."

My parents visited me in school on a fall Sunday. The tension between Dad and me did nothing to brighten the occasion. Mom brought cookies and clothes. It was a pleasant day. I showed them the campus and told them about my plans for the future. Mom was concerned that I would be drafted and shipped to Europe to fight. My dad and I hardly spoke to each other. He seemed to harden up his personality when he spoke to me.

Carl and I had taken a chance that could have gotten us thrown out of school. One night after the 10:00 P.M. bed check, he and I slipped off to Rome, Georgia, the closest town. We lived in Friendship Hall at the time, and each owned a bicycle.

We were returning at 4:00 A.M. down the long, straight, three-mile stretch to the school campus. Before we arrived at the shop and gym building, Mr. Seymour, the night watchman, turned on his headlights pointed in our direction. We were a quarter of a mile away and ducked into the bushes to the left of the road. Quickly he drove down to investigate and passed us. He got out of his car and looked into the woods with his flashlight.

Jumping back into his car, he drove around in the direction of the dairy barn to head us off there. He thought we had cut through the woods.

We saw his lights and peddled like crazy for the gym.

He knew he had missed us and headed for the way we had come.

We dragged our bicycles up into the balcony of the gym and from a window watched him search for us in the shrubbery with his flashlight. Soon he gave up and left.

We rode our bikes back to the dorm, lay down in our clothes and slept for an hour. At breakfast and in class, we were still sleepy.

Next day Mr. G. H. Emrick called me in and showed me a handkerchief with my name on it.

"Is this yours?" he asked.

"It's got my name on it," I said.

"It was found on the country road last night."

"Because of the school laundry, we often get things that belong to other students," I said.

G.H. looked me in the eye with a half smile and asked, "Did you or did you not go into Rome last night?"

I couldn't tell a barefaced lie even when a *yes* answer would bring punishment.

"I did go to Rome last night," I said.

Mr. Emrick responded, "Ha! Ha! Ha! That will be an E on conduct. You may go. Take the incriminating evidence with you," he said and handed me the handkerchief.

I smiled and said, "Thank you" and departed, knowing I was lucky he didn't ship me.

Some classes became more interesting as the war news increased. Those with a current-event application were my main concern. I loved the discussion classes and was always ready to make a contribution.

The war in Europe sparked my interest and that of my classmates. In civics class we learned the names and titles of the people who ran the world. We were interested to see how these world personalities fit into the current-event information we received from the newspapers and the radio.

Mr. Robinson, my civics professor, asked the class, "How many of you know why Hitler is such a danger to the free world?" I raised my right hand. "All right, let's hear from Mr. Jones."

"Many times Hitler said he wants to get back those German lands lost after World War I. No one is sure if he will stop with the conquest of those lands. He might want part of the United States. He's already taken Denmark, Norway, the Low Countries, most of the Balkans, some of Russia, and some of North Africa."

"When do you think he will stop this aggression?" Mr. Robinson asked.

"When he loses his power over the German people, or when someone kills him. Mr. Winston Churchill, the prime minister of Great Britain, doesn't trust Hitler. Mr. Churchill had direct contact with Hitler. I am willing to believe him as a free-world leader."

"Jones, you may not be right about many things, but you are right about Hitler," Professor Robinson said.

The headmaster at school, Mr. Emrick, was teaching my senior economics class. When I reacted with enthusiasm to one of Mr. Emrick's questions, he asked in a voice loaded with irony, "John, what do you plan to do with all the education you have acquired?"

"I just got it. Do you expect me to do something with it

now? That is a sobering question. In what direction should I point my life. There is so much out there to do. Until I grow up, I am in no rush to take on responsibility. Maybe later, after college or marriage," I continued. "Seriously, I want to be an architect."

"The quicker you can decide what you plan to do, the more likely you are to make a success of your life."

A note arrived from Mandy. She wrote, "Sorry about Sunday, but I do have a test. Perhaps later."

Under my breath, I said, "You had your chance."

At the boarding school, the teachers kept us busy. Before I realized it, December had arrived. Christmas vacation presented a chance to go home and visit the family.

Abruptly, on December 7, 1941, the Japanese bombed Pearl Harbor. "A day of infamy," President Roosevelt said.

My roommate, Carl and I heard the news on his radio in our room at school. He turned to me and said, "War! This is war." He wrote the three letters, W-A-R, on the radio.

"Do you know what this means?" he exclaimed. "It means that the draft board will have you and me in the armed services in a very short time."

"You're right," I replied. "Wars usually last about four years; you can bet we will be drafted. Are you ready?"

"John, this is your chance to be a hero," Carl said. "You are hero material. Now you have the chance. I want to make a lot of money. Look around you. You want something better than this dormitory room—two beds, two chests of drawers, two study tables. This is lean living. Somewhere out there, you and I are going to make it. I want to be one of the richest SOBs in this country."

"Most heroes get killed, Carl. That's not part of my plan.

"Just to prove my dad wrong, I would like to amount to something. To do something useful, something which would contribute to my economic well-being and be good for this country, that would make me happy. I plan to be an architect. Now the Japanese have come along and loused up my schedule. I'm gonna have to put off my career until after the war."

From that moment our lives changed, not abruptly at first. Slowly the news began to sink in. People we did not know were to rob us of our innocence and involve us in earth-shattering events. Ready or not, we were living in a history-producing era.

Home for Christmas, I witnessed a nation preparing for war. Many young men were in uniform. President Roosevelt had had the foresight to start training civilians as early as 1939.

Before I left school, Mandy had given me a note in which she indicated she would be spending some of her Christmas vacation in Atlanta. She gave me her aunt's number and asked that I call. She accepted my call and request for a date. My dad allowed me to borrow the car.

Mandy Hamilton was an exquisitely formed girl with long, curly, black hair. Her blue eyes looked out on a world of adventure. Away from school, she was mischievous enough to want to do all those outrageous things that I would never dare. I thought she was marvelous and couldn't take my eyes off her.

When I knocked, she opened the door and said, "Welcome to the Atlanta apartment of my aunt and uncle."

Her aunt Rose said, "Hello, we are delighted that you could visit Mandy."

After shaking hands with Uncle Martee, he wished me a Merry Christmas, and he and Aunt Rose retired to another part of the house. Mandy and I were alone in the living room.

After her aunt and uncle left the living room, she walked around the room and turned off all the lights except the one at the couch. This girl was making a hit with me. She was saving electricity. The lamp near the couch contained a magenta-colored bulb. In the soft red glow Mandy appeared to be the most beautiful and desirable creature to walk the streets of Atlanta. I stood in awe of this dream girl.

We had exchanged correspondence at school. We had not yet dated. Mandy could not work me into her schedule. However, her letters were friendly. My letters were intimate and sincere. My poems were accepted with some appreciation.

Mandy said, "I saved all your letters in a little cedar chest, and here is the key required to open the lock."

Alarmed, I said, "Mandy, my letters couldn't be that good. You gave me no indication that you even liked me, still I'm glad you thought the letters were good enough to keep."

"John, please recite that last poem you wrote for me and use all the feeling you must have felt when you wrote it," she said as she looked up at me through her long lashes.

A command performance was not on my schedule. Would I be able to live up to her expectations of me as a budding poet? Mailing a poem in a letter is different from having to deliver it in person.

Panic seized me! I couldn't remember the poem. My memory was a blank. Searching my mind for a solution, I was about to speak when she said, "Sit here close beside me. Don't be bashful."

Her conduct was new to me. I had always been the aggressor.

"To do the poem justice with expression," I pleaded, "you must let me see the lines."

Mandy opened her cedar chest and brought out the letter with the poem. With the words, I read the lines of the poem with all the feeling I could muster.

Then I looked into her misty eyes with a long searching look. Something told me the time was now. I put my arms around her and pulled her to me. She cradled so naturally against my chest. I planted a lingering kiss on her rosebud lips and felt ten feet tall. With a running start, I could jump over the Empire State Building.

Again, panic seized me. Snapping back to reality, I turned her loose like a hot potato. Mandy's relatives were in the same apartment just down the hall.

Mandy read my face and recognized my concern. She said, "Don't worry about my aunt and uncle. They trust me."

"They don't trust me," I said.

She nestled against me on the couch and turned her face up to be kissed. It was a fantastic evening. She liked my company. She seemed to like everything about me. My confidence high, I tried for a more intimate relationship, but kissing was as far as Mandy would go.

Back in school in the new year, 1942, Carl said, "Carol Lombard, the movie actress, died in a TWA-plane crash on a flight to Los Angeles. Clark Gable, her husband, was inconsolable. It's dangerous to fly even when someone is not shooting at the plane."

What did the future hold for me? With a war under way and high-school graduation coming up, I felt that life was taking me downhill fast. Life was becoming hardball, grown up and complicated. Decisions, decisions. I would have to make decisions that could get me killed or get me through the war in one piece. Was I capable of making those decisions?

The coming of World War II was not a happy occasion for anyone. Wars kill people and create shortages. People are required to sacrifice and put their private lives on hold. For me, a kid just about to graduate from high school, war would mean getting away from home and traveling. That could be fun. I tried not to think about people getting killed and the possibility that I too might be unlucky. This war caught me just at an age too young to have any experience that would qualify me for a deferment, but old enough to be a desirable candidate for frontline fighting. I had to stay alive and become a success to prove my dad wrong. Getting killed wasn't a happy option anyway.

I would try to stay in college as long as possible. However, forces were working against me and soon my life would be taken over by the changing world.

My graduation from high school in June was low key. Mom and Dad didn't attend. Mom did send me a little cash and wished me well. I didn't hear anything from Dad. It was just as well. Now I would show him what I was capable of.

The job I was to get at Brookley Field in Mobile, Alabama, was an essential job in an essential industry, but it wasn't enough for me.

CHAPTER FOUR

I knew it was summer. My roommate brought back my cough medicine and borrowed my suntan lotion. In my private moments of thought, I worried about my involvement in the war. Would the draft board take me and louse up my life?

In the summer of 1942, I would become eighteen and be required to register for the draft. Having just graduated from high school from boys' boarding school in June, my plan was to start college in the fall. For the summer, I would work, save money and have my share of fun. Living a regimented life is great for accomplishment but having fun is also important. The restraints placed on me by the boarding school became tiresome.

From the bunk in my room I said, "Carl, tell you what I'm gonna do. I'm gonna get an essential job in an essential industry and profitably work my way through the war. Worse things could happen you know. It would be nice to have money to spend. Being poor is no fun."

"Yeah," Carl said as he shifted his chair at his study table and looked my way. "Poverty imposes an unwanted, austere lifestyle. Maybe with a little effort we can change things. It's hell to be poor."

"Working my way through school as an apprentice brick mason and carpenter has prepared me to do something useful. With these talents and skills I can contribute to the war effort and make some money. My skill with a hammer, a saw and a brick trowel should land me a well-paying job," I said.

"You can do a lot of things, but what will you do this summer?" Carl asked. "Remember we had the same conversation last year. This year you have a high-school diploma. It should be easier to get a job. I didn't do well last summer. Loading half-rotted cow hides was a stinking bad job."

"My job with Southern Dairies was not much better. I did have fun living in that boarding house. You wouldn't believe how many girls live in Atlanta.

"College in the fall will require additional cash even though I am working my way," I continued. "My folks have less money than they had last year, and they didn't have much then. I will have to provide my own funds for college. Why couldn't I have been born rich? Having to work is tremendously inconvenient when the time could be used for having fun."

"It's the same with me," Carl lamented. "Don't have any money either. Why not go with me to Mobile and get a job this summer? It could be fun. You could live with my mom and me."

Carl's suggestion to go to Mobile for the summer fell on fertile ground. The idea sprouted and grew. Carl didn't have to be too convincing because I really wanted to go.

I called Mom and told her what I was doing. Carl and I packed our suitcases, thumbed a ride to Mobile and made application at Brookley Field for work. Carl received employment as a storekeeper. Because of my carpentry experience, the Army Air Corps assigned me to a much-better job as a senior packer. I crated items for shipments, everything from small shipments of special bolts to airplane wings.

Carl's mother's house was in Fairhope, Alabama, near Mobile, and she allowed me to live there for minimal rent. The arrangement was very satisfactory to everyone involved.

The house was old and needed paint. There were five rooms but no bath. A side and a back porch gave it a cool look among the big live oak trees. The floors were tongue and grooved southern pine. The walls were wood paneling. However there was no inside plumbing except a kitchen sink to raise our comfort index.

A delightful small town, Fairhope is the center of a farming community. Tourism is also big. The small stores and streets are busy during the summer. Loads of girls come over from Mobile to attend house parties on the beach. All these house-party girls were looking for boys. Carl and I were looking for girls. We found plenty. The finding made for an exciting time.

Glad to be alive during this summer of great expectations and adventure, I loved my lifestyle and scheduled it to satisfy my candy-store appetite. I wanted to experience life to its fullest. The shortage of boys in Fairhope became a bonus for Carl, Byron, another friend, and me. Byron was the owner of an ancient '34 Ford that would do sixty miles per hour in second gear. This car not only helped in getting about, it became a magnet for girls. We almost always triple-dated. The reasons for our success were not difficult to determine. The lack of competition, the car, and our availability, all worked to make the three of us the most popular young men in Fairhope.

Some sort of psychological change affects girls during a war. Apparently the "war psychology" dictates when men are in short supply, girls grab one while they can. Whatever the reason for our popularity, we loved it and played the part. In a single night, on days off, we would schedule two dates, an early date lasting until 10:00 P.M. and then a late date from 10:00 P.M. until the wee hours of the morning or as long as the chaperon for our dates would allow the girls to stay out.

Because of my ambition, I promised myself that I would not be the reason for some young girl to name me as the father of her unborn child. However, the temptation and opportunity were there.

"Carl, I'm convinced I've been fun starved but not anymore," I said. "We play on the beach, swim in the bay, dance at Lacarona and the Legion Club. We've both become good dancers. Before the summer is over, we will be experts. Some nights we danced all night."

"Yeah, you are right," Carl said. "To hold a girl and keep time to the music is a delightful pastime. I've fallen in love seven times already during this summer. We've learned a lot about girls."

"You certainly had the opportunity," I continued. "We must have dated two dozens."

The recreation facilities in Fairhope were unsophisticated, even somewhat crude. The lack of proper places for recreation was not a handicap. We loved these existing facilities. In some places we danced without shoes, in shirts and white pants. Both boys and girls loved the casual look. The casual look suited our pocketbooks, lifestyles and, above all, facilitated having fun. The fresh salt smell of the sea, the full moon over the water and the weather-beaten, sun-bleached pier and buildings provided the intoxicating ambiance for romance.

I quickly forgot Mandy in this parade of female pulchritude. We did exchange a few letters. Soon the interest dropped to zero.

Then I met Sara Wilson.

A group of girls at the Municipal Pier were playing in water off the low pier. I was relaxing on the high pier, getting a tan and feasting my eyes on the bathing beauties in the water. One girl in the group was outstanding. She was kidding the other girls about their boyfriends. Even from a distance, her wit and charm were obvious. Lively and vivacious, she swam circles around her friends. It appeared the other girls were coming out second best.

Because she had enjoyed a joke at the expense of her friends, they all converged on her. Water was flying in all directions as they splashed and called her Sara. Some of the girls disappeared below the surface of the water, and there was more kicking and splashing. As quickly as the commotion had started, it stopped. One of the girls held up the bottom part of Sara's two-piece suit.

I yelled, "I'll help!" and hit the water. Using my most impressive overhand stroke, I swam over to where the girls were bunched up. They immediately closed ranks and shooed me away. Retreating to a safe distance from the yelling females, I assured them my intentions were not honorable. I wanted to create a little more tension and see how their fun and games would end.

"Sara, come over after you retrieve your swimsuit. I'll give you my autograph," I said.

Sara's natural blonde hair had a hint of brown, coupled with her curls and obvious good health, it gave her a striking appearance. Her face was heartshaped, with regular features except for a slightly turned-up nose. Her blue eyes met my admiring gaze with a good-natured challenge. I got the impression she was looking me over and "setting me up." She flashed the quizzical look and caused me to forget everything I had learned. My experience as a girl chaser became lost in the confrontation with this blue-eyed beauty.

Sara approached me, wearing both pieces of her two-piece bathing suit. The shape and presence of this gorgeous creature filled me with awe. As she walked toward me on the upper pier with a catlike grace, I became totally awed by this provocative female. Vacationers and other bathers walked by. Oblivious to anything except this pretty girl, I waited until she stood close.

Mother Nature had been generous with her in passing out physical attributes. I fell in love with this girl immediately.

Sara looked me over and asked, "What makes you think I want your autograph?"

"My signature and ten cents will get you a cup of coffee," I replied.

"I don't like coffee."

"I knew we had a common interest the moment you appeared. I don't like coffee either. My name is John Jones. I am Mrs. Jones's little boy."

She started to walk away.

"What else do you not like?" I continued.

"I don't like boys who are stuck on themselves."

"Me neither. How long are you here for?"

"Just the weekend. We are members of a girl's club in Mobile, but only ten girls could make the retreat here in Fairhope. Our rented house is down the beach. It's complete with a housemother who came with us."

"How about a date tonight? We could go dancing on the pier. They have a jukebox there with some good records. I'll even treat you to a hot dog. Now that's something you can't turn down."

"I'm sorry. We are not allowed to date by ourselves."

"Perhaps we could meet you and your girlfriends here on the pier. I'll bring a couple of my friends."

"Okay, I will try to get them down. Don't hold your breath or take any bets."

"With your charm, you won't have any trouble. Good-bye until tonight."

Carl, Byron and I were there at the appointed time.

The wood building rested on pilings driven into the sand. The outside was southern yellow pine bleached to a nice gray patina. Inside was a bar, a place to dance, some booths and tables and a row of coin-operated slot machines.

Our girls had not yet arrived. Two other girls without escorts were playing the slot machines. I walked over to see how they were doing. They were playing the nickel machine and had lost a couple of bucks.

The girls were in their early twenties. One was short and the other was about five feet eight inches. Both had dark hair.

"If you girls are tired of pulling that handle, may I try my lucky nickel?" I asked. I knew the machines were ready to pay off. The girls had put in several dollars worth of nickels and hadn't received anything more than three nickels at a time. The odds were in my favor.

"Buddy, it's yours," the taller girl said. I flashed a smile, dropped in a nickel and pulled the handle, and the plums lined up. The machine coughed out twenty nickels. It was difficult to suppress a look of triumph as I scooped them up and put them in my pocket.

The girls who had given up the slot machine walked over to our table. Gradually we learned they were ladies of the evening and wanted to sell themselves.

"How much do you charge?" I asked.

Dot, the taller of the two, said, "Ten dollars."

"Where can we go?" Carl asked.

"We have an apartment down the beach. We can go there, or we can walk down the beach. We can also go to your place. You have a car and five of us can go together."

"I don't have ten bucks, but I have two," I said. "What will that get me?"

"A smile and you already have that."

"How did you girls get into this business?" I asked.

"It's something we like doing, and we get paid for it," the blonde said. "If I didn't get paid, I'd be doing it anyway."

"Doesn't it bother you that you might catch something?" I asked.

"We are careful who we do business with," the tall brunette responded.

"Call me if you decide against being a professional. I'm available," I said.

These girls knew they were wasting their time and strolled out on the pier to look for other prospects.

The dates I made, came in a crowd. All ten girls showed up. I introduced the boys, and Sara introduced the girls. We pulled two tables together and ordered a round of Cokes. The girls came in all sizes and shapes. Their ages were sixteen to eighteen. We considered ourselves fortunate to have three and one-third girls each for a date. Sara received my full attention.

She was wearing shorts and tennis shoes with no socks. Her blouse was knotted at the waist, exposing some skin. Her hair was alive with a spring in the curl. Her expression was the same and seemed to say, "You said you were good company, now prove it."

I did make a special effort to impress her.

I walked over and placed a nickel in the jukebox and punched in "Don't Sit under the Apple Tree with Anyone Else but Me."

"Sara, how about a dance?" I asked.

"Delighted," she said.

The dance floor was uneven and rough, but holding Sara close was a tremendous incentive to dance. After a slow start, she learned the cadence of my step and did well. The more we danced, the better she became. Her movements were sure and on the beat.

Later I said to Byron, "To hold that sweet young thing and

move to the rhythm of the music was a bit of heaven. Even the rundown dance place took on a glow as the sun set on the horizon. Because of her, the warm light and deep shadows made magic on the ancient pier and her face. I'm in love."

The Municipal Pier ran one-half mile out into the bay. The Lacarona was built on pilings to the right of the Municipal Pier. In the twenties, trucks came out from local farms to load produce on to boats. The produce boats motored the fresh food across the bay to Mobile. The same boats also unloaded processed goods for the customers in Fairhope.

The Lacarona was of weather-beaten unpainted wood on the outside with a wood-shingle roof. The inside was sealed with board and battens with a bar on the right side from the entrance door. Along the wall to the left were booths made of boards with tables made of three two-by-ten planks nailed together from underneath. Five tables with chairs occupied the open space near the bar. The open space in the center was empty and was used as a dance floor.

Carl and Byron also found girls they liked and were now dancing. Four of the girls without male partners formed two couples and were also on the dance floor. Everyone seemed to be having a good time.

I looked down at Sara and asked, "Aren't you glad you came?"

"Yes. What else do you have in your bag of tricks?"

"Who, me?" I exclaimed. "There are no tricks up my sleeve or anywhere else. Why don't you and I walk to the end of the pier for some fresh air?"

She looked up and smiled. "I've been warned about you and your desire for fresh air. We girls have to stay together. The housemother said, 'There is safety in numbers.'"

"You are safe with me. How can you live under such strict rules?"

She smiled again.

We danced until 10:30 P.M. and then walked the girls back to their bungalow and met the housemother. Sara left the next day.

As Carl and I walked away from the house, I turned to him

and said, "Just when I meet someone, who is both intelligent and nice looking, she quickly walks out of my life."

"You don't run her off," Carl said. "She has other obligations. You're right about Sara. She is one fine-looking girl."

Carl carried his 190 pounds well on his six-foot-one-inch frame. His regular features and easygoing personality set him apart. Most girls liked him. His white, even teeth and a bright, mischievous smile added to his allure.

"Carl, with your youthful attitude of 'I don't give a damn,' no one ever discovers your high IQ," I said. This attitude seemed to be very acceptable to the girls.

"You have been taught differently," I said. The 'I don't give a damn' mental characteristic must have been inherited from your father, that hard-rock miner from the mountains of North Carolina. Your Danish mother is dedicated to having you make a success of your life. Which one will win?"

"I'm trying to have fun, and you want to be serious."

"Brookley Field put us on the graveyard shift," I said. "Our shift works from eleven o'clock to seven the next morning. Are you sure that's something we ought to do?" I asked.

"We can adapt to that schedule though," Carl said. "We can leave home for Mobile about seven in the evening, party in Mobile until eleven o'clock, and then go to work. It is a rigorous schedule. We will need all the sleep we can get."

My job was in a large warehouse with roll-up doors. The items to be crated were sitting against a long wall. When I came on shift, I checked the items for priority and selected the ones to be crated. My two helpers and I prepared the parts for shipment. The items ready for shipment were picked up and loaded on a truck, freight car or plane, depending on size and priority. We stumbled in at Carl's mother's home around 8:00 A.M. I went to bed immediately.

"If I go to bed," Carl said, "I might miss something."

"Please tell me what I missed," I asked and said goodnight.

Carl had an annoying habit of practicing his trumpet after I was well asleep. He would break out his brass noisemaker and blow with enthusiasm. Several altercations erupted and ended with me telling Carl where he could place his trumpet. With a relaxed personality, Carl required less sleep than the average person. The horn blowing was recreation for this music lover. However, I helped him work out a more suitable playing schedule.

Carl's mother's house didn't have inside plumbing. Even for pioneer types like Carl and me, inside plumbing had its allure. We talked with Carl's mother about the possibility of a bathroom.

"If you boys will furnish the labor, do the building and install the fixtures, I'll buy the materials," she said.

"John, are you willing?" Carl asked. "You're the one with building skills. A bathroom will mean you won't have to take a cold shower with the garden hose when the cold weather arrives in November."

"It's something we can all use," I said. "I'll be happy to donate whatever skills I have to this worthwhile enterprise."

Carl and I went to work. First, we dug a ditch to the property line from the city sewer and turned up a pipe in the location of the bathroom. Then we connected the water pipe from the kitchen area. The water pipes were galvanized iron and had to be cut and threaded. We borrowed a thread cutter and vise to cut and install the pipe. Using the same construction technique, we brought gas to the water heater in the bathroom. In less than two months, we poured a slab, built the walls and roof and set the fixtures. It was a pleasure not to have to go out to the outhouse. The building program did cut down on our social life. We continued to work our full shift at Brookley Field.

The year 1942 was a bad year for the Yankees baseball team. The Cardinals won and ended the New York Yankees' sixteen-year World Series winning streak. Johnny Beasley was the winning pitcher.

Carl and I saw *Bambi*. The movie stimulated our young

minds. We thought about our future, the war and what it might hold for us. On August 24, 1942, Walt Disney claimed it was the best picture ever made. It appealed to all ages but especially young people just starting in life like Bambi. The main character was a brown-eyed, white-spotted fawn whose progressive discoveries of rain, snow, ice, the seasons, man, love and death made for a wonderfully sensitive, full-length, cartoon movie. *Bambi* was a movie of hope and established order as to what life could be. The movie satisfied some of our need for direction.

"I'm not about to give up my independence to some army sergeant," Carl said, "but if the cause is great enough, I will."

"Has anyone asked you?"

"No, but I'm doing well with my job," he said. "I've learned the business and am looking forward to a promotion. I'm an attractive catch."

"Yeah, hope you get what you deserve."

As the summer passed, I became tired of the routine; the parade of female pulchritude. I felt something missing in my life. My friends were joining the service and going away to training camps and to the war, and to high adventure. Crating airplane wings lost some of its appeal. To leave this good job caused me some concern about my quest for success. The grudge, against my dad, made me want to stay and work toward a promotion. Torn between something I wanted to do and something I thought I should do, kept me on edge. For weeks this split dominated my life and caused a conflict between my feeling and thinking. The split made me indecisive and ill at ease.

"Is something bothering you?" Carl asked.

"Yes. I'm glad you brought it up. Carl, earlier we talked about getting an essential job in an essential industry and working our way through the war," I said. "That isn't enough for me anymore. I want to be involved. I want to be where the action is."

"What do you mean, 'It isn't enough'? You are involved. You are serving your country by working in the war effort. When they need you, they'll call. There is a thing called the draft."

"I know, but I'm not getting shot at. I'm not putting my life at risk as other boys are doing. If my grandchildren ask, 'Granddad, what did you do in the war?' Can I tell them I spent the time crating airplane wings at Brookley Field in Mobile, Alabama?"

"You could do worse—you could volunteer and get killed."

"I don't want to get killed. Getting killed would sure mess up my plans for the future. I want to be a success. I also want to help win the war; being in the service can make a difference. War is exciting. It should also give me some memories."

"You can remember how much money you made during the war. John, you're hero material. You've made up your mind to volunteer. I wish you the best of luck. I'm going to stay right here until they draft me," Carl said.

Some of my friends came home on leave. They talked about their lives in the service, glowing tales of training camps and girls away from home. Life in the armed forces sounded interesting and adventurous. This would be an opportunity to find out if my dad was right: Was I worth a damn?

In early fall, I walked into the army recruiting center in Mobile and enlisted. I asked to be assigned to the Army Air Corp. The army shipped me along with five other boys to Fort McPherson, in Atlanta, Georgia, for processing. The night we arrived, a sudden cold spell dropped the temperature. We were assigned to a barracks and a bunk.

After the long train ride, I was tired and felt the need to freshen up. Grabbing a towel, I headed for the crowded latrine and was busy soaping up in the shower. A fellow of medium build in his GI shorts was shaving nearby. He stopped shaving and opened the window. A blast of cold air hit me. I gave the guy a dirty look, walked over to the window and closed it. The guy shaving walked over, raised the window again and gave me a dirty look.

He asked, "Do you know who I am?" Without waiting for a reply, he said, "I'm Sergeant Johnson."

I had been sworn in but was still in civilian clothes, and I said, "Sergeant, if you raise that window again, you are going to lose some of those pearly white teeth that look so good in the mirror." I closed the window again. Sergeant Johnson's bluff had been called. The window remained closed.

I discovered that Sergeant Johnson was the duty sergeant for the barracks. Next day after placement and qualification tests, I was first on the duty roster for KP.

The wood-frame barracks did have a wood floor, and no interior finish. Bunks were located on each side of a central corridor. At one end there was a latrine, and at the other the sleeping quarters of the barracks noncommissioned officer.

Sergeant Johnson had his radio on. The station was playing 1942 Hit Parade songs such as "Praise the Lord and Pass the Ammunition," "When the Lights Go On Again All Over the World" and "My Devotion." However, the song that topped the record for popularity was Irvin Berlin's "White Christmas" sung by Bing Crosby. With a war in progress, the uncertainty of the future became a burden on the spirit. "White Christmas" lifted spirits and made people optimistic. The words of the song formed a promise that soon peace would be a reality.

Everyone seemed tired of rationing, shortages, and long hours, they wanted a future with promise. "White Christmas" vocalized that promise. One could still dream. Bing Crosby with his mellow voice and convincing manner inspired everyone to look to their inner strength, and the extra effort necessary for victory.

I too looked to my inner strength. My time in the service had been short, but already I had antagonized a sergeant. I was glad I never saw him again. This sort of talent could keep me in trouble.

I was soon to learn what army basic training meant.

CHAPTER FIVE

The best way to stay out of the army was to join the Army Air Corps. Because of my high score on the general qualification test, the army placed me on a "stop order" for a group assigned to the Air Corps.

While waiting for this shipment, I printed information on the back of individual service records. For two weeks, I practiced lettering. My drafting experience also helped me stay out of the infantry.

Two weeks later my group left for Keesler Field near Biloxi, Mississippi. Could the Air Corps expect this group to start playing soldier immediately? They damn sure did. The change of pace became abrupt and serious. Could I measure up to Army Air Corps standards? I would try.

In Biloxi uniforms were the first order of the day. The supply sergeant said, "Well, Jones, how do you want your uniform? Too little or too big?"

"Too big," I said. "I haven't stopped growing yet. Hey wait. I'll never grow that big," I yelled.

"Ask your grandma to alter them."

The Air Corps was not difficult. Already in good shape from sports and hard work at the boarding school, I could also accept discipline. Following orders had also been a big part of my life in a well-run boys' boarding school. The school had equipped me with experience and education to do the expected. Eager to make a success in the Air Corps, I worked hard to become as good as they could make me. The Air Corps conditioned and trained me for combat. When the sergeant told me, "What you learn here may save your life," I listened.

"By the way Jones, what were you in civilian life?" Sergeant Carlton asked.

"Happy," I said.

"Smart ass. We'll correct that right away. You are assigned to twelve weeks of basic training. We'll reshape your attitude."

The military service training became everything I expected and more. Basic training stretched a fifteen-hour day. Up early, we fell out for reveille fully dressed and waited in line for breakfast. After breakfast, we marched to the training area where we experienced another wait. The routine became hurry and wait. This nonessential activity ravaged my nervous system. As a trainee, I had looked forward to making an efficient contribution to the war effort. To relate our boot training to winning the war required an elastic mind. Some boys wanted to skip basic training. If they knew what the future held, they would not have been in a rush.

Sam Long occupied the bunk next to mine. "What's the worst month for basic training?" he asked.

"The long March," I said.

"Jones, you're smart enough to be a corporal," Sam said as he flopped down on his bunk.

Taking orders was a large part of training. There seemed to be plenty of noncommissioned officers to give those orders. Training included marching on the parade grounds, hiking for miles, running the obstacle course, listening to lectures, doing calisthenics and watching filmstrips.

A big bully-type drill sergeant pulled together and dominated the routine. He had been selected for his obnoxious personality and his ability to browbeat other members of the human race. Our Sergeant Carlton gave us what I thought to be good advice: "Keep your mind and your bowels open, drink plenty of water, and volunteer for nothing."

Not many people liked the tough training that was designed to prepare the GI mentally and physically for combat. The routine was accepted because each trainee knew the knowledge might help him survive.

In the past, the United States Army logged a tremendous amount of time, training people for combat. The system worked. The drill sergeant thought for the recruit and told him what to do. The training was continuous and punitive until the trainee followed orders without thinking.

Dan Johnson said, "Sergeant Carlton, I want to complain about the slop from the dining hall they call food. That stuff is terrible. They serve such small portions too."

"Come by my room at five o'clock in the morning, before you go on KP, and I will tell you all about the healthy diet you are receiving at this health resort."

Some pretty tough guys in the service were molded to the army's behavior pattern. The training did mold my thinking. It taught me teamwork and competence. It helped me later to do my job, to give as well as take orders.

The drill sergeants worked us hard for three months of basic training. When it was over, my memory of those three months became a big blank. I remembered the crawl under the barbed wire with the live ammo overhead, the trip through the gas chamber, the removal and clearing of the gas mask and some of the inspections. The remainder of the activity is hazy. My tired body responded, and I developed into a well-trained soldier. The days came and went like a dream.

In a class on the M-1 Rifle, the sergeant said, "The projectile from this M-1 will shoot through two feet of solid wood. Jones, when you are crawling under the barbed wire, keep your head down."

Sergeant Carlton, the drill sergeant, had years of experience in turning raw recruits into organized fighting machines. Thirty and well built physically, he knew his trade. The sergeant's speech and manner were uncouth. Accustomed to shouting, he did it with an enthusiasm indicating he liked his job. I also had the feeling he derived some satisfaction in the discomfort of others.

Sergeant Carlton had been in the army before the war started and had come up the hard way. He did everything by army regulations. His vocabulary contained technical army words mixed with his own brand of bad English. He was six feet tall with big hands and forearms, and his face and eyes were hard. If he ever smiled, he did it in his room. A smile would have cracked his face.

The sergeant browbeat the squad by browbeating one of its members. He'd pick someone a little stuck on himself, take him apart and generally make him appear an idiot. Sometimes this technique backfired.

At roll call one morning, Tom Muse did not sound off at the proper sound level and with the precise military clip he had been taught.

Sergeant Carlton said, "Private Muse, let me hear that again."

Tom said, "Here," in a medium voice.

The sergeant said, "Muse! Get the shit out of your mouth and talk like a man. You sound like a queer. Now let me hear you again."

"Here!" Muse responded a fraction louder, but it was not good enough for the sergeant.

"Muse, we are all standing here waiting for you, a queer, to talk like a man," he said. "Now sound off loud enough for the colonel to hear you in the next compound."

Muse's "here" was just a little louder but still not good enough for the sergeant.

The sergeant said, "I want you to admit before the entire squad that you are an asshole. So I want you to say, 'I am an asshole' ten times."

In a very composed voice, Tom Muse said, "Sergeant, I'm trying to be a soldier. You are rough on me. I haven't done anything wrong. I don't understand why you are picking on me. It's not nice to call someone an asshole. I can't say that. I am not an asshole."

He said, "Private, if I want an opinion out of you, I will ask. If I say you are an asshole, you are an asshole. You are at attention and will not move or speak until I give you permission."

Everyone stood at attention through the several minutes it required for this confrontation.

Carlton said, "Muse, step out of formation and come up here."

Muse did as he was told and stood before the sergeant.

He continued, "I am putting you on the dirtiest, nastiest detail I can find. You will be sorry you ever met me. From now on your ass is mine. Before I am through with you, you will beg to be called an asshole. You remain at attention until I return. At that time, you and I will have it out."

The sergeant allowed Muse to rejoin the formation and the school schedule later, but he was a challenge to the sergeant. The sergeant had every intention of breaking this man.

For insubordination, he ordered Private Muse to take a five-mile hike with a full pack after the training routine for the day. Muse dressed out, waited until the last minute, then went in to see the sergeant.

"Sergeant," he said. "The regulations state you can't send me out alone. You are required to go with me."

Much to his dismay, Sergeant Carlton also made the hike.

Sergeant Carlton wasn't the best-liked drill instructor. His loud voice and overbearing manner did little to ingratiate him to his squad.

He stepped particularly on the toes of Sam Long, a friend of mine who had worked as a photographer before joining the Air Corps. Sam and I put our heads together to decide how we could cause the sergeant embarrassment and not get caught. If we could photograph him doing something which was not manly or would lower his image as a drill sergeant, we would consider that a success.

We formulated a plan whereby we would have some ugly girl come, throw her arms around him and kiss him, so we could photograph the action.

Sam and I didn't know any ugly girls. In fact, we didn't know any girls at all except the one I met in the PX. Perhaps I could talk her into calling Sergeant Carlton and setting him up for our scheme. However, the girl at the PX was rather nice looking.

This prank had to occur while the boys were on a pass in town to facilitate the photograph with an ugly woman. We would have to get the sergeant drunk. First, we would have to find an ugly woman and bribe her. This prank was taking on the characteristics of hard work and high adventure. There was some doubt we could pull it off.

"Let's photograph them separately and put them together in a patched-up photo," Sam said.

Sam was able to get a photograph of the sergeant with his arm around the shoulder of a friend. The friend was cut out and the ugly woman cut in. I spent hours looking in a rundown section of Biloxi and finally settled on a woman with no teeth, stringy black hair and a wart on her nose. She was perfect in all details. Her dress was a disaster area. Her sagging breasts were held up by her potbelly. This unwholesome woman would not let anyone forget her feet and legs. A sagging stocking on her left leg and high-top tennis shoes on her feet gave new meaning to ugly. I'd seen ugly, but this was ugly, ugly.

Sam cut in the picture so that Sergeant Carlton still had his arm around a friend. After the pictures were glued together, we needed a photograph made of the paste-up. Sam called on his friends at the base photo lab and took them into his confidence. They happily processed five eight by tens of the sergeant and the girl Sam had cut into his picture.

To maximize the impact of our prank, the five photos had to be posted as quickly as possible after the day's routine but before chow.

Sam and I took three other guys into our confidence that had received ill treatment from the sergeant. Each agreed to post one photograph, and Sam and I took one each.

When the sergeant walked into the shower, I sprinted to the mess hall and posted one picture there. The photograph stood out among the printed material. One was posted in the compound on the south end of our building, one on the bulletin board on the north end of the building, one at the base theater, and the last one was put up in our barracks.

With all the pictures in place, the pranksters waited for the excitement to occur.

Sergeant Carlton missed the bulletin board in the barracks. The squad fell out and marched to the mess hall in formation. In order to get into the mess hall, the recruits had to pass the mess hall bulletin board. The sergeant didn't see the picture but the men from his barracks did as they filed past. They were laughing and pointing to the sergeant. He came over to see what had caused the disturbance.

When the sergeant saw himself with his arm around that ugly woman he said, "Some SOB! Some SOB is going to get it!" He opened the display, took out the picture and tore it into small pieces. Then he looked at his squad.

"Did any of you men have anything to do with this?" he asked.

Everyone shook his head. One boy said, "It was here before we arrived at the mess hall."

Sergeant Carlton would have believed that story if he had not seen the same picture on the bulletin board at the north end of the barracks. When he got around to the south bulletin board, there was a crowd around it, laughing and speculating as to how it got there.

One recruit made the mistake of saying, "She's not half bad, Sergeant."

He said, "Wilson, you go on KP at five o'clock tomorrow morning."

The sergeant destroyed that picture.

When he came into the barracks, he met the same scene with everyone laughing and speculating as to how the picture appeared from nowhere. Then the sergeant suspected his own men.

He called everyone in, and the squad lined up on each side of the central corridor the length of the barracks between the bunks. After calling us to attention, he said, "Men, now listen up and listen good. I'm gonna find the SOB who did this. If I don't find him, you SOBs are gonna stay here all night at attention. Now make it easy on yourselves and tell me what you know."

His authoritative voice was strong and loud enough to be

heard anywhere in the barracks. For the next forty-five minutes, Sergeant Carlton walked up and down the corridor, giving the squad hell, spewing out army language like a pro. No one cracked. Very few people knew about it. Those who did were involved.

After an hour, the sergeant got tired and said, "At ease, dismissed." He said, "I will find out who did it, and when I do . . ." But the sergeant never found out who originated the prank.

Long lines were a part of army life. Waiting in line was standard procedure for almost everything. There was a line at the shower, a line at the mess hall, a line at the PX. In fact, a line became a must for all those functions necessary to life in the service.

Waiting for anything is stressful for most people. If someone ducked in line to shorten his wait, he would suffer a hard time. Most fights in the service started in the chow line. Sometimes a recruit had to fight just to stay in the line. If the other fellows thought someone wouldn't fight, they would push him out of line and force him to go to the rear. It became necessary to have a scrap now and then just to show the troublemakers you owned a pair of balls.

My time to be tested in the chow line arrived. Virgil Vanic, a recruit back of me, pushed me out of line and yelled, "Jones, you can't break in line in front of me." The other guys around knew I had not broken in line but would not take sides. I had two choices—go to the end of the line, or fight. I tried to get back in line. Virgil pushed me out again. He was heavier than I and a lot meaner.

Pushing back, I tried to stay in line. Virgil grabbed me around the neck, threw me down on the ground and held me there. My right arm became free. I used it to pound Virgil in the face. My fourth punch got him in the nose, and it began to bleed. He turned me loose. Virgil got up and stood with his hands by his sides made into fists. Blood was running from his nose down his neck onto his clothes.

"Jones, you want fight," he said. "You know it. I know it. If you want to fight, just hit me. I'll give you the first punch."

The more Virgil talked, the braver he became. He said, "If you want to make something out of this, just hit me."

I swung hard and put the weight of my shoulder in the punch. Virgil went back on his ass. Then he got up and looked around for something to use as a weapon. At this time some of the boys urged Virgil to go back to the barracks and wash the blood off his mouth and face. The fight had drawn a crowd of the GIs in line. No one of authority had been alerted. Luck was with us. The incident blew over. No one tried to push me out of line again.

One of the most outrageous indignities ever forced on a GI was the short-arm inspection. All recruits lined up, naked in single file, and moved up one at a time to an army doctor.

The doctor said to the recruit, "Skin it back and milk it down."

The logic behind this degradation was that if the person had venereal disease, there would be pus that could be detected. A canker sore is also an indication of VD. Very few cases turned up in these inspections. If a GI had VD, he usually turned himself in. Penicillin had been invented, and treatment was available.

Sam Long said, "These monthly short-arm inspections are a great waste of time. Even the physical examination every three months is too much. Do you realize how much of our time in the service is spent naked? We take it off more often than a stripper, and we do it for nothing."

"Sam, every time I show my balls for this Air Corps routine," I said, "I lose some modesty. This constant exposure leaves me less concerned. With each inspection, I am less and less embarrassed. When someone says, 'Turn your head and cough' while they feel my balls for a hernia, it no longer causes me distress."

Our first barracks inspection was scheduled. The barracks became a beehive of activity. The Air Corps had no positive incentives to ensure performance. However, they had many penalties and could take away the few privileges available. If someone were gigged in the barracks inspection, the whole outfit had to suffer. The people who cared did a little inspecting on their own to make sure the goof-offs would pass.

"Sam," I said, "let's have an inspection before the inspection. We'll pick three other guys and make an inspection to make sure we don't all get gigged for some stupid mistake by one of our own."

We called the squad together in the barracks before lunch. "The desire to avoid punishment is a good reason to get together guys," Sam said. "I think it can work. An inspection is about cleanliness and order. We'll scrub the inside walls and floor with soap and water with GI brushes. The windows will be spotless. The bunks will be made in military fashion so that when the blanket is pulled tight, a coin dropped on the blanket will bounce. Shoes will be shined and footlockers organized. Each recruit will stand a minute inspection of his person—eyes shall always to be front and center. Any inspection of the inspector's team is not permitted. Any man's indiscretion that can earn a gig will be eliminated. Unless the inspecting officer wants to be an SOB, we'll be in good shape."

Our barracks passed with some margin. However, on a later inspection the barracks was gigged because Bob Watson wore his hair too long.

After the hike and the other punishment, Sam Long said, "You are the offender, Bob. We'll give you a haircut short enough to satisfy the most discriminating drill sergeant. Bob," Sam continued, "we notice you are reluctant to bathe and walk around with a noticeable body odor. While we have you down on the latrine floor, we also plan to give you a bath with GI soap and a scrub brush. It will be two weeks before your skin loses its healthy red glow. Bob, we expect your personal hygiene and grooming to improve tremendously. May we have your promise on that?"

"Yes," Bob agreed.

In my spare time I read. The year 1942 wasn't bad for books. Lloyd C. Douglas wrote a bestseller, *The Robe*. Daphne du Maurier spiced up the bookstore with *Frenchmen's Creek*. Sergeant Carlton's radio was playing "Begin the Beguine." The Hit Parade was on with Dorothy Collins singing. The music could make one homesick.

George Shelton dropped down on the adjacent bunk and said to me, "What are you thinking about?"

George was above medium height and weight but not fat. With his GI haircut, the sharp angles of his face gave him an austere look. He had a nervous habit of scratching his right ear.

Startled, I looked up and said, "Thinking about my family and school chums. Would they really miss me if I got killed?"

"You aren't worried about getting killed, are you?"

"I'll worry when I see the Grim Reaper up close.

"My mom would cry. It's not in my plans to get killed. I've so much planned to do. It's very important to prove my dad wrong. Can't do all those things if I get killed."

George said, "You are in the Air Corps. You are safe. Air Corps people live way past the next cocktail hour."

"Tell me about your life before you came into the service," I asked.

"There isn't much to tell," George said. "I've got one mother, one father, two brothers and a sister. Just graduated from high school and was working as a soda jerk in a drugstore when the word came from Uncle Sam. Jobs were hard to get. I was delighted when Uncle Sam came along and said, 'Boy, we want you.' A great relief, the summons gave me a chance to get out of that rut. I would have tried to go to college, maybe as a co-op student. That drugstore became a drag. However, occasionally, good-looking chicks came in to brighten my day. For them I would show off with something extra. A banana split was my specialty. The ice cream, nuts, syrup and whipping cream were enough for two."

"You sound like you're glad to be in the Air Corps."

"I am."

"Do you miss your family?" I asked.

"Sure, but I don't want to go back to that damn drugstore."

"How do you really feel about being in the Air Corps? Are you afraid of how you'll act in combat?"

"Don't even think about it. You can bet your ass that I'll do everything possible to dodge those German shells and inflict as much pain on the enemy as possible."

George was like most guys I met in the service. I was with them for a short time, and then they were transferred.

The army required exercise. The instructors developed formats and positions. They did it by the numbers. They exercised us until our tongues hung out.

On the exercise field the squad was doing side-straddle hops by the numbers. The drill instructor had the great idea to match up alternate rows of troops by having them face each other and engage in some friendly hand-to-hand combat.

The instructor yelled, "Now try your jujitsu on the GI facing you."

Most GIs looked upon this friendly combat as a chance to goof off. I thought it might be fun to try my talents in a real situation.

My 160 pounds was all muscle, and I had received some training in wrestling. Working as a tile setter's helper one summer from high school with Larson Key, a second cousin, I received some experience in how to protect myself. Larson was a wrestler. Not high on the professional level, he had made a few bucks by winning matches in his class.

"Larson," I said, "when you put your hands down by your sides you are shaped like a human wedge."

"That is because I have overdeveloped my arms and shoulders," he said. "We will be alone together a lot this summer. While we are waiting for material or for a project to be ready, I can give you some lessons in wrestling which will be helpful in later life."

"I'd be happy to learn anything you could teach me," I said, not completely sure I wanted to take the punishment that came with the lessons.

Larson needed practice, and I was the only person available. I learned both the devastating effects of a body slam and how to protect myself in the event one was applied. To anticipate a person's movements and to use this knowledge against the challenger was part of my summer education.

The GI I now faced was six feet two inches and must have weighed 190 pounds. Arms out front and bodies arched forward, we circled each other, looking for an opening. With my left hand, I pointed down and to the left. My opponent looked in that direction. I reached out, took his left hand by the bottom of the palm with my right hand and my thumb inside his fist. I yanked him fast forward to my left and threw my right armpit over his shoulder, simultaneously lowering my shoulder on his, raising and twisting his arm.

My opponent fell face down in the sand. He yelled his displeasure as I applied the leverage to this arm. My attack had been fast and aggressive. It had not been my intention to hurt my opponent, but I had. Easier to overcome than I anticipated, my feeling of mastery and well-being was short lived. This guy with a hurt ego and sand on his face would have to be released.

The instructor blew the whistle to break. With my opponent loose, I now realized the danger. My mind had not followed the event through. Now I was in serious trouble. My opponent had sand on his face and blood in his eye.

The big guy spat sand out of his mouth and said, "You son of a bitch, I'll get you next time."

There wasn't time for me to apologize. We were back in line again and doing our left face, so we could try again this friendly practice of the martial arts. My health would not be in jeopardy if I broke away for a fast five-mile run. It required guts to remain in the area and take the punishment that was sure to come.

With a scowl on his face, my opponent became eager for combat and jumped just ahead of the whistle. Sensitive to the danger, my mind raced. How could I get out of this fight and not have my body broken into small pieces?

The big fellow came at me like a bull with his head down. I jumped to one side. The weight of his plunge took him to the ground. Concerned for the family I planned to have some day, I decided direct action was necessary. Other parts of the world looked safer. Darting through the formation out of his reach and sight seemed advisable.

Later, the instructor blew the whistle and once again troops lined up. This time I was in a line across the field facing a short, slow boy who had no desire to distinguish himself as a master of the martial arts. Combat with this soldier did not appear to be hazardous. He was content to posture and so was I.

The instructor blew the whistle again and yelled, "Dismissed."

My peripheral vision picked out my first opponent looking for me. He seemed very eager to make contact. I fell in with some friends and walked casually back to the barracks and was delighted that I never saw this big guy again.

George Shelton asked, "John, are you ready for graduation? Soon they will pronounce you a soldier. You should be proud."

Back in the barracks our drill sergeant gave his farewell speech. "You guys have been fed wholesome food in a controlled environment with rest, plenty of fresh air and exercise. You have responded to this training and are in better condition than you were when you came to us. We did what we could for you. Now it is up to you. We wish you the best of luck."

We were in better health. Our attitude hadn't changed much. We knew now we would have to do it the Air Corps way.

With basic training behind us, we trainees could move on to more specialized training. At the same base, I took a ten-week course in airplane mechanics.

George Shelton said, "The army has a different idea about schooling. The student is given tests to determine what he can do and how well. If the student doesn't learn the subject being taught, it's the instructor's fault. The rationale is if the student has the ability to learn as shown by the test, the teaching process should be tailored to develop interest and learning. The material to be learned is broken down into digestible segments for easy assimilation. It has to be the fault of the instructor if the student doesn't learn."

"Bull. You're kidding. It's up to the individual to develop his own interest and study the material," I said.

"That's not the Air Corps way," he said.

"In the classroom, the instructors were well trained. The airplane has been dissected into systems to make the subject simple," the instructor said. "The flap-lowering mechanism is an example of how the flaps could be moved down or up. The system is hydraulic, electric or manual. The prime system and the back-up systems are illustrated. Each system is made into a mock-up and attached to a board, a wonderful way to learn fast."

"Well I've learned fast. How about you, Sam Long?"

"Me, too."

"Mock-ups are an easy way to learn," I said, "but how about those tech orders?"

"Those tech orders are for the birds," George Shelton said. "A set of tech orders are available for each type of aircraft. Carry one around with you. The exercise is the most important thing you will receive from a close association with the big book." He continued, "They were written for the air force by Phi Beta Kappa. Nothing was omitted. They were intended to be easy to read, instructive, and useful. Most maintenance people know to read them only as a last resort and with skepticism."

"I can agree with that. The army routine of getting up, having breakfast, going to class, spiced with five-mile hikes, calisthenics, filmstrips on VD and marching is a big pain in the ass. Why the hell do we have to march everywhere in formation? It's exhausting and guaranteed to give you the red ass. The instructor says 'it's useful for our future army experience.'"

"Don't know," George said. "I plan to learn as much as I can. They do teach teamwork—doing things together." "Teamwork with a bunch of GIs is not the highest or most enjoyable use of time," I said. "Teamwork does serve a purpose. The training received in the air force is a good foundation in discipline and can be useful for a guy's future. The discipline learned here could make it possible to compete when you look for a job."

"Cousin Elmo told me," I said, "A three-year hitch in the army is like college without an English department."

Turning to George sitting on the next bunk, I asked, "George, tell me we are not stuck forever on this base. Surely, an airman's life is not all blood and guts training. We should have some free time for adventure of other sorts. When do we get a pass into town?"

George responded, "One of man's greatest adventures is his contact with the opposite sex. I'm not about to miss out on that adventure when opportunity knocks. I understand leave will be granted this weekend."

The time passed quickly. Soon mechanic's school was over, and we were on orders to attend gunnery school in Laredo, Texas. I was eager to shoot at something.

Elevation in rank came quickly. When someone yelled, "Sergeant," I looked around for the sergeant. With an increase in rank came an increase in pay. We all could use the extra money.

To keep the public informed, President Roosevelt made little speeches on the radio he called "fireside chats." He spoke in eloquent terms about making the world safe for democracy. "We are depending on our boys in the service to defeat the enemy," President Roosevelt said.

If the world depended on me, it was in bad shape I thought. Oddly enough, the world really did depend on me and a few million other GIs like me.

I felt the excitement of the time as the days slipped away and my turn at combat approached. Would it really be as bad as we had heard?

At our next base near the Mexican border, I learned that the area contained more than a gunnery school. A trip across the border to a brothel was educational.

CHAPTER
SIX

Laredo, Texas, was our next base for training. It's the only place in the world where the wind blows dust around during a rain. There is nothing to obstruct the view but a few cacti. The sky comes down with a bang and smashes the horizon into a thin gray line almost obscured by the blowing dust. It is a country of big sky and sand.

Before entering, I looked around at the air base at Laredo. The temporary buildings had a hot and dry look. The outside looked as though someone planted grass and only cacti came up. The construction and landscape were austere and naked, sharply outlined by the strong midafternoon shadows. The place looked deserted until the troops filed out of the barracks.

Next day, we continued our routine of exercising and marching. Machine guns, both thirty and fifty caliber, turrets and their maintenance were included in the class. Here again the Air Corps training routine was applied. The classes were small with mock-ups and cut-aways to show how each piece of equipment operated. Sergeant Runson, our instructor in this phase, was thirty and typical army cadre. He was well qualified in his subject.

"It is good of you to come," Sergeant Runson said.

"I only came to find out when vacation starts," I said.

"Jones, we have made this course so simple even you can understand the presentation," the sergeant said. "We will be using mock-ups of the turrets and the guns. You will learn to assemble and disassemble these guns blindfolded. You will also learn the names of all the parts and their functions."

"Sergeant, could I switch to female anatomy? Then I could really develop an interest in learning all the parts and their function. These machine guns leave me a little cold."

"Jones, keep your mind on the subject and research the female parts on your own time."

Ed Daughtry, a boy I met earlier in my class, was small and outspoken. He was from South Carolina, and a silly grin lit up his pointed face when he said, "The schooling is interesting and the procedures are easy to follow, but God, that's a hell of a lot of stuff to learn in a short time. We only get twelve weeks. What are we gonna do?"

"Show the sergeant how smart you are. Learn it all," I said as I got up from my bunk and walked around.

Spare time was available just before lights out. The trainees used this time for bull sessions and letter writing. The bunks were lined up three feet apart, perpendicular to the central corridor with a footlocker at the corridor end of the bunk. The closeness facilitated conversation, and the boys talked freely of the day's events while reclining on their bunks.

"Sergeant Runson will have to get it through his head, we can be pushed only so far," another student, Ron Bloom, said from his bunk. Ron was tall, soft spoken and from Lynn, Massachusetts.

"Some shinola, he is going to push as hard as he damn well pleases," Crimes added from two bunks down. "This is the Air Corps. Make up your mind to get your ass in the learning mode." Crimes was a rough-looking, ex-rodeo rider.

"Crimes, how do you know so much about Air Corps teaching?" Ron asked.

"My mom told me."

"You mean this is not the Boy Scouts of America? I joined the wrong outfit," I said.

Back in the barracks, John Roberts, a lanky boy from the Kansas farm country, said, "Have you guys seen that girl down at the PX? She's really great. She has milk jugs the size of large grapefruits and is good looking too. That's a girl you wouldn't kick out of bed."

Sam Brown, from Ohio, spoke up, "That's nothing. My girl is prettier. She has tits the size of eggs."

"Fried?" I asked.

"You don't need any more than you can get in your mouth," Sam said.

Roy Edwards, a boy from South Carolina, spoke up and said, "Just got a letter from my girlfriend. She wants to get married."

A loudmouth from the other side of the group yelled, "Roy, who the hell would want to marry you? She must be ugly."

"She's not ugly," Roy responded. "She's just a little bit pregnant."

Moose asked, "How the hell could she get pregnant with you in the service?"

John Roberts said, "It was done by proxy."

"I don't understand that word, proxy." Roy answered. "I've been away six months and this is the first time she brought it up."

"You have a friend in your hometown," continued John. "He helped you."

"When it comes to screwing, I don't need no help," Roy said. "But I sure do like that girl."

Sergeant Allen, the barracks chief, walked in. His personality was smooth for a training sergeant. His military bearing and physical build indicated basic army cadre.

Roy said, "Sergeant, we sure are glad to see you. When can we go into town?"

"Shit. Roy, you just got here, and you want to leave," Allen replied. "You don't like our little home away from home? It'll be at least two weeks before you can be trusted in town. Besides, you might want to go across the border and get some of that Mexican stuff. There's a good chance if you do you'll get a case of VD along with it. Edwards, can you handle that stuff? Your pecker will rot off up to your belly."

"I don't want nothing to happen to that thing. It's the only one I got," Roy said as he looked up at Sergeant Allen standing in the middle of the barracks.

"If you want to keep it safe, you had better keep it in your pants," Sergeant Allen said. "Wait 'til you see the VD films again. It'll remind you of the danger. Lights out. Get your asses in the sack."

The next day on the firing range, Sergeant Allen said, "Today, to train the eye and the hand, you will shoot trap skeet with a shotgun with a double-pistol-grip mount on the stock. The gun is mounted with a swivel on a post, to simulate the waist gun on a B-24. Learn as much as you can. It may save your life."

After shooting two boxes of shotgun shells I became good at hitting the clay pigeons they threw out. This was fun, and it didn't cost me anything.

Sergeant Allen found our group of ten students and said, "Next, you will be placed in a pick-up truck and driven through a skeet range. Clay pigeons come at you from all directions from underground traps. We ask that you shoot and shoot quickly. Don't shoot the boys operating the traps and don't shoot each other."

The pick-up truck drove slowly through the skeet range full of bunkers, and I fired 175 rounds of ammo from a handheld, twelve-gauge shotgun. This one day of recreation left my right shoulder black and blue. This type of shooting was great fun. I learned to shoot well. My eye-and-hand coordination improved.

"Hey! This shooting is fun. It's new and different, but wait for the excitement of flying around in a two-place trainer and shooting at a wind sock towed by another trainer," Daughtry said. "Runson, our flight sergeant, is gonna tell you not to shoot the towing plane. If you shoot the pilot of the towing plane, you make a B on the course. I've heard the pilots of these planes are very nervous people. They let the wind sock out on a long, long cable—how long. Now it takes them two days to fly by."

Back in the barracks after a full day of flying, Daughtry said, "Did you shoot down any friendly aircraft, John?"

"No," I replied from my horizontal position on my bunk. "I couldn't tell if my tracer rounds were going under or over the target. I almost stopped sighting and started hosing the target. How did you like flying?"

"Great!" Daughtry said as he sat on my footlocker and looked at me. "Shooting that sock was a breeze. I could have done better but couldn't get my eye back of the gun to sight properly."

"What kept you from getting your eye back of the machine gun?" I asked.

"The gun mounted on the front rim of the rear cockpit couldn't be moved. In order to shoot at the sock from the side, I had to put my leg out of the cockpit to sight down the gun barrel."

"Daughtry, that gun is mounted on a ring and can be moved to any point. The mount has a lock that will hold it in any position."

"Damn! I wondered about that," Daughtry exclaimed. "I had to unfasten my gunnery safety belt and risk my family jewels to hit the target. Cold air blew up my pant's leg, causing icicles on my pecker."

"Well, if you made it today, you will do better tomorrow," I said, trying to talk through my laughter.

"My pilot was a little bored with the whole idea of training and did a few slow rolls before we came in to land. This maneuver made the plane turn like a corkscrew.

This was the first time I've flown in an airplane," I said. "The shock of looking straight down, upside down out of an open cockpit strapped in only by a seat belt, was less than reassuring. This was something to write home about. My fingers made dents in the metal that surrounded the cockpit."

As I became accustomed to flying, I looked forward to the time in the air. As the course wound down, I loved being in an airplane. Then my pilot took the plane up to nine thousand feet and did an inside loop. Stalling out at the top, we dropped several thousand feet into a flat spin. I was dizzy as my maiden aunt. I could see the ground coming up like a freight train. My hand was on the seat belt for a quick release, but it wasn't required.

The pilot kicked the right rudder and brought the plane out of the spin and the fall. I felt the skin on my face pull down and the blood drained out of my head for a quick black out as the pilot pulled back on the stick. Over the intercom to the pilot, I said, "There is a little pile in my pants that belongs to you."

Normal flying excited me enough. This pilot almost wrecked my newfound confidence. Later I asked the pilot why he saved that special treat for me.

"Just wanted to see if you could take it, and you took it very well. With a little training you could be up there flying the plane yourself."

"Do they also let you pull the target?"

"You bet," he said. "The second time I pulled that thing, tragedy missed its opportunity. Some gunner put four holes in my tail section. I let the cable out another two hundred feet and insisted that the gunner who made the holes flunk the course."

Our training group had been cooped up on the base for a month. Finally, we were issued passes to go into Laredo, Texas. The boys were excited. Interesting tales about available women across the border were circulated in the camp. These sexually deprived boys stood around with their mouths open, listening to this local trivial nonsense from the permanent cadre.

Training films were shown before passes were issued. The group scheduled for passes into town were assembled and shown pictures of the advanced stages of syphilis and gonorrhea. The film made me sick as I watched. The entire lesson was designed to kill all desire for sex. Once in town we quickly forgot the film. The Air Corps' concern didn't stop there. The sergeant gave each trainee the pro-station location, so a GI could get a prophylactic after sex if he were lucky enough to score.

A prophylactic is a process performed after sex and will prevent VD. Those GIs who get drunk don't always avail themselves of this protection, and some suffered the indignity of VD. Because of the films, most GIs ran to the nearest pro-station. No one in his right mind wanted to see his organ rot off.

Ron, Daughtry and I wanted to change our luck and soak up some Mexican culture. We took a taxi into Nuevo Laredo.

An English-speaking pimp asked, "Want to see a show, Joe? Good show. You like. Guarantee you like."

"What kind of show?" Ron asked.

"Girls with no clothes act. Make you sexy. Make you want sex bad. You be surprised at good show. Cost little money. How about it?"

"Might be worth a look," Ron said.

We three walked to a rundown part of the city with the pimp. The housing was like barracks and was called Boys Town because of the clientele. The inhabitants were mainly prostitutes and their pimps.

"I'm looking for a girl with a Coke-bottle figure," I said.

"Prepare yourself for Miss Milk Bottle," Daughrty said.

We were asked to wait in a dimly lit room with four other GIs. I looked at the wooden walls. Deposits of grime from the last century decorated the surface. Everything suggested disorganized squalor. The four dilapidated sofa chairs were dirty with a slick look to the fabric. A soiled mat lay on the wood floor near a wall. Five minutes later two rough-looking women came in and sat on the mat. The onlookers stood in a semicircle, watching the action before them with great expectation.

I chose not to sit on any of the chairs and avoided contact with all surfaces. A record player with a scratched record provided music for the occasion. The beat was Latin with a good tempo. The girls swayed to the music and took off their clothes, which wasn't much of a surprise or even a treat.

One was about twenty, the other closer to thirty-five. Both were short and dumpy with dirty black hair, sagging skin and dark, heavy, Indian features. The girls looked as though they had not bathed for several months.

"What do you think, Daughtry?" I asked.

"Well, let's put it this way, if they had a beauty contest, no one would win."

"This house and the women look like crap and have done nothing to excite me," Ron said. "Why don't we go? If this is all we get to see, I'm ready to go now."

"Look!" I said. "There's no expression on the faces of the girls. They never smile and look at their brown stained teeth. They need to spend three hours in a beauty shop just to get an estimate."

The girls played with each other to build interest. One girl strapped on a rubber pecker. The other girl played with the rubber pecker and placed it in her body several times. Then one of the girls put an egg up her twat and squeezed it out. "Anyone for scrambled eggs?" the older girl asked.

As the grand finale, they licked each other in the crotch.

"The show, the girls and the surroundings destroyed all my desire for sex for some time," I said. "What did it do for you Daughtry?"

"I enjoyed as much as I could stand," Daughtry said.

We made our way to the door. Turned off by the dirt and squalor, I did not even touch the doorknob as we departed but waited for someone else to open the door.

On the way out, the pimp had asked, "How about it, boys? Are you ready for one of these girls?"

With a deadpan look on his face Daughtry said in a voice filled with irony, "Thank you, kind pimp. We have been overstimulated. The show completely satisfied us. We are now going back to the Air Corps to rest up for two weeks."

Ron scratched his head and adjusted his cap. "Man, I've never seen anything like that. A little goes a long way. Never want to see it again. My skin crawls when I think about those dirty women."

Relieved to be outside, we decided to have a drink. Daughtry said as we boarded a bus back to the base, "If the girls had been pretty, if the place had been cleaner, if they had omitted the egg, if the girls could dance, and if there were real music, the situation might have been to my liking. It may surprise you, but the better a woman looks the longer I look."

Back on the base, the crew thought about graduation scheduled in two weeks. The time passed quickly and gunnery school was over. At Salt Lake City, our next destination, they would assign us to 2ND Air Corps training bases for our third and final training phase.

In less than a week, orders were cut, assigning our class to Sioux City, Iowa, for our final training. Would all of this training bring me closer to death in combat? I wondered.

We would love Sioux City. The girls were nice. Just because a girl allowed me into her bed didn't mean there was sex involved.

CHAPTER
SEVEN

In the middle of the Corn Belt, Sioux City was home to one of the best bases in the 2ND Air Corps. Sioux City's leading hotel, the Corn Husker, gave some indication of what people did in Iowa.

The land was rich, flat, free of trees, and ideal for farming. The banks and businesses was farmer oriented. The local people were friendly and generous with service men and welcomed us into their city and into their homes. These loyal Americans worked hard in the war effort and appreciated our contribution in the military.

When our class arrived, we were assigned barracks, fed and allowed one good night's rest. Next morning, the Air Corps routine continued. The training staff gave us a chance to apply all we had learned. We did march and exercise, but now the greatest emphasis was placed on preparations for combat, which meant flying the planes we were to take into the air war over Europe.

My class and I were assigned to ten-man crews: four officers and six enlisted men.

The 2ND Air Corps final-phase training was no nonsense. Restricted to the base because of the intensity of the training, we continued to learn. This training gave us a chance to get to know the members of our crew and the plane.

"Daughtry, we've been here two days, and we are already two weeks behind." I said.

"Yeah, ain't it the truth. Hell! We took off at two in the morning and flew for eight hours—four hours out, we bombed an imaginary target, then flew the four hours back. We are wearing out our asses learning to find the target, make a bomb run and return to base."

We had just landed, gathered up our gear and headed for the barracks. The weather was cold, and the wind was blowing at twenty knots. We had parked the plane on a hardstand that was some distance from the operations building. As we boarded a truck to take us in, Crimes punched me in the ribs with his index finger and said, "Hey, pal. Wouldn't you like to hold one of those pink, corn-fed, Iowa girls? Wouldn't it be nice to walk into a bar and pick up one of those sweet things?"

"Never been in a bar, and I'm not looking for bad girls."

My upbringing had strongly conditioned me against drinking hard liquor and associating with the wrong kind of women.

"A good girl is good, but a bad girl is better," Crimes continued. "They can't keep us on this base much longer without giving us a pass."

"Bull!" I exclaimed. "This is the army, Mr. Crimes. They can do what they damn well please. Still, I would like to go into town. Might see something worthwhile."

"I like the flying," Daughtry said as we walked into the barracks. "It's inspirational to watch the sun peek over the Iowa farmland. The first light is a glow which changes from gray to azure, then pink, then to warmer tones as the sun presents itself in the east for a new day."

"You sure talk funny," I said. "The pink is very poetic. The best way to fill out a pink slip is with a beautiful female body."

"Jones, the way to make your girlfriend into an outstanding beauty is associate her with a crowd of ugly people," Daughtry said as he dropped down on his bunk and stretched out. "Boy! They sure keep us busy with the training program," Daughtry continued. "Being restricted to the base is a drag. Day after day we train without a letup. My ass is tired."

"Cheer up," I said. "There's a break coming up. Passes will be issued for tomorrow. I haven't seen a girl in months and am so deprived of female companionship just looking at a girl will be a treat."

Next day, Ron Bloom and I caught a ride into Sioux City. When we arrived, we looked for something to do and decided to go to the drugstore and have a milkshake, then perhaps take in a movie.

On the way to the drugstore, we came face to face with two Iowa farm girls. Quick to note their obvious rosy glow of health and well-endowed female attributes, I said, "Hi." However, to be attractive to Ron and me did not require they be models from *Playboy* magazine. The girls were nice looking and seemed to possess all those characteristics that make women attractive to men.

As we met on a ten-foot-wide sidewalk, the girls moved to the right to avoid a head-on collision. Ron and I moved to the left to avoid the same confrontation. All four pedestrians came to an abrupt halt, facing each other.

Ron stood to one side. I said, "This doesn't make any sense. We should all be going in the same direction anyway. We are headed to the drugstore for a milkshake. Want to come along?"

Our genuine smiles and reassuring words seemed to convince the girls we were nice boys and good company. The girls giggled.

The pretty blonde one said, "How do we know you are nice boys?"

"I have a letter from my mom in my pocket," I said with a smile. "She recommends me highly. Would the Air Corps employ bad people to do their job?"

The blonde said as she looked me up and down, "I guess it's okay. My mom did tell me not to talk with soldiers."

"We are not soldiers," I exclaimed. "We are airmen. There is a difference."

I took the blonde by the arm and squired her down the sidewalk in the direction of the drugstore.

"My name is John. I am Mrs. Jones's little boy. Please tell me your name."

The blonde with the pink complexion said with softness in her voice, "I am Nancy Erickson, and my mom doesn't feel an obligation to recommend me. I stand on my own qualifications. The girl with me is Sara Nash."

"Your qualifications look more than adequate to me," I said. "I will accept Mother Nature's recommendation. The handsome boy you see here behind us is Ron Bloom."

Nancy was a pleasure to behold. Her blue eyes, perfect complexion and white teeth were part of a combination of things that worked with nature to produce a wholesome, pretty face. When I was able to look past her face, I saw her body was well formed. Here again, nature had been generous. Her tiny waist and full bosom received my immediate seal of approval.

Nancy said, "We live thirty miles from Sioux City on a corn farm. Usually we go home for the weekend, but now we are working part-time at the Krystal Restaurant and attending Sioux City College. We are both freshmen at the college and live in a rooming house off campus."

It surprised me that Nancy was only seventeen and Sara eighteen. They were my kind of girls. If Ron and I had not seen any girls for a long time, it also appeared that both girls had not been out with boys recently and had a healthy interest in male company.

After a milkshake and several Cokes, the girls seemed reluctant to let us go. We had no plans to deprive them of our company.

"What shall we do?" Nancy asked.

"Let's fight, so we can kiss and make up," I said. "If you are against fighting, I suggest the four of us see a movie together."

"Yes," Nancy said. "That's a good idea." She smiled her approval.

It was difficult to remember the movie or who played in it. It was easy for me to remember Nancy's hand in mine as we watched the movie. Contemplating what could happen later that evening, I got goose bumps on my skin. Holding her close and kissing those slightly puckered, peach, blush lips was also a part of my fantasy. When the movie was over, we walked the girls back to their boarding house.

"Sara and I and another girl occupy this large room with a private bath. There are no kitchen facilities, but sometimes we do bring food to the room. We also have our own outside entrance on the left side of the house." Nancy said.

The two-story Victorian-style abode was across the street from a large house which sat back from the street with a low stone wall at the sidewalk about two feet high ideal for sitting. We all sat down on the low stone wall. The night air was cool, and I snuggled close to Nancy to keep warm. Nancy appeared to like the closeness.

Ron's friend, Sara, said, "It's cold. I am going up to the room. Do you want to come along?"

Ron made up his mind quickly. Standing up, he and Sara walked arm in arm across the street and up the stairs. I watched them as they entered the door to the stair.

I wanted to give Ron at least an hour of privacy before I came up with Nancy, but this became a test of will. The cold stone cooled my body parts in contact. To snuggle together with Nancy on the cold stone wall was not unpleasant. I kept my arm around her. Her warm angora sweater tickled my nose as I kissed her ear and neck. Somewhere on that Iowa farm, this girl learned plenty about kissing—a kiss that turned up my toes with its warmth. That kiss made me forget my silent promise to give Ron privacy.

Nancy said, "I'm ready to go up. We will freeze to death if we stay here much longer."

Thirty minutes by my watch had passed since Ron and Sara had left. If all the conditions were right for Ron to score, he already had.

When Nancy and I entered the room, the lights were low. The right corner of the room contained a double bed. Ron and Sara were stretched out on top of that bed. On the right, near the door, were a dresser, a closet and some chairs and a table. Diagonally across the room from the double bed was a single bed.

Ron appeared to be asleep and didn't speak as we came in. He was on his back with one arm around Sara. His shirt and shoes were off, but his pants were on. The room had the look of a dormitory. The furniture was old and the draperies were bland beige. The sheets on the bed were very clean.

Nancy said, "I will slip into something more comfortable. In the meantime, make yourself at home."

She pointed to the single bed on the left side of the room. My blood pressure jumped ten points. I took my cue from Ron and removed my shirt and shoes and lay flat on the bed. Nancy returned from the bathroom, and the sight of this pretty girl in nightclothes provided an unanticipated treat. Everything about me seemed warm. Lady Luck had been kind to allow this generous gift into my life.

She was wearing a pair of blue pajamas of semitransparent material that molded her gorgeous set of boobs and telegraphed with undiminished clarity the size and perfection of Mother Nature's gifts. The dark pink of her nipples were obvious through the fabric. My thoughts had already created an embarrassing bulge in my pants and made me thankful the lights were low.

Nancy cut out the last light and stepped over me, I was now lying flat on the near side of the bed. She lay down close, pulled the covers over her but did not press her body against mine or kiss me as she had on the stone wall outside.

Ron and Sara continued to act as though they were asleep. In the darkness, I slid my hand under the cover toward the pink nipples. Nancy gently but firmly held my hand and moved it back on my side of the bed. I tried other subterfuges to get a hand over and around her defense. Each time she rejected my overtures. She made me feel as though I were betraying a trust. Perhaps after Ron and Sara were asleep, she would be more cooperative.

Miserably, I lay wide awake in the dark for another hour and tried again, this time a little more aggressively. Those beautiful tits felt soft yet firm, just as perfect as they looked.

Nancy sat up in bed. In a loud whisper she said, "I thought you wanted to sleep."

"Sleep? I can never sleep with you in my bed." I continued, "Okay. I'll go, if you want me to."

She said in an intimate whisper, "No, don't go. It's nice having you here. I love being with you. Please stay."

Hope and optimism were born anew. I lay down and looked at the ceiling some more. After Nancy had gone to sleep, I made more advances. It appeared I was making progress. Then Nancy woke up.

Turning over on her back, she said in a sweet voice, "You are very persistent. Forget about sex and go to sleep."

"I can't forget about sex. Mother Nature did not prepare me to deal with this 'so near and yet so far' situation. I will leave and make you happy."

The thought of giving up without success crippled my thinking and will to resist.

How much longer could I hold on? My pants were wet in front with pre-seminal fluid, and my balls ached. I made two more attempts that she gently but firmly rebuked. Finally, at 5:00 A.M., I got up, put on my shirt and quietly shook Nancy awake.

"Good-bye, love," I said and started to leave.

In a loud whisper, she called me back. "Give me your address, and I'll write."

"Better still," I said, "on our next pass, I'll look you up."

She said, "Okay," and kissed me good-bye.

I pushed myself off the bed, collected Ron and headed for the base.

Ron said, "How did you do?"

"A man can never tell about a girl until he is alone with her, and after that he shouldn't," I said.

"Ah!" He said.

At the first parked car, I reached down and tried to lift the front end. The effort made me feel better.

I didn't look forward to a rematch. I had been defeated at my own game. Perhaps a new conquest should be considered.

Never in my life did I expect to be involved in a minor airplane crash with Jimmy Stewart, but the unexpected happened.

CHAPTER EIGHT

I developed some confidence in my crew and in flying, but something happened and shattered that "feel good" feeling.

Another group was getting their third-phase training at our base. Further along in their training, they wanted to show off. One of their squadrons had returned from formation flight training. They wanted to show the world how good they were, and they buzzed the field in formation. The lead plane pulled up too abruptly, and his wingman clipped his tail with his props. The lead plane flew straight up until it lost air speed and dropped back to earth, killing all ten airmen.

I was on the flight line and witnessed the accident. Deeply moved by the knowledge that ten men could die so quickly, I felt tears running down my cheeks, and I was glad our crew seemed to want to pull together now that the assignments were complete.

The first pilot, Brecovitch, set up a meeting of the crew on the hardstand near our plane. Brecovitch set a no-nonsense tone in all matters related to flying. The crew honored his approach in these training activities. We were serious about what we were doing. In spite of several incompatible personalities, we functioned rather well as a crew.

"Since we'll be flying together to destroy the German war machine, perhaps we should get to know each other," Brecovitch said as he stood erect in front of the group seated on the grass. The weather had turned cold, but there was no wind, and the sun was out. "I'll tell you about myself and expect each of you to tell us about who you are. I grew up in the coal-mining region of Pennsylvania. If my personality seems abrupt, it probably is.

Physically, I am six feet tall and in good shape. My skin is rough from the world of hard knocks. I am not afraid of this thing they call the B-24 airplane and am thoroughly dedicated to flying. In fact, I enjoy a little adventure. My obligation to get us there and bring us back is a responsibility I do not take lightly. No one on this crew will be allowed to interfere with that obligation. I am a good Joe, which is my first name." He sat down and pointed to the copilot.

"I am your copilot, and my name is Mike Murphy. You also know I'm Irish and a little uncomfortable flying this B-24 now. I expect my confidence to improve as I gain experience.

"If you see me in the mornings with the plane's oxygen mask pressed tight against my face, you will know I drank too much the night before. Pure oxygen," Mike continued, "is the best thing in the world for a hangover. It oxidizes blood sugar quickly.

"Thirty-two years old with sandy hair, I am cursed with that Irish look: thin white skin with freckles. My medium build is plagued with the beginning of a round stomach," Mike continued as he patted himself on the stomach and ran his hand through his thinning sandy hair. "Hundreds of girls across the country could attest to my ability as a charmer. I am such a loser, health foods make me sick and aspirin gives me a headache."

As he stood to speak, Roy Watson said, "I am your navigator. I'm five eleven and overweight, but you know that. A mouth full of marbles is not the reason for the way I talk. My teeth are stained from chewing tobacco. However, I am smart and a good navigator. There will be occasions you will be happy I am good at my job. Knowing where we are is a comfort, even if we want to be somewhere else.

"First we thought the world was flat. Then we decided it was round. Now we know it's crooked," Roy said and sat down.

Lt. Rufus Graffhen said as he sat erect and looked at the group, "I am your bombardier and not the regular mama's boy you may think. Don't be fooled by my out-of-shape look. Expect me to change that as I run and work out. You noncommissioned crew members are required by Air Corps regulations to call me 'sir.' Please do not precede this 'sir' with an adjective of lesser value. You may say Rufus has no military presence. That's not important. I am smart and good at my job. Give me your cooperation, and I will do my best to hit the target.

"This is a dangerous world we live in. No one gets out alive." Rufus said.

"I am Bob Jackson, your radio operator. At thirty-two and a train engineer before the service, my medium frame is not built for all this rough stuff we experience in the service. Got married before I left home but have no children. Out of place in the Air Corps, I want to get back to the ease and comfort of running a train in the States. My opinions are not strong about anything. However, if you push me I can and will react with vigor."

"John Jones is the name," I said as I stood up. "I am your chief engineer and occupy the top turret during combat. My hundred and sixty-five pounds are in good shape. I intend to stay in shape and do the best job for you possible. My mom recommends me highly."

"I'm glad someone recommends you," Daughtry said with pride. "I'm your ball turret gunner and assistant engineer and proud to be from South Caroline. I worked in an auto parts store. Some of you knuckleheads suggested when I left the auto parts store to come into the service, I forgot some of my parts. That's not true. I'm a good guy and want to be a good friend to all of you.

"I'm lean, excitable and short," Ed said. "My one hundred thirty pounds made me the ideal ball turret gunner. However, I feel uncomfortable in the ball turret. The first flight in the ball turret scared the shit out of me. I'm over that now. I've had a shower. The turret is comfortable to operate. I lay on my back and sight between my legs. The shell of the turret is of one-fourth-inch aluminum, which can stop most of the flak except a direct hit. The turret is designed to be opened from inside the plane in the waste sections with the guns pointed straight down. After entry, the turret is lowered so the door to escape and the guns are below the airplane. In the event of a hit, the turret door is designed to fall away. The safety belt can then be released, and I can bail out of the turret. It is comforting to know I can wear a parachute in the turret.

"On one occasion, I was frightened out of a year's growth when the door came loose but did not fall," Daughtry continued. "On that occasion I did not take my parachute into the turret with me. The turret requires a seat pack."

"Daughtry," I said, "You have just told us more than we wanted to know."

"That's okay. With every conversation, we learn something about our individual crew members and what makes them function," Brecovitch said.

Speaking a very nice-sounding version of the English language, the New England sound, Ron Bloom said, "You may think me slow in my movements, never in a hurry, but I get things done. That's my nature. I am your right waist gunner.

"From Lynn, Massachusetts. I am lean with a slightly uncoordinated look. My six-foot frame makes me overly conscious of my height. My shoulders are hunched to get me down to the operating level of my fifty-caliber machine gun. I can move fast when the situation warrants. If you see me pulling my blond hair and my movements are wild gestures, you will know Daughtry has asked me to get him out of the ball turret again."

"I am Sam J. Logan, the best tail gunner on this crew and love flying. Married to a beautiful tall girl, I miss home and all things that are a part of the good old U.S.A. You know I will not go out with other girls. It is an arrangement I will keep for the duration. You fellows can derive comfort from having me in the back where most attacks are directed.

"I want to make you proud of me and my ability to shoot. Walking with a swagger is my way of saying I'm good. My dry sense of humor is sometimes difficult to understand, but my heart is in the right place. You can depend on me."

"My position is the left waist gunner. I am Crimes. Don't

any of you try to receive credit for my kills because I'm good. Been married and fathered a child and I know the penalty for nonpayment of child support. For thirty days I sat in that dirty jail and hated every minute. My ex-wife came by to enjoy my discomfort and squeeze some more money out of me.

"The jailer asked if I wanted to see her, and I said, 'Yeah, bring her up here, so I can bash her head in against the bars.'

"The judge gave me another thirty days.

"To escape the sentence, I joined the Air Corps. I never graduated from high school and trouble seems to follow me around. I am very good at picking up girls and taking them to bed. If you guys want any pointers, let me know."

"Thank you for being frank with us about what you did before you came to the Air Corps. Do your job, and you won't have any trouble with me," Brecovitch said with concern. "You are dismissed."

The movie star, Second Lieutenant Jimmy Stewart, was our squadron operations officer. Later he was promoted to squadron commander and then group commander.

For the next twelve months, the crew was to see a lot of Lt. Stewart. He led our squadron on air raids over Germany and occupied Europe. Because of his reputation for doing things right, the flyboys felt safer when he flew in the lead aircraft. However, everyone became curious as to his personality traits. He worked hard and tried his best to keep the group plugging for the war effort. It wasn't easy keeping a group of young men inexperienced in combat directed down the same path.

Jimmy Stewart seemed to want to forget his celebrity status. Some people could not. Walking across the compound one day in Sioux City, I witnessed two young girls asking for Jimmy's autograph. He refused and gave them a chewing out.

"I am here as an officer of the Army Air Corps to help in the war effort and would like to spend my time doing just that. Forget about Jimmy Stewart, the actor, for now."

According to gossip around the base, Jimmy Stewart in his private life appeared a loner. To my knowledge, he had no close friends. For recreation, he would get a two-day pass, go to the Officer's Club, drink lots of hard liquor, then go back to the officers' quarters and go to bed. When on the job, he was all business and used the same discipline and dedication that made him a great actor, to become an effective contributor to the war effort.

The crew continued to fly at all hours. We got out of the sack at 3:00 A.M. in the cold night air, dress out, had breakfast and were in the air at 4:30 A.M.

"Today we will fly out, bomb a target, and then fly back," Brecovitch said. "We will repeat our standard practice of selecting a destination to bomb. We will fly there, find the target, bomb the target with imaginary bombs and fly back. There will be no flak and no fighters. The lesson is to repeat the procedure until everyone knows his job. You can't make a hit if you have no aim in life."

The crew continued to learn about the airplane, its fuel-consumption rate, and how much of a bomb load it could get off the ground on runways of different lengths. All information about the plane became important to survival in combat.

"You boys gripe a lot about everything, but our training is high adventure," Logan said as Daughtry and I sat across a table facing him in the NCO Club. "Never in the normal course of living would we be able to do the things we are doing. You guys can feel good about yourselves. You should. You are special. You are Air Corps. You know it and the enemy will soon.

"We have a damn good crew," Logan said. "We have all gotten to know each other. We are learning to work as a team. We train together, eat together, sleep in the same barracks and generally enjoy short leaves together. We know each other's weaknesses and strengths. For the most part, we feel a mutual obligation to the crew for its survival."

"Logan, we will get you a date with a Sioux City girl, so you can get your testosterone level down and talk like the rest of us," I said.

Later the six enlisted men from our crew walked into the NCO Club and sat down at a table. The club was located in a temporary frame building with wood floors, walls and ceiling, a bar on one side, tables and chairs on the other, with a dance floor in the center. As the ranking noncommissioned officer, a technical sergeant, I began a discussion of the abilities of the four officers who made up part of the crew. These officers were the pilot, copilot, navigator and bombardier.

We sat around a round table and made our own drinks from a bottle of Old Granddad, now half empty on the table. With inhibitions lowered by the alcohol, a crew member would likely express his true feelings.

Logan sat up straight and looked at the faces around the table and said, "Don't know about that copilot. Murphy was a fireman who sat on his ass all day, waiting for something to happen. Looks like he is doing the same thing now. Doesn't seem to know what he's about. I would feel better if Brecovitch would let him do a few more landings and takeoffs. I think he is afraid of the airplane."

"Murphy is not as bad as our bombardier," said Ron Bloom with a look of condemnation. "Did you ever see such a mama's boy? That bastard is so soft he looks like a corn-fed pig. How did he ever get to be an officer? The U.S. Air Corps is hard up for qualified people. He is a washout. How is he gonna act in combat?"

"How about our pilot?" I asked. "Do you like him?"

Crimes scratched under his left armpit and piped up, "He damn sure wouldn't win a beauty contest. His complexion looks like he took a shotgun blast in the face. He does seem to know what he is doing in the cockpit. He handles the plane well."

Daughtry laughed his crooked laugh and said, "How about that lard-ass navigator, Roy Watson? He talks like he has a mouth full of shit. So far he has been able to get us back to our base."

Logan responded, "If I'm any judge of brains, Roy has them. When we fly across the Atlantic we will need all of his faculties."

Daughtry said in a sincere voice, "Hey, fellows! We are talking about our crew. Our pilots, navigator and bombardier may not be the best, but they are ours. Lighten up. We are probably not the best either. Think I'll have another drink."

"Daughtry, you're just being modest," I said from the other side of the table. "You know we are a good crew, as good as or better than most of the air crews we've met. Perhaps with a little training, we can improve the performance of every member. I don't have the remotest idea of how my performance will be in combat, but I will be there trying and so will each of you."

"Gentlemen, may I change the subject. We have exhausted this crew confab. We are fortunate to be stationed in Sioux City," Logan said. "It is a marvelous city to be near, big enough to have hotels, stores and restaurants but small enough to be friendly. The people are nice to soldiers."

"In cities with a large population of soldiers, I have found it difficult to meet girls," I said. "The kind mothers would approve. There is no one to handle an introduction. No cousins, aunts, or uncles to make things easy and pave the way for an easy relationship. There are dances at the USO and the Red Cross, but their functions never coincided with my leave. The only way to meet a girl is to go out, find out where they are and pick one up. Sometimes this requires talent and can be fun and adventure."

"Meeting new people and seeing new places always proves adventurous for me," Logan said. "Exploring the area around the base, I met some interesting people, some of them girls. No, I didn't talk about sex. You dumb ass. We talked about the weather."

Ron Bloom and I received leave and again went into Sioux City. Where to go and what to do must be decided on short notice. In the farm belt, recreational facilities were limited. Being off the base was important. If nothing else, we wanted to dress up and look around. We might find someone we liked.

"Do you like bathing beauties?" Ron asked.

"Don't know. I never bathed any."

Again, we tried the drugstore. The design of the seating in the drugstore was horseshoe shaped with booths around the shoe.

An ice cream bar operated out of the open end of the shoe. The décor, modern late thirties with some marble and lots of chrome made the place sparkle. The twenty feet from side to side inside the booths provided plenty circulation room.

Two good-looking girls were seated in a booth across the horseshoe from Ron and me. They smiled back when I looked at them.

This was an encouragement. However, the drugstore was full of people including an air cadet in training for a pilot. Ron and I wanted to approach the girls, but it would be embarrassing to be rebuffed in front of all these people. It would take real nerve to approach the girls.

The air cadet got up, walked over to the girls and said, "Do you have a match?"

One of the girls said, "Yes," smiling sweetly and giving him one.

The scene touched me and promised success. I was delighted when the cadet said, "Thank you," and walked off.

Walking over to the girls' booth, I smiled my brightest and said, "We have just learned that you carry matches. I am making a survey of girls who carry matches. May I ask you a few questions? Please permit me to tell you why. Mom doesn't allow me to smoke. May I sit down?"

The youngest girl responded, "You want to tell us why you don't smoke or why you carry matches?"

"Both."

Everyone in the drugstore heard and saw what was going on and laughed. Some applauded.

The girls were cute. They were short but very wholesome looking.

"With me I have another member of the armed forces," I said. "His name is Ron Bloom. You really should meet him. He is somewhat of an expert on smoking and matches. He smokes and came from a town where they make both matches and cigarettes. He can speak with authority on matches. He read so much about the harmful effect of smoking he stopped reading."

The girls moved over and made room for Ron and me in their booth, and the youngest girl said, "My name is Doris Sorenson, and this is my sister, Sue. It is nice to learn about something from an expert. Are you from our local air base?"

"Yes. We are receiving our third-phase training there," I said. "It is one of the nicest bases we have been assigned. We like Sioux City also."

"Sue has a job, and I have just started to the Iowa State College." Doris said.

Doris was the best looking, so I gave her my undivided attention.

"Now that we've met," I said, "may we invite you to have a Coke and maybe a movie later?"

"How do we know you fellows are nice guys?" Sue said.

"You can really tell by looking, but Ron here has just been declared Mr. Nice Guy at the base by our commander, Colonel Terrell."

"With such a sterling recommendation we accept your offer," Sue said.

"Sergeant Jones, what are you doing for the war effort? Doris asked. "You seem talented for almost anything you choose now or after the war."

"Following orders has been my outstanding talent. Thanks for your confidence. It is my fondest hope that I don't get used up during the war. If there is some left of me when the war is over, I will make my big effort toward a successful career then."

After the movie Ron and I walked the girls home and met their parents. Meeting a girl's parents was usually a bore, but Doris's mother and father were very nice. They accepted us into their home and served cake and ice cream. We enjoyed the evening and were very careful, however, not to tell the parents how we met their daughters.

The parents were around fifty. Doris's mother dressed as a housewife in a cotton dress and sandals with no stockings.

A local bank employed Mr. Sorenson as a bookkeeper. He looked as though he had just arrived at home and removed his hat, coat and tie. He and his wife were not outstanding personalities. They did have the look of solid citizens.

These were girls Ron and I wanted to see again. Sometimes our luck did not bear fruit, and we ended up with girls of questionable reputation. As the poet said, "There is a little girl who had a little curl right in the middle of her forehead. When she was good she was very, very good, but when she was bad, she was marvelous."

Phase training progressed, and the crew scheduled a gunnery range mission out near Casper, Wyoming. The purpose of the mission was to learn to strafe with the ten fifty-caliber machine guns aboard our plane. A gunnery range had been marked off in a remote area. We were to fly to Casper, spend the night and hit the gunnery range on the flight back. Everyone got a chance to shoot. We could tell where our shots were going because they kicked up dust on the range.

On this particular mission, our operation officer, Jimmy Stewart, was flying copilot. He made the trip to evaluate the operation of our crew.

Now a first lieutenant, he had been a pilot before the war. His reputation as a no-nonsense officer would cause him to rise in rank and become group commander and later a two-star general.

Tall and skinny, Jimmy Stewart wore his uniform well. He did not show the doubt or casual behavior of the actor. He was all business and a smile seldom broke the serious expression on his face.

We landed flat broke in Casper, with a rare chance to go into town. Jimmy Stewart came through with a twenty-dollar loan for each of us. After an evening visiting the bars in this wide-open, friendly, western town, the crew returned to the base before midnight.

On the return trip, the pilot flew low. The crew saw a wild and unpopulated country and spotted wild horses by the hundreds.

Upon our arrival in Sioux City, a thunderstorm was in progress over the field. Normally, the pilot flew a pattern for landing at one thousand feet. The pilot lined up with the runway, flew downwind, keeping the lights of the field in view, then turned and flew upwind to land. Jimmy Stewart elected to land the plane from the copilot's side. Because of low visibility, the pilot, Jimmy Stewart, remained in close to keep the lights of the field in view. With the plane at one thousand feet, and in close, the approach angle became steep.

On the final approach, I called off the air speed, as a precautionary measure to let the pilot know if the aircraft's flying speed dropped below eighty miles per hour, the stalling speed with full flaps. The flaps were fully extended with the approach at a steep angle. Just before the plane touched down, a flash of lightning made the night into day. Then night again. The plane hit the ground on the nose wheel just as I called out 150 miles per hour. The plane rocked back on the strut under the tail and became airborne again. To keep the plane on the runway, Jimmy pushed the stick forward. The nose came down and touched the pavement. The nose wheel had been knocked off. The plane skidded down the runway on its nose and the two landing wheels.

Sparks generated by the metal sliding over the pavement made the plane appear to be on fire. The people in the tower did think we were on fire. Any minute I expected to feel the plane blow. However, Lt. Stewart kept his cool and the plane on the runway. I turned off the generators and electrical system so as not to contribute to the already-critical fire hazard. We had no release of fuel.

It was raining hard during the accident. When the plane stopped, the rain stopped. The crew piled out of the airplane in a hurry. Three fire engines rushed to the plane. The fire did not ignite.

The group commander, Col. Terrell, also appeared. He said, "Are you hurt, Jimmy? Is anyone hurt?"

Jimmy said, "Only my pride."

My knee had banged against the armor plate back of the pilot. Happy to be on terra firma, I ignored the pain. The bruise did not require medical attention.

Only one person appeared slightly injured in the landing. Crimes stood up during the final approach to turn on the overhead light in the waist section. He did not follow instructions. The rough landing threw him against the bulkhead at the rear bomb bay. All crew members were assigned positions for seating during landings. Crimes did not act in a responsible way.

The Air Corps placed the airplane in Class 26 and never flew it again.

The army announced late in the afternoon of October 21, 1942, that Captain Eddie Rickenbacker's plane had been lost somewhere in the South Pacific, with only enough gasoline for one hour's flight. Twenty-nine days later, they found Eddie alive, floating in the Pacific, six hundred miles north of the Solomon Islands.

On November 23, from the radio we learned that the U.S. forces had landed in North Africa to help the British. The U.S. Marines smacked the Japs in the Solomon Islands.

Daughtry said, "Can you believe the number-one song on the Hit Parade in 1943 is "Sunday, Monday, or Always," a promise to wait for the boys to come home?

"Paper Doll," "Put Your Arms Around Me Honey" and "Pistol Packing Mama" were also on the Hit Parade."

Crimes said, "Jones, look at this. The English and Americans under Field Marshal Montgomery pushed the Germans out of North Africa into Italy."

Things were not going well for the United States in the Pacific. However, the country continued to build ships, planes and other implements of war. The military experts expected the tide to turn soon.

The grudge with my dad continued to live in my subconscious. For now, my quest for success was on hold. The Air Corps scheduled me for combat in the not-too-distant future; I was not sure how I would react to the tension. If I acted in a cowardly way, I would not be able to live with myself.

We had finished our formal training and were restricted to the base. The officer in charge did allow me to bring my girlfriend to visit.

CHAPTER NINE

The last night before the overseas flight became a time for celebrating. The 445 Bomb Group had finished phase training. We were ready for enemy contact. This is time for sober contemplation of what combat will be, I thought. Tomorrow we would begin our flight to our theater of operations, Great Britain, to do the job we were trained to do—to kill the enemy. Some airmen remained in the barracks and wrote letters home. Others drank in the NCO or Officer's Club. Restricted to the base, we all felt the excitement of the change that had to occur.

I couldn't go into town to see Doris Sorenson. Perhaps she might be able to come to the base.

"Can my girlfriend come to the base?" I asked First Sergeant Mathews.

"The regulations say you can't go into town; they don't say she can't come to visit you at the base," Mathews said.

I was there to meet her taxi just inside the main gate. Doris made a positive response to my telephone call. After paying the taxi driver, we walked to the NCO Club. For a while we danced to the jukebox.

Doris and I had been seeing each other as often as we could. Her good looks and straightforward manner attracted my attention. On each date, I tried the subtle game of seduction with no success. The more she rejected me, the greater an attraction she became. Since our first date, our relationship had warmed up. She was a girl easy to like. Her sweet disposition and agreeable nature caused me to want to place all I owned at her disposal. I even thought of marriage.

Doris lived with her parents and invited me out to her parents' home on several occasions. They lived in a Victorian-style house painted white with green shutters. The front porch covered the entire width of the house and came complete with a swing and rocking chairs. The house had a comfortable look. The occupants were homemakers.

The Victorian style continued inside. The rug, the draperies, sofa and other furniture were of the same style. Even the light fixtures matched the decor.

Doris was short, not more than five feet three with dark hair and eyes. Everything about this girl attracted me. Her face was a reflection of her serious but flexible personality. I loved the shape of her pink lips as they put together words. Her eyes were alert and at times playful but also registered her convictions.

"Doris, you are a born homemaker," I said. "Are you looking for someone to be the other half of a proposed family?"

"Yes," she said with some feeling as she looked at me through her long eyelashes. "However, I am not sure you are the one," and she emphasized "one." "You have many things going for you. You don't seem ready to settle down."

"Things are too unsettled to make plans of a permanent nature," I said. "I find it difficult not to be drawn into your tender trap. You are a very desirable girl.

"Your parents seem to accept me and by their conduct encouraged my relationship with you. On each visit they go all out to see that I enjoyed the visit. Your mom cooked things she knows I like. Your dad treats me with great respect and consideration. I feel at ease with them."

"I'm glad you like them. I do too."

Doris's conversation seemed animated. She could talk about almost anything with conviction. She was either for something or against. I wanted to know how she felt about the future.

Seated in the NCO Club in a quiet corner I looked into her deep blue eyes and said, "Doris, if you could have anything you wanted, what would you ask for?"

She leaned forward, looked into my face and said with her

look of concern, "That's easy. I would wish the war would be over and all the killing stopped."

"That's noble," I responded. "But what about you? What do you want out of life?"

"It would be nice to have an exciting life, to live to the fullest. 'To cut a broad swath,' as Henry David Thoreau suggested. However, that is really not necessary for me. I want to marry someone who loves me, make a life together, have children and then watch those children have children. It would be nice to have grandchildren, to watch them grow into useful and healthy adults."

"Don't you have any desire to make the world better or make a lot of money?" I asked.

"Not really." She laughed with a musical quality in her voice.

"You are not even married and already you are talking about grandchildren. You have condensed your life. You've gone from an upper teenager to old age in less than fifteen minutes. Is that good?"

"We are all going to grow old and die. What we do along the way will make a difference to someone."

"That is too much reality for me. I do not want to think about dying while I am still young. We have plenty of time to think about old age," I said. "If I survive the war, I might think about old age when I'm old."

The experts say, "Man's strongest motivation is the desire to perpetuate the race." Tonight, I felt this urge stronger than at any other time in my life. Perhaps Doris might feel the same way, I thought. She did come to the base, and that was an indication of her feeling.

We danced a short time to the jukebox in the NCO Club and drifted outside hand in hand. It was no accident that our walk ended at the gym. A very secluded spot, deserted and remote from the other activity buildings, the place was also dark. We sat on the built-in benches located at the side entrance. In a close embrace, I felt the warmth of her body. She was returning my kisses with equal enthusiasm. My time was now. I slipped my hand under her sweater and worked my finger under her bra to the very firm nipple. She responded with a slight shiver through her body. Doris wasn't easy, but surely the magic of our last night together would work in my favor.

Doris and I petted for another thirty minutes, warming the air around us. Although she had been matching me kiss for kiss, I had not been able to keep my hand on anything that would foretell success.

Stretched out on the bench with the upper part of her body in my lap, Doris was supported and cuddled by my arms. We were face to face. I looked into that sweet face, those half-closed, tantalizing, blue eyes and said, "You are not going to let me go to war without something to remember you by, are you?"

"You will remember me like this. When you come back, we will get married and, you can have all you want."

This wasn't the answer I wanted. This girl was desirable and knew it. I wasn't upset by her refusal. She lived up to her set of values and earned my admiration.

Trying a new tactic, I said, "Don't you love me?"

"I have the distinct impression you don't love me. If you did, you would not want to make love to me without being married. Do you have another girlfriend at home? You wouldn't want to love me and leave me, would you? What if I got pregnant? Would you claim the baby as yours? I've known you for a short time and feel that you have some things going for you that might be interesting to share."

I could not argue with that logic and stood up, pulled her to me and kissed her again.

"We should be getting back," Doris said.

As we were walking back of the gym, I tripped her and pinned her to the grass. She was very calm and not at all alarmed or angry.

Doris said, "Let me up, or I will scream."

I let her up. She brushed off her dress, and we walked back to the NCO Club. Her manner was so direct, and she knew exactly what she wanted. It wasn't illicit sex.

"John, what do you want to do when you get out of the service?" she asked.

"We have already discussed my future one time. I have been regimented for so long, being a bum and hitchhiking around the U.S.A. might be fun."

"John, be serious," she said. "There must be something you want to do badly, something you could do very well."

"You are serious, and I am jesting," I said. "My dad once told me that I would never be worth a damn. My greatest desire is to prove him wrong. I really want to be an architect."

She directed my interest in sex to a conversation about me. For the next hour, I entertained her by multiplying large numbers in my head, something I learned in business arithmetic in high school. She thought I was a genius.

Time passed too quickly. I felt sad. She might slip through my fingers. Her taxi arrived. I had not scored, had not even gotten to first base, but the evening had been enjoyable, nevertheless.

As the taxi waited, she stood on her tiptoes and kissed me full on the lips.

"Be careful and don't get killed," she said. "Come to see me after the war."

I was touched by the contact with this wholesome, pretty girl. Her honesty and integrity were readily apparent.

After she was gone, I thought of a thousand things I could have said to have made her glad she came. Tomorrow was another day—the big day. My mind switched from my love and admiration for this pretty girl to the reality of war, and the long trip to Great Britain. I headed straight to bed.

Flying across the Atlantic by the southern route would also be adventurous and dangerous.

CHAPTER
TEN

With our phase training over, the group was ready to go. A new plane arrived with our crew's name on it straight from the plant in Michigan. It was the latest B-24G with nose, belly, top and tail turrets. The plane could lift eight thousand pounds of bombs, hold 2,300 gallons of high-test gasoline and cruise at 150 miles per hour. We were delighted with the new airplane. The crew felt the pride of ownership.

"Daughtry," I said, "isn't she a beaut?"

Daughtry laughed. "She looks like a pregnant duck. I hope she will get us there and through our tour of duty. I would feel safer if she had armor plate all around, not just back of the pilot and copilot."

The crew took her up for a test flight. She performed beautifully. Everything was new and in perfect working order.

The B-24G had a stubby fuselage and twin rudders. The Davis wing was high and the main landing gear under the wings supported the belly of the plane thirty inches off the runway. The nose wheel of the tricycle landing gear folded up into the nose section back of the bombardier and the nose turret.

There was also a belly turret that would retract into the waist section. This was Daughtry's position. My position was the top turret over the flight deck.

Brecovitch said, "Jones, I want you to be readily available to me in the event something goes wrong with the aircraft that can be repaired in the air. The aircraft is designed with backup systems. If one system is shot out, I want those other two systems working and ready to use."

I studied the airplane until I knew it and all its systems and how to activate them. On several occasions the crew and I would be thankful for this knowledge.

"John, how do you feel about this trip overseas?" Ron asked as we walked back to the operations building.

Before I could answer, Logan responded, "This is high adventure. We have a pilot who had never flown across a large body of water and a navigator who has never tested his skills on a long journey. Doesn't that build your confidence? The rest of us are just along for the ride."

Radio directional aids had been set up along the route to keep us on the straight and narrow. On one occasion, these aids kept us out of trouble on the flight leg into England.

We said good-bye to Sioux City before dawn next morning. With a full tank of gas, we headed southeast for Warner Robins Air Force Base near Macon, Georgia.

The trip was uneventful and would have been boring had it not been for the beautiful countryside. We were flying at low altitude, sometimes at three hundred feet. I sat in the nose turret and watched for hours as the flat, fertile farmlands of the Midwest changed into hills after we crossed the Mississippi. The Appalachians of Tennessee and north Georgia looked rugged as we made our way southeast.

People were at work in the fields, cars were on the highways and trains were snaking their way across country. All this activity had a purpose. I wondered about my own purpose. Did God have big plans for me? Would I survive this trip—this war? Just ninety miles north of Macon was my hometown—Tucker, Georgia. It pained me to think I might not see my family again. Ennui overcame me, and I went to sleep pondering the weighty questions of my future.

"In a few minutes we will land at Warner Robins and will be welcomed by the ground crew," Brecovitch said over the intercom from the pilot's position. "Other planes from other groups also passed through Warner Robins. These boys know where we are headed. See those wood-frame, single-story buildings? They looked a lot like the other temporary barracks we occupied in Sioux City. The mess hall will feed us well. At least that's what the man in the tower said."

The crew took off at 7:30 A.M., the regimented rows of buildings on the base were obvious as we flew south to Morrison Field, Florida, and caused me to speculate about my own regimentation in general. I tried to focus on the job ahead. There was plenty of time to worry about my education later, if I made it through the war.

Seated in the copilot's seat doing pilot navigation, I picked out landmarks located on the chart. The Saint Mary's River, the Okefenokee Swamp in Georgia and Lake Okeechobee in Florida were easy to spot.

"Morrison Field has a sameness about it," Daughtry said, "like the air base we just left. Jones, do you realize this is the last of our home turf for a long while? Departing Morrison Field is a sad event, like leaving a well-attached girlfriend."

Borinquen Field, Puerto Rico, was our next destination. Puerto Rico is a beautiful little island and blessed with good weather and rich soil. The quaint architecture, the palm trees and tropical vegetation were new to the flight crew. After landing and checking into a barracks, we were issued passes and caught a bus into town. Our first surprise occurred when I asked for rum and Coke and received more rum than Coke. The effect of the extra rum was sudden and mind deadening. Some bizarre activity occurred, but everyone except Crimes limited his drinking to a reasonable amount. Crimes drank himself into a stupor and had to be helped back to the base.

Bob Jackson remarked, "I could spend the rest of my life here with the rum, the sugar cane, and the girls and not be bored."

"We won't have time to be bored," I said. "We take off tomorrow morning at seven o'clock." Our destination: Atkinson Field, British Guyana.

Crimes asked as we stood around in the operations building, "Where the hell is British Guyana?"

Our navigator, Roy Watson, pointed to it on the map and

said, "Guyana is a country on the northeast coast of South America. It is about the size of Idaho and has about as many people. About one-half of the population is black and most of the remainder is East Indians brought to Guyana to work on the plantations. Georgetown is the capital city with a population of more than eighty thousand. English is the official language.

"Someone beat us here," Roy continued. "Some European explorers came to Guyana in the late 1500s. They found Indians living in the area. The Dutch founded a colony. The French and English also claimed the area. In 1854, the British gained control and formed the colony of British Guyana."

"That's interesting," Crimes said. "Can you tell us about the other places we're going?"

Second Lieutenant Roy Watson said, "I will try but give me some time. It would make a lot more sense to tell you about a country as we arrive."

British Guyana gave us the feel of the tropics. The jungle was all around. The barracks were located in a clearing. The lush green foliage came up to each side of the landing strip. The weather was clear when we arrived, but during night it rained hard.

The base was operated by less than twenty service people. The station officers had the few available good-looking girls booked on a permanent basis. Even the lady killer, Crimes, could not change the situation. We were not allowed into Georgetown and restricted to the area surrounding the base.

The crew filled the plane with bananas and other tropical fruit and decided that Georgetown was a drag. We left without regret and flew low over the northern part of Brazil. We could see the native villages spotted in the rough terrain below. When not sleeping, I watched from the flight deck, looking through field glasses at the countryside. We were surprised to find that the northern part of Brazil, except for the coast, was mostly desert. The landing at Belem, Brazil, was a relief after the long, uneventful flight.

The base at Belem was austere. Construction of facilities and amenities had been cut to the minimum. The airstrip had been dug into the desert, and the weather was hot and dry. The barracks were typical with insect screens and no windows. Long overhangs at the eve line kept the rainwater from blowing inside the building. In the event of strong winds, shutters were located near the window openings.

"Fifty men and no women operate the base," Daughtry said. "That's a disappointment. However, they do provide the basic services for flight crews on their way to Great Britain. The food is not all that bad. There are some tropical fruit dishes mixed in the regular army menu. They have provided us with clean bunks and hot showers. What more could a traveler want?"

"Something is missing at this base," I said. "Girls. How about some girls?"

"You will see some when you get to England," Daughtry said.

Roy Watson continued our education with information about the area. He said, "Belem is on the north coast of South America. Almost a third of the population of Brazil lives in the northeast section. There is some desert in this section. The climate is hot the year round. Life is hard for the people of this region, and the per capita income is very low, but the girls are good looking. The natives have been living the same way for hundreds of years.

"The Portuguese settled in Brazil," Roy said. "Because of the treaty with Spain in 1494, Portugal was allowed to keep the eastern part of South America. Portuguese is the official spoken language."

"That's all very interesting. It is great all that stuff happened years ago," Ron said. "I'm ready to fly out of here."

After the airplane's tanks were filled with 90-octane gasoline, it was ready to travel. So was the crew.

Perhaps there would be more to interest us in Natal, Brazil, our next stop. The city of Natal is located further east in the coastal region. Again, we were restricted to the base. Fruit was plentiful and again the crew loaded up the plane with pineapples, oranges, coconuts and bananas, enough to last until England, and some to give away.

In Natal we took an extra two days to pull a twenty-five-hour inspection on the airplane before making our long over-water flight to North Africa.

The long over-water flight had the crew worried. If we ran out of gasoline or if something went wrong with the engines, we would all be killed. I worked with the crew chief to check everything that could be checked—several times. Normally, a twenty-five-hour inspection is a minor inspection. The long over-water flight made it very important.

The pilot, Brecovitch, came by while I was making the inspection and said, "Sergeant, how does she look?"

"From what we can see so far, she is better than when she rolled off the assembly line at Willow Run. We have checked the engines, the generators, and all the systems. We have even checked for potential leaks and other things that might go wrong."

"Remember, we can't land to change an engine out there in the wide blue ocean," he said.

George Noland, the crew chief, was concerned about good maintenance and went by the book. George had been an auto mechanic before the war and loved his work. The maintenance of the plane was important to him; more so because he was also a passenger. We treated this B-24 like it was ours. When we finished, I looked around for some adventure.

Again we were restricted to the base. However, we learned that a native village was located nearby. Where there were people, there were girls. Crimes, Bloom, Daughtry and I dodged the MPs, climbed the fence and took off in search of romance.

We found a fat old woman who promised to fix us up with some good-looking girls. She had a sinister look and took a liking to Daughtry.

"The near encounter with the MPs has scared me," Daughtry said. "That old woman might want to rape me. I'm headed back to the base. She has caused me some concern. See you fellows back in the barracks."

Because of our high sex drive level, Crimes, Bloom and I would not easily give up our search for romance.

The vegetation was sparse and low. In the moonlight, the dwarf trees looked like mesquite. The sandy soil barely supported the cacti and other tropical desert vegetation. After the hot days, the cool night air was pleasant. The smell of the desert, the full moon and the night shadows contributed to the romance of the evening.

"I'm not about to return to the base until I have investigated the female situation," I said.

"I feel the same way," Ron said.

When the girls came they were very young and short with Indian features. When we gave the old woman our money, she asked us to pick a girl.

I picked a girl who looked like a beauty queen in the soft moonlight. She was sixteen to eighteen and could not speak a word of English. Her hair was very dark, and her eyes were black, but her skin was smooth, soft and brown. There was no bra under her peasant-type blouse, and her breasts were well formed and soft. She had a pretty profile all the way down. Her figure was harder to ignore than a ringing telephone.

She unfolded her blanket and spread it on the ground and motioned for me to sit down. For a time we sat side by side on the blanket, touching each other. This Indian girl was passionate and appeared to like what she did. The time passed quickly. Soon Ron was calling me to go back to the base. I could have spent the night in this unusual desert and wanted to come back the next night. The girls really liked us and let us know in a way we could appreciate. However, the crew had a job to do in Great Britain. We took off the next morning across the South Atlantic.

The flight to Dakar, Africa was 1,500 miles all over water. The crew sweated as we climbed to ten thousand feet, leaned back the fuel mixture, reduced the rpm to 2,200, manifold pressure at twenty-five inches and coasted. The dependable Pratt and Whitney R-1830 engines performed superbly hour after hour. I checked the gasoline consumption. The four engines together burned 171 gallons per hour, the best fuel economy ever achieved in our flying experience. Flying combat formation, at times, the plane used 340 gallons per hour. Saving gasoline would insure plenty for the crossing.

In mid-ocean, from our radio, we learned that Hitchcock's *Shadow of a Doubt* played at the movies. The movie *The Outlaw* aroused the interest of the nation. It was a Western produced by Howard Hughes with the lead female part played by an unknown bombshell, Jane Russell. This physically blessed actress became the delight of all GIs I knew.

"Dakar is a tremendous disappointment," Crimes said as we rested on our bunks in the transit barracks. "The landing strip and base are located a thirty-minute ride from the city and everything else because the town is a cesspool."

"Yeah," I said.

"Just take a deep breath. The native village we passed through on the outskirts of Dakar on our way to swim in the Atlantic disappointed us. We smelled Dakar before we saw it. The houses were huts with thatched roofs. Flies were everywhere. The stench under the tropical sun was awesome." Crimes continued. "Men and women sleep in the streets. The streets are disaster areas. Trash and garbage are everywhere. Most natives, both men and women, relieved themselves in the street. Boy, they can have it."

"Are you saying you don't like Dakar?" I asked.

"Yeah!"

"Dakar is located on the western-most point of Africa in the country of Senegal. That's our reason for placing a landing strip in this uncivilized country," Roy Watson said. "Dakar served as a trading center."

"Roy, you don't have to tell us anything about Dakar. I've seen enough and don't want to know anything else," I said.

"I plan to tell you about the region anyway," he said. "The population of the entire country is near three and a half million. Dakar is a tropical paradise except for the people. You will see young girls walking around with nothing on above the waist. Stark-naked children are everywhere. Flies were all over the children, on their sores, eyes, mouths, and genitals. This display of nudity and squalor was a shock to me." Roy continued. "You guys probably wonder why these people have not taken better care of nature's gifts."

The beach remained beautiful and clean. Mother Nature cleaned it every day. We swam and played in the water. Using our bodies as surfboards, we rode the waves in and made the most of our outing. When the sun was near the horizon, the crew piled into the six-by-six truck and made our way back to the base.

The Air Corps constructed the airstrip in an area of no trees and a few waist-high bushes. The soil was sandy and dry. The barracks and mess hall were of the same architecture and construction as the other bases we visited. The accommodations were primitive but clean.

Next morning the crew was up early at 5:00 A.M. We were glad to leave Dakar. The take off for Marrakech, Morocco was without regret. The natives in this city were Arabs. They were cleaner and better looking.

The culture of Marrakech, a short step from the Middle Ages, interested us. Masonry buildings and their method of construction were as old as the Bible. Sun-dried mud brick or stone formed the thick walls of the houses. The Arabs used wood to frame the roof. Many of the buildings were covered with galvanized corrugated metal. Other buildings used clay tile roofing.

Our first experience with floor toilets surprised me. Floor toilets were not comfortable to use but did their job.

Crimes said, "How do you use these things?"

"Back up to it and squat. Be sure you don't fall backwards," I said.

The weather was hot and dry as we walked around the city of Marrakech. Logan looked around and said, "This simple, unadorned, utilitarian architecture reflects a lifestyle that is slow and easy. I like that. This Arab society must have learned through the ages to cope with shortages, war, and hardship by using the land and material available. In spite of limited resources they were able to maintain this low level of culture they have experienced for ages.

"The prevailing attitude of 'Why bother?' has kept progress to a minimum and the entrepreneurs out." Logan continued. "Everything seems to work to discourage any extra effort which would lead to improvement."

"With their history of conflict, you didn't expect it to be like the United States, did you?" I asked, impressed with his evaluation.

The crew bought souvenirs and spent a few days looking the city over. The most interesting part was the Medina or the native quarters. Houses were close together with small windows. The bazaars or open markets were filled with stalls operated by individual owners. The fresh meat hung in the stalls and attracted flies, but the vegetables looked edible. In this market there seemed to be a land of plenty. Almost everything appeared for sale in the local market.

"How can so many people live so close together and not go crazy?" Daughtry asked. "By American standards, the Medina is dirty, but the dry air, extreme heat and bright sunlight seemed to sanitize everything. Sanitation here is better than in Dakar," he continued. "The smell is not as bad."

To our delight our radio operator had sex with an Arab girl. The crew had something to tease him about.

"Hey, what goes?" I asked. "Usually you are so conservative and careful you wouldn't look at a strange woman."

"This city of Arabian nights has sparked my interest. I do want to make the most of this situation of plenty. The bars and the women seem to have also attracted the attention of you guys," Bob said.

Stops were always short, and next day we took off for England.

"Our flight plan for England is to take off from Marrakech and fly the Atlantic around Spain and Portugal and then to a base in southern England," Roy Watson said from his seat at the navigator's table. "I'm following a radio directional beam set up for U.S. military aircraft along the route," Roy continued. "We also are receiving a second strong signal of the same frequency from a questionable source. I am now checking its location with celestial navigation. The heading that routes the plane over water around Spain and France is the one we're taking. The other heading would take the plane over northern France and into the hands of the Germans."

The crew made it to jolly old England and landed at St. Morgan after nightfall. It was comforting to know the navigator could find this little speck on the map. The navigator earned our confidence. The trip across the Atlantic to England from Marrakech made us comfortable with his navigation.

The next morning the crew was rudely awakened by a loud-mouthed old Limey. He said, "Drop your cocks and grab your socks."

He pulled the covers off my bunk; I counted ten and then hit him. For the sake of international cooperation and goodwill, I apologized.

The day was November 17, 1943. That same day, the crew took off from St. Morgan and landed at the permanent base at Tibenham, England. We were the second plane to land on the base. The group commander, Colonel Terrell, was already there.

When we landed, Logan looked around and said, "Look at these primitive accommodations, and it's raining. Everything is wet and damp. I'm ready to leave."

"That is not to be but very funny. Ha. Ha," I said.

Our arrival sparked my interest to learn more about this powerhouse of a country. A history book from the base commander's office introduced me to Great Britain's proud tradition. England, Wales, Scotland and Northern Ireland make up the nation of Great Britain. Their commanding position and their navy were powerful enough to control India, the Middle East, and the Far East with only a few officers with swagger sticks.

"The barracks on this base are corrugated metal huts with no inside plumbing," Crimes said. "These metal huts are equipped with small charcoal heaters vented through the roof. The toilets and showers are a good five-minute walk across the base.

"Hell! Did you notice that the airstrip could not be more than three thousand feet long? This length worried me."

This base was to be the home of the 445th Bomb Group, a group made up of four squadrons including a group operations squadron.

At full strength, with fifteen crews per squadron, together with the cooks, MPs and support troops, the base contained approximately seven hundred people.

Most days, for a mission, a squadron could put up twelve planes. If each squadron did that well, the total for the group would be forty-eight planes.

Later our crew would participate in one thousand plane raids over Germany. This would mean that twenty-two groups sent out their maximum participation.

Now that we were in Great Britain, we wanted to see it. "Nothing doing," Col. Terrell said. "You'll get a chance later. Now we must think about our missions over Germany."

Already I thought about those flights, and the thinking did nothing to lift my spirit. I chose to allow my mind to dwell on subjects of a non-serious nature.

We continued to fly around England for practice and agonize about our first mission. Getting firsthand information about combat became of prime interest to everyone who flew. After twenty-five missions we would be sent to the States for rest and rehabilitation.

Our wait for combat was short. The 445th Bomb Group was called for a general briefing. The next day the group would fly over Germany and receive its baptism of fire.

After only thirteen months training for war, it was difficult for me to believe that I was ready to face up to the German war machine.

"Don't take it personal," Daughtry said. "This is the way war works. You can be well trained but never prepared for the blood and guts of war. Growing up, I would never pick a fight. Because I am small, I learned to talk my way out of difficult situations. You can bet I would go to great lengths to stay out of a fight.

Now you and I both are in an impersonal fight with the Germans. They never gave me a chance to talk with Hitler."

"How do you know all this?" I asked.

"My mother told me," he responded.

Mandy surprised me with a letter. It had gone to my old base in the 2nd Air Force and caught up with me in England. She was casual and entertaining in her letter. I would not have been impressed except that three more arrived the next day.

With the first mission coming up, I had some thoughts about flying.

CHAPTER
ELEVEN

The imminent danger of our first combat mission caused me to think that I should be serious about my life. I should also try to be brave and not let the tension of the flights get me down. Every day we went through the same routine in our training. Tomorrow would be different. Excited about that first mission, I would play it cool and do the job I had been trained to do.

I wasn't a fighter, but I found that I could when I was challenged. Some fights are necessary for a boy. When other kids know you will fight, they will usually leave you alone. Only two fights were required to get me through high school.

My well-developed muscles on my medium-built bone structure didn't frighten anyone but allowed me to defend myself. I learned to take punishment even though I didn't like it. Learning not to be afraid or overwhelmed by severe or unfair treatment was part of my training. I also learned too much sympathy is not good. It lowers an individual's opinion of himself and his ability to perform. The lessons I learned at the boys' school were a great help in doing the job the air force required of me.

"We don't have enough recreation around here?" Daughtry said from a seat on his bunk in our new barracks, while with his right hand he pulled at a clump of hair that stood straight up on his head.

"I'm glad you brought up the subject," I replied. "We fly combat starting tomorrow."

"I know all about that," Daughtry said. "I asked about recreation. Will they issue us tea and English cookies before takeoff? After our return, will we have croquet on the airstrip? Will a jolly old time be planned?"

"By George, I think you've got it," I said, seating myself on Daughtry's bunk. "Forget about recreation. You're gonna be so damn tired dodging those German shells when you return, you will hit the sack without chow."

Later that day we landed from a practice mission and changed clothes. On our way to our Quonset hut, I heard airplanes overhead in the clouds that had just moved in. The planes were trying to land before ground fog made it impossible. Then I heard a crash and a loud swoosh and then an explosion as the two B-24s hit the ground. Daughtry and I ran in the direction of the nearer explosion, about a mile away.

A fire truck's siren was turned on full blast as the driver rushed to the crash site. Because of the fire, we couldn't get near the airplane.

Off to our left, an English farmer pointed out the location of two men who had fallen free of the planes.

We walked over to the first airman. He had fallen and hit with such an impact that his body dug itself into the soft earth. His parachute harness for a chest pack, and his flight clothes were intact. His head was smashed and looked flat. There was very little blood. We could do nothing but look as the ambulance people pulled his body from the soft earth and placed it in a body bag and then into the ambulance.

Not far away we found the other airman. He had fallen through the roof of a chicken house. Apparently his body broke through the clay tile roof. His face had hit the roof and smashed his head and body into a heap of human flesh on the chicken house floor. He took out a two-by-six-foot section of the roof.

The ambulance driver then ran us off and asked that we go back to the base, or he would report us to the base commander. With our first mission tomorrow, we didn't need the stimulation. We knew that planes crash and people were killed in these crashes. This was the first time that we actually saw the dead victims and fully understood what happens to the human body when it makes the sudden stop at ground level.

Don, Daughtry, and I walked slowly back to our barracks. As we walked, Daughtry said, "Damn, with all these planes flying around in the fog, I can understand why they collide."

"The air bases are so close together it is easy for a plane from one group to stray into our airspace. That plane did take out one of our crews," I said.

"Shit! I had rather have the Germans shoot at me over Germany than try to land in that fog," Don said.

"We may get caught in the fog when landing. Particularly if our missions are long. There is no way the forecasters can predict the weather for a long period of time, even in summer," I said.

"This is dangerous business," Daughtry said. "I want to go home."

In our walk back to the barracks, I became depressed and couldn't get the two dead airmen out of my mind. The sound of the collision of the planes in midair was awful. The debris made a whooshing sound on its speedy indirect fall to the earth.

Hell! I would have to get into an airplane tomorrow morning and fly over Germany. The Germans would do their best to knock us out of the sky. Was I afraid? Damn right! The two-plane crash was an example of what happens when your bomber gets a direct hit from the ground antiaircraft fire or the machine guns of an enemy fighter plane.

Blessed or damned by an unusual ability to visualize a situation, this could happen to me, I thought. I won't go. I'm scared to death. Maybe there is a way to avoid the mission tomorrow.

My pals thought I could do most anything. However I never

felt confident enough to brag. Did anyone know I was quaking in my boots?

I knew my crew was thinking and feeling the same thing. Somehow I had to resolve this conflict. I felt the need to be alone and walked away from my friends towards the showers at the Headquarters Squadron.

To be completely honest with myself, I searched deep within my conscious mind and asked, are you really afraid of that mission tomorrow?

During my childhood many things frightened me. I was afraid to ride a horse; afraid of the dark; afraid of heights, afraid of being beaten up by a more aggressive kid. One by one, I had overcome these fears. The mission tomorrow was a greater fear—the fear of death.

As I continued my walk toward the showers, I felt alone. A flashback memory of my youth troubled me. My mom was permissive and my dad strict with his discipline. My mom made excuses for me and insisted that I suffered ill health.

Trading on these kind words, I appeared to be a sissy until I got away from home and depended on myself.

The need to reach outside of my normal pattern of thinking for something of substance, for something to use in my present situation became necessary. I did not believe in asking God for favors and decided not to pray for my safe return. I did ask that the Lords' will be done.

Earlier a fight in the chow line with a larger guy built my confidence. I smashed his nose and won the fight. For my fear of heights, a walk through the bomb bay on a twelve-inch-wide catwalk at ten thousand feet with the bomb bay doors open didn't cure this fear. The exercise did make me more confident, in the event, I had to do it in combat.

My loss of nerve would affect the other members of my crew and perhaps others. Then thinking about my dad, if I didn't make the flight and was sent home in disgrace, he would say, "What did you expect?"

When I was a child, my mom said, "Son, do the best you

can. Then no one can complain." I made that decision, stood up straight, and with my head high, I walked into the barracks with a smile on my face.

The war economy provided no recreation on the base. Drinking and playing darts at the local pubs in town was better than nothing. Soldiers were sometimes innovative and made their own recreation. However, we still looked for something more than reading and letter writing to relatives and girlfriends. My personal recreation outlet was hunting near the base. I checked out a skeet shotgun with shells and roamed the countryside, looking for game.

When things really turned bad, the airmen drug out their old recreation standby, the bull session. Two people would start a ridiculous conversation in the barracks about some subject no one knew anything about, such as the sex life of the Arctic tern.

"I understand the Arctic tern take turns in their sex life," I said.

"Not so," said Ron. "The Arctic tern exercises complete abstinence."

"If that be true, how do they manage to produce slight terns?"

"They produce left turns. There are no right turns in the Arctic I am told," said Daughtry.

"But listen to this," I said. "There were two upper-class Englishmen at the club. One said, 'Did you hear?' The other Englishman said, 'Ear what?' 'Hopkins was ousted from the club.' 'Oh, I say, why was Hopkins ousted from the club?' 'Hopkins was caught having relations with a goat.' 'A nanny goat or a billy goat?' asked the other club member. 'It was a nanny goat, of course. There is nothing irregular about Hopkins.'"

Ron said, "Next time you feel compelled to tell a joke, don't. It is time for us to turn in. The Arctic tern already had a turn."

Ralph Peters, from the Saunders crew, said, "Home and girlfriends are what I want to talk about. Boy, I miss them both.

I really didn't know how well off I was until Uncle Sam said, 'I want you.' My girl, Nancy, promised she might just come around to my way of thinking. Didn't even get to kiss her good-bye. She had to go out of town. Now she tells me she will meet me at the dock when I arrive in New York, if I make it."

"You sure she isn't coming to meet the boat loaded with other GIs?" Ron asked.

"The *Stars and Stripes* newspaper says, 'Night and Day, You Are the One,' sung by Frank Sinatra, made the Hit Parade." Don said. "George Burns observed his fortieth birthday. Maulding of the *Stars and Stripes* said, 'He probably won't live very long smoking those big black cigars.'"

"Bet old George will never give up cigars just to live to be a hundred," Daughtry said.

Like millions of other young men in the U.S. military, we followed instructions and did our job conscientiously with only an occasional slip. We had no illusions about how average a cog we were in the American Fighting Machine. However, we lived with the feeling that our actions, however modest, were helping to win the war. This knowledge lifted our spirits and the spirits of our buddies and made us willing to face the danger.

All these young men knew the damage our bombs would be doing. They understood the necessity to hurt the enemy. There was no doubt in our minds, even in the darkest hour, that the United States would win the war.

Sitting on my bunk in our metal hut, I looked over at Daughtry and asked, "With the first mission coming up, Daughtry, do you worry and speculate as to what might happen?" I asked. "A combat mission could be deadly."

"There is no useful purpose in a bunch of speculation," Daughtry said. "I know the danger is there, but that big worry, along with a bunch of other stuff, is stored in the back of my head bone. How about you, I want to live up to the confidence you guys have in me?"

"Do I worry? Well, some, but I keep busy and try not to think about getting killed." I said. "My grandmother told me, 'If your time comes, you will go. Don't worry about it.'"

"I can accept that philosophy," Daughtry said. "What if it's the pilot's time to go? Where would I be then?"

"I don't seriously worry about getting killed," Crimes said as he joined the conversation from his bunk. "If the Germans aren't shooting at me. There is no merit in worrying about things that arc not imminent. When danger is imminent, there is no time to worry anyway. It's not fair. The boys on the ground have all the fun."

People are killed in combat and can cause some fear in all of us. This ever-present concern can be shoved in the background by a positive attitude and a busy schedule, I thought. However, this persistent threat caused my logical sense of reasoning to become distorted. This distortion began with me in gunnery school in Laredo, Texas. The trainees were firing fifty-caliber machine guns mounted on a post at a wind sock drawn by an L5 airplane.

With the training session over, Sam Turner, a gunnery student, asked the training officer, "May I use my last shot to shoot at a hawk circling out about a hundred yards?" "Sure," the officer said. "Lead him." Sam knew he had only one shot. He studied the hawk's pattern of flight, led him and fired. The hawk died with an explosion of feathers and dropped to the earth—what a luck.

The next week, Sam Turner and his crew died in a training accident. I shunned good luck and wanted no part of it and felt better when my luck was bad.

The night before our first mission, we played poker with our buddies in the barracks. McGreggor was one of the players. Mac had been winning a few hands. His confidence was high. The cards were dealt. Everyone received a good hand, and again the pot grew above two hundred dollars. When the betting stopped and the players laid down their cards, Mac won the hand with a royal flush. The next day Mac flew his first mission and didn't come back.

Good luck was not welcome. If I earned a profit or praise, I loved it. Unearned good luck frightened me.

Earlier I fantasized about being a hero and going home with a chest full of medals and a proud smile on my face. Somehow being a hero didn't seem important any longer. The important thing now was for me to return to the good old U.S.A. alive with not too much damage to my epidermis.

"It would be a shame to have the nice skin Mother Nature gave me punctured with shrapnel," I said, warming my hands against the outside cold on the small coke stove in our hut. "Worse than that, it could be painful."

From a horizontal position on his bunk, Daughtry said, "The odds for survival on a combat mission over Germany are low. I am concerned for my ass. Allow me to do a few lower-math calculations that will add to your agitation. Flying at one hundred fifty miles per hour, a B-24 Bomb Group would be in the target area for a minimum of ten minutes. With three hundred fifty flak guns firing sixteen shells per minute, the gunners would have fifty-six thousand chances to knock us out of the sky and send our planes hurling the twenty-three thousand feet down to Germany. The temperature will be negative thirty-five degrees Celsius. A very uncomfortable place to be. Even the cold could kill you."

"Are you trying to scare us?" Crimes asked as he sat down on my footlocker. "If you are, I don't scare easily."

"I can understand that," Ron said. "It takes some smarts to be afraid. Just look at the thing we will be flying."

"Are you about to tell me that you are gonna hide under your bunk tomorrow morning?"

"No, but how about that thing you will be flying in?"

"The manufacturer said, 'The B-24 is a workhorse. It can carry a heavier bomb load, fly higher and faster. It has gun turrets in the nose, tail, top and the belly. A gun is also mounted at each waist window.' That is the plus side. Just look how big and slow that sucker is."

"Fellows, after the general briefing today, we damn well know that tomorrow's flight is not just another training mission," I said. "Flying over Germany is not my favorite destination. Being a target is not an attractive option, now or for the future. The risk could permanently limit my plans. I am less than enthusiastic for a plane ride over Germany, but I will always be there to do my share."

Our first mission was scheduled tomorrow.

CHAPTER
TWELVE

The radio operator, Bob Jackson, shook me awake. The day was cold, damp and foggy, a typical winter day in England.

Bob yelled, "Time to get up. This is the big day."

I sat up alert. Funny, it felt like any other day to me, except for one small shard of fear which poked its unwelcome way through my subconscious. Reaching for my long johns and wool socks, I said to myself, I will deal with it later.

Bob and the other members of the crew must have been up for more than thirty minutes and were partially dressed. Daughtry walked around in his long johns.

"Build a fire, Daughtry," I said. "I hate to get up in a cold room."

"Off your ass," he said. "You ain't gonna have time to sit by a fire."

"It's hell living in these fucking barracks." Crimes said. "Twelve enlisted men or two crews lived in one metal hut and two crews of four officers and eight men occupy the adjacent hut. There are six cots down each side of the hut with three feet between each bunk. It's the same every place we've been. The footlockers are at the foot of the bed off the center aisle. We have no inside plumbing. That small coke stove with a chimney out the top just barely takes the chill off the air, and those raw light bulbs swinging on their service wire don't provide enough light to see crap!"

"This is our first mission, and you are griping about our having better accommodations," Ron said. "Jesus Christ, you're crazy."

I tied my shoes and looked at my watch. It was 4:36 A.M. The ball turret gunner, Daughtry, had also been slow. We walked out together into the still-dark morning.

"How did you sleep?" Daughtry asked.

"Fine," I replied. "Moments after my head touched the pillow, Bob was shaking me into consciousness."

Daughtry was short and walked with a swinging step. The easy smile on his pointed face gave no indication of his quick temper. His less-than-medium-size body would back up his anger even when there was little chance of winning a physical encounter. Almost without a chin, the boy had spirit and a good nature, most of the time.

Daughtry's voice was calm when he said, "Your ass is mud if we get a hit and you bastards don't get me out of that turret. I'll never speak to you again."

"You are in better shape than any of us," I said. "All you have to do is tilt that turret and fall out of the bottom."

We increased our pace and caught up with Ron Bloom and Crimes.

"Watch me today, boys! I plan to bag me an ME109," Crimes said.

Crimes manned a single fifty-caliber machine gun in the waist position. He had been a rider in a rodeo, and his 170 pounds had bounced on both horses and steers. He loved horses and saddles. Crimes and I had already experienced several encounters which were not exactly fights but tests of strength and will. Crimes tested me as he tested other members of the crew to see how far he could push without a fight. He had been careful not to push too hard.

Now he yelled over his shoulders, "Ron is a mama's boy."

"Ron," I said, "Crimes is trying to tell you that he had rather be here than stateside in the bed with some ugly broad. You know he's lying. He just loves ugly broads. Remember the last one? She was tall with sloping shoulders, a big ass and legs and short arms. She looked like something put together with spare body parts."

Crimes said, "Jones, why do you have to butt in and screw up someone else's conversation?"

Ron said with his voice soft and slow, "You know, Crimes."

Ron never seemed to be in a hurry. His long, lanky frame curved with a slight bend in the shoulders. His regular features and good skin gave him a pleasant appearance.

We four airmen walked into the mess hall with Sam J. Logan, the tail gunner, and Bob Jackson, the radio operator, went through the food line and sat down together.

The mess hall was another corrugated metal Quonset hut with a kitchen at one end and the chairs and tables at the other end.

Bob said, "Don't you just love this variety? This is the same stuff we ate yesterday. That's enough to frost you? I'm gonna tell you what—you will get the same thing tomorrow! The air force doesn't want to surprise you."

Logan laughed. At twenty, Logan married his childhood sweetheart before being drafted. Pictures of his wedding, near his bunk, showed the bride about three inches taller than the groom. We worried less with Logan guarding our tail in the rear turret.

Looking around the table at the faces of my crew, it occurred to me that their thoughts were the same as mine. They were concerned as to how they would react to enemy fire.

Crimes noisily slurped his oatmeal. Some dripped on his chin. "Hey! Hey!" he said, "Eat your heart out guys. I met a blonde in the Fox and Hound last night. She had tits the size of grapefruits and a figure like Betty Grable."

Everyone laughed.

"Not again, Crimes. You have used that line before," Logan said, smiling. "When you down two mugs of ale, it louses up your twenty-twenty vision. The last beauty you introduced us to had broken teeth and stringy hair. She is the one who downed seven beers, and her round belly popped her skirt at the waist."

Crimes's face twisted into an expression of anger, and he said, "Sam, you wouldn't know a woman if you saw one. You haven't had a piece of ass since you left your wife in the States. You probably can't. You don't have any balls."

Bob emptied his coffee cup, swallowed his last bite of powdered eggs, pushed back his empty tray and rose to go. "You guys talk crap for breakfast. I am forcing myself away from this uplifting conversation. If they call the war off, I will be at the radio briefing."

We rose as a group to leave. Ron looked at me with a side glance. "How do you feel about today's raid? You have been quiet all morning. Are you afraid?"

"Isn't it smart to be afraid?" I asked, speaking with more confidence that I felt. "Isn't that a sign of intelligence?"

"Well, yes," Ron admitted.

Ron and I walked to the briefing building, a double-skin, corrugated, metal structure on a concrete slab. The building appeared shaped like a barrel and cut in half the long way with windows in each end. A speaker's platform was located up front in the briefing room. Folding chairs were placed on each side with an aisle down the center.

A pot-bellied coal-burning stove took some of the chill out of the air. The vague, gray, metal folding chairs and pocked wooden desks did little to improve the austerity of a dreadful building.

The exposed incandescent light bulbs hanging from the ceiling on their service wire provided enough light to see but not enough to read. Over the raised platform, where the maps were located, the light burned brighter.

"Why do we have to have a briefing?" Daughtry asked. "Why can't we just take off and bump the hell out of the Germans?"

Logan piped up, "Daughtry, they want to give you all the facts and scare the hell out of you first."

"They can save their breath," Daughtry said. "I'm scared already."

The airmen shuffled around finding seats. The low murmur generated by the men as they exchanged quiet conversation indicated the importance of the meeting.

The group commander, Colonel Terrell, with his squadron commanders and operations officers along with the briefing officer, Major Apple, walked in. Someone yelled, "Attention!" Everyone stood. With his graying temples and tight, concerned expression, the group commander looked like a college professor who took his job seriously. A little overweight for his five-foot-ten height, he appeared well rounded in body and personality.

He said, "At ease. Be seated."

Gradually, the noise level dropped as everyone found a seat.

Major Apple began, "Today will be your first mission. You have been in training for over a year. Your preparedness is high. You have been cleared by the inspecting general for operations over enemy territory.

"Your target today is Bremen, Germany," he continued. "You will take off at eight hundred thirty hours, in twenty-second intervals and assemble around the lead airplane. Colonel Terrell will be in that plane. Watch for green flares shot at thirty-second intervals. As the formation builds, you will have no difficulty finding your place in the formation.

"The group will have fighter cover by spitfires from Great Britain until you make your landfall on the Dutch coast," the major continued. "From there, P-38s will take you to within two hundred twenty miles of the target. You will be on your own to the initial point. The group will then turn to a heading of one hundred thirty degrees and be over the target in four minutes. The P-38s will meet you coming out at this point approximately two hundred fifty miles from the target and be with you until you cross the coastline. Your target is the railroad marshaling yards and the steel mills outside of Bremen. You will be flying at twenty-three thousand feet. At that altitude the temperature will be negative thirty-five degrees Celsius. Gentlemen, that is cold! Anything exposed will freeze! Go to the toilet before you leave the ground!

"It is my suggestion that you remember your training. Check your electronically heated suits and your oxygen masks. Please also check on your belly turret gunner and your tail gunner to make sure they are functioning. They will not be much help to you if they are frozen to death."

Major Apple turned to the colonel's party. "Colonel Terrell, would you like to make a statement?"

"Yes, thank you," the colonel said and stood up. "We have trained together, and I know most of you by name. I wish you the best of luck. Remember your training. Remember that you are America's finest. Remember why you are here, and when you do your job, we can all go home.

"After you have dressed in your flight clothes, there will be trucks to take you to your hardstand. You already know the lead plane takes off at eight thirty. You also know your order of takeoff. If you are shot down, remember to give only your name, rank, and serial number. Good luck and God bless you."

The sincerity and tension in his voice indicated his concern.

The airmen filed out into the locker room and began the dress routine. The long johns and ODs we were wearing were the dress foundation; over these we pulled our electrically heated suits. These suits were long johns with wires sewed in. Next came our summer-weight flying coveralls. The ODs and the long johns were worn in the event the electrically heated suit malfunctioned.

As the crew stepped aboard the truck to take us to the hardstand, I looked at Daughtry and said, "Hey, buddy, you look like a well-dressed Eskimo. Thinking about a trip to the Pole?"

A smile broke over Daughtry's troubled face. He said, "Up

your ass, John Jones. Get out of the way of this modern warrior."

Logan piped up, "I hated the part when the major said, 'The P38s will take you within two hundred twenty miles of the target.' What do we do for the fighter cover from there to the target and after the target? Boy, we are exposing our ass today."

Before the crew arrived at the airplane, the crew chief had already started the engines and checked out the major systems. It was my job to check after him. The pilot also had a preflight checklist. With so much checking, it was inconceivable that anything could go wrong, but airplane parts malfunction without notice, and on several occasions I had to deal with these failures.

Still a little foggy and very dark, the truck driver had difficulty finding the hardstand. But the fog had started to clear. Fog frightened most airmen in Great Britain.

Brecovitch, the pilot, asked, "Sergeant, have you checked the airplane?"

"Yes," I said. "She is in great shape."

Brecovitch was a thorough and careful pilot. He had guts and was not afraid of the airplane. A bond of confidence formed between the two of us.

Loaded into the bomb bay were six one-thousand-pound bombs.

"This load dropped in the right place could make a big dent in Hitler's personality." Lieutenant Murphey quipped.

Ron said, "Gosh, that is three tons of TNT. In our group alone with forty-eight planes we will be carrying one hundred thirty-four tons of explosives."

Mike Murphey, our skittish copilot, said, "Climb aboard, guys. This is the Bremen Express!"

As we climbed aboard, Lieutenant Rufus Graffhen, the bombardier, said, "This entire war looks bad from any angle."

Second Lieutenant Roy Watson, the navigator, came aboard. He looked at me, winked and said, "Are you ready for combat?"

"I'm the best Uncle Sam has got. You will be over Germany for lunch. Flak and scrambled fighters are on the menu. For dinner you will be back here for drinks at the Officer's Club."

Our squadron got the signal, and Brecovitch pulled the plane up to the end of the runway in line for takeoff with the other B-24s.

Our turn came. The pilot shoved the throttles forward. The RPM climbed to 2,700. The pilot removed his foot from the brakes, and the plane moved down the runway. The flying boxcar gained speed. I could feel the wings take the load of the fuselage. The copilot closed the cowl flaps. When the aircraft became airborne, he raised the landing gear and then the flaps.

The crew felt the turbulence of the previous airplane and for a moment, one wing dropped. The pilot pulled back on the throttle and lowered the manifold pressure.

The plane climbed to altitude and found its place in the formation. Now some time later our plane was over the target.

Good sense dictates that anyone should try to make the best of a bad situation. What could anyone in a sitting duck position do to improve his lot?

Three and a half hours into the flight, I shifted my fanny, numbed by cold and prolonged sitting, and looked out. Mustering the small amount of objectivity at my disposal, I thought of the fastest route to get my ass out of the flying boxcar loaded with six thousand pounds of bombs and 2,300 gallons of high-test gasoline in the event of a direct hit. The gasoline alone was dangerous and so volatile it would ignite with a hot breath. The sudden appearance and disappearance of another German airplane diving through our formation with guns blazing diverted my attention.

I found him in my gun sight, lead him and fired. Quickly he was below the sight line for the top turret.

Shells were bursting all around me. The sky was black with smoke. With each burst of flak, I felt an inclination to duck. Ducking was unproductive. There was no place to hide. Hey! This could be dangerous!

I felt alone as the barrage hammered away at the formation

of B-24s. Turning the top gun turret, I looked for enemy fighters. Keeping busy kept my mind off the exploding shells.

Those puffs of black smoke meant death and destruction—my death and destruction. The reality of combat shook me all the way down to my long johns. Sitting still required an effort.

Pressing the intercom button in the turret, I called, "Top turret to belly. ME109 coming your way at one o'clock, high. Daughtry. Get him. Over."

The twin fifty-caliber machine guns in my turret barked in short bursts at a second ME109 coming in high. The plane passed quickly below the top turret sight line.

"Hey!" I said. "Belly turret, another one is on his way. Do you read that yellow-and-red flak? Pretty, huh? The Germans are measuring our altitude. Those bastards!"

"Look at that smoked up sky," Logan said. "Those gunners below are making a substantial contribution to my discomfort. This is not the scenic route. I plan to complain to my travel agent."

Over the target, with the flak coming up thick and fast, I looked down and saw Bob standing in the flight deck door near the bomb bay. The bomb bay doors were open. He used a gray English aerial camera to take pictures of the havoc wrought by our exploding bombs.

Suddenly, Bob looked up. His eye watered, and the tears froze into little balls of ice which clung to his eyelashes. His comic appearance was so out of place, I laughed hard in my oxygen mask.

The fighters continued to harass our formation of B-24s.

The bombardier in the nose yelled over the intercom, "Twelve o'clock low; three FW190s coming with guns blazing. Now they are peeling off right and left. Shoot them! Daughtry, you wanted a 190. Now is your chance. Get those bastards!"

In seconds they were gone. I looked up at the sun. A small speck came out of the sun, diving down at the formation with all guns blazing. "Top turret to left waist. 109 coming out of the sun. Nine o'clock high. Let's nail him."

The German plane dived through the formation and missed "D" for Dog but got the plane in the box below.

I ducked lower in the top turret only to realize that the aluminum skin on the airplane offered just about as much protection against flak as the skin I wore. After that, ducking was involuntary and little comfort.

The trip prepared me to answer the question in Mom's last letter, "Son, how was your day?" Well, Mom, one I hope to remember. Today I forgot to take my vitamins, wash my ears and stay on the ground.

How would I react to the danger associated with combat? That thought crossed my mind on numerous occasions. Could I do my job and be a credit to my country? Would I be unable to function under pressure? Now, I had my answer. I could function. The military training and discipline made it possible for me to do my job with some confidence.

Now back over the North Sea, the pilot had already begun to let down, to begin our descent to ten thousand feet. Someone lit a cigarette. The smoke had a wonderful smell. It also meant we were out of enemy territory.

The statistics of the mission were simple. The date was December 16, 1943, to Bremen, Germany. We took off at 8:30 A.M. and returned at 3:30 P.M., a seven-hour flight. The temperature was—35ºC. We flew at an altitude of twenty-three thousand feet and lost eleven bombers from our group of forty-eight, a twenty-two-percent loss.

What a thrill to be alive. The joy of having come through uninjured excited me. I felt my body parts; they were still there and in good shape except my legs and feet were numb. My electric-heated suit went out, and my ass got cold.

Bob, the radio operator, looked up at me and asked, "After

we left the target, you were laughing like a hyena. What's so damn funny?"

"The little balls of ice which formed on your eyelashes are gone now," I said. "Were you able to sing 'Jingle Bells' to the tinkle?"

"I had difficulty seeing any damn thing. Hope I got some good pictures with that camera."

The plane rolled to a stop on the runway. Everyone aboard felt the release of tension. As a crew, we had experienced enemy fire and passed the test. We were combat experienced.

For me this was a time of mixed emotions. Happy to have returned in one piece, I felt tired from the long hours of flying and the tension of combat. Slapping a brake on my emotions, I decided to forego kissing the ground, which seemed like something that should be done. However, the plane required attention.

Excited, Daughtry came running to the flight deck just outside the pilot's cockpit. "John, did you see that ME109 dive through the formation just off our wing?" he asked. Daughtry spoke fast, and the words spilled out.

"That German boy must have been in a hurry!" Daughtry continued. "He came in from above and raked the formation with his guns. Did you see the airplane back of us get a direct hit, catch fire and go down? Some of the boys got out. I saw only three chutes. Was that the Saunders crew in our barracks?"

"I'm not sure," I said.

We turned off the runway to taxi to our hardstand back near the tower. I saw a plane come in with only three props going. A closer look revealed a large hole in the fuselage back of the pilot. It looked like a shell had made a direct hit and took out the armor plate back of the pilot.

The plane pulled around on the hardstand near ours. Ambulances met the plane. The tail turret had been shot up. The tail gunner had been hit from below in his ass. I could see that he was dead and that part of his body was damaged as they lifted him out of the plane and into the cold meat wagon.

The other crews were experiencing the same feeling of euphoria. The excitement in the locker room overflowed. The animated conversation spewed forth. Everyone tried to talk at once. We had release in conversation. The airmen were talking it out.

Logan said, "Now that we know what combat is like, it won't be so bad next time."

"Ha, ha," I responded. "For me, it is worse to know what to expect."

"We didn't see enough fighter planes," Crimes said. "We had to go through all that flak. My ass ate up the cushion I sat on. Those Germans knew about me, and the bastards wouldn't come out and fight."

We were debriefed as a crew. The questions were detailed: When did you first encounter flak? Was it on the right or left side? When did the fighters show up? What direction did they come from? Did you have flak at the initial point?

The questions continued until the crew members were tired, and the debriefing officer had milked us of all useful information.

By asking these questions, the debriefing officers were able to pinpoint the location of the flak guns. On the next mission to the same target, hopefully we would be routed around those guns.

From the debriefing officer, we learned the Saunders crew was back of our plane in the deep slot. The plane caught fire and went down, and only three chutes were observed. No one said anything, but the news hurt.

The airmen dressed and headed for the mess hall. Fried porkchops and baked beans were on the menu. To my surprise, I was very hungry. Because of the tension, I forgot about food. Now my body needed it. I ate with an appetite.

"What are you thinking about, Jones?" Daughtry asked as we slowly walked back to our barracks. "You are thinking about those poor guys who didn't make it, the members of the Saunders crew."

"It wasn't as bad as I thought it would be," Logan said again.

"It's worse than I thought it would be," I answered. "I saw five planes from our group go down and parachutes pop out. The total losses from our group for the day was eleven aircrafts. That is a twenty-two-percent loss. These losses are frightening. With those odds, after five missions we won't be here either."

We stepped inside the almost-empty barracks. At the other end of the building there were six empty bunks made as per air force regulations from this morning. The reality hit us. Our buddies were gone—killed with one direct hit in the right place except for the three chutes observed. There was little chance that those three made it.

With tears in his eyes, Daughtry said, "McGregger won a big pot with a royal flush last night but his luck ran out today."

Logan's voice choked up as he remembered Diego Ramirez, the boy who came all the way from Colombia, South America, to join the air force and fight for the cause of freedom.

Ron said, "They were a good bunch of boys."

Ron walked outside the barracks, ashamed not to have his emotions under control. I also felt the loss of good friends. Nothing is forever. During a war, time is always short. I turned to join Ron and saw Crimes going through McGregger's personal things.

"What the hell are you doing?" I asked Crimes.

He looked up at me. "I am taking the valuables. If we don't steal their stuff, the people in supply will."

"Crimes, we are not going to steal from the dead. Put it back," I said.

He looked at me and said, "Go fuck yourself."

I grabbed Crimes by the shoulder and spun him around and

said, "Put it back. Put it all back, or I will knock your goddamn teeth out the back of your head."

Crimes gave me a dirty look and walked over to his bunk and lay down. Sooner or later I would have to fight Crimes and didn't look forward to that event.

The crew took each dead man's valuables, made a list of the contents and turned them over to the headquarters people to be sent to the families of these airmen.

The crew talked for a while in the barracks and wrote letters home. Then we took a walk to the shower. Walking back, I looked at the sky. The fog was all gone. I felt great to be alive. There was safety for today. Tomorrow became a question mark. One down and twenty-four more to go before we were to be sent back to the United States.

Would we make it? We were born in the best American tradition and would learn to tolerate much more than had been thrown at us today.

I learned that near our base there were other things to do. Hunting was one.

CHAPTER
THIRTEEN

A small cluster of homes, called Tivietshal, was located near our base in England. One had to walk to Tivietshal to catch a train or have a drink. The countryside nearby was spotted with farms, similar to ones in the United States, only smaller, with hedgerows dividing the land.

The area around Tivietshal had not been touched by German bombs because there were no factories or concentration of people. The countryside was beautiful and alive with small wild game.

On my grandfather's farm in North Alabama, I loved to hunt quail, rabbits or any other small game and missed that relaxation in the service. With a skeet shotgun, checked out from base ordnance, I roamed the British countryside, looking for game. On hunting trips into the hinterland, I met some English people. They raised no objection to my hunting.

I gave the game I killed to the local farm families. They were happy to have the red meat because the local shortages extended to almost everything, even shotgun shells. The local hunters were not able to thin out the rabbits that multiplied, well, like rabbits. The farmers were also grateful that my hunting was successful.

At war since 1939, the British were short of everything. They had been bombed and beaten down but not beaten. They worked long hours, and some of the work was disagreeable. They would not, however, give up their spot of tea at 10:00 A.M. or at 4:00 P.M. They never appeared to be in a hurry, yet things were accomplished. Cheerful and optimistic, they were delighted to talk with Americans. American flight crews felt at ease in their country.

Before the base was built, Tivietshal had been a small country village. All the local people knew each other, and things were slow to change. In general, these good people led lives uncomplicated by machinery. To most of the people in the Tivietshal area, the bicycle was a complicated device. Cars were rare and petrol to run them unavailable. The local people walked a great deal.

On one hunting trip, I had the good luck to meet the occupants of the Yew Tree Farm house, the Wilson family. Their house was at the end of the Tivietshal base runway. On most occasions, the flight crews took off into the prevailing wind and over the farmhouse, just barely clearing the chimney. I saw the house and wondered who lived there, and if the occupants were disturbed by the noise from our planes as we took off. The construction of the house was stucco with a steep-pitched roof of red clay tile.

After killing two rabbits on their farm without asking, I decided that the owners should have the rabbits. I walked up to the house, knocked on the door and said to the lady inside, "I shot these rabbits on your farm. May I give them to you?"

"You surely may. My name is Sara Wilson. I live here with my husband, Major William Wilson. We have a daughter, sixteen, and a son, eight." Mrs. Wilson accepted the rabbits with many thanks.

Sara offered me tea. It was without sugar but warm and stimulating.

A young girl entered the room. "This is my daughter, Ruth," Sara said. She was five foot two, and her thin body made her appear small. She was somewhat ordinary in looks, but the blush of youth made her face wholesome and agreeable. "Ruth, what do you do?" I asked.

"I'm only sixteen." Ruth said with spirit. "However, I have finished the U.S. equivalent of high school and am employed by the British Rationing Office. Every day, I walk down to the train station at Tivietshal, catch the train to Norwich and return on the same train in the afternoon. So you see I am quite busy."

The chat with the family pleased me greatly. I told them about my family in the U.S.

"Success in the U.S. is relative," I said. "The more success, the more relatives."

The Wilson's gave me some local history. "May I come by to visit Ruth?" I asked.

"That would be agreeable," Sara said. "Please understand that Ruth is too young to go to a pub. She is too young to drink. Do you agree?"

It would have been impolite and improper to disagree. "My family doesn't believe in drinking at any age," I said, "that is everyone except my drinking uncle Joe."

Charles, the eight-year-old boy, came home from school, and we met. He saw my shotgun and became interested in what I had been hunting.

Alive with enthusiasm, Charles asked, "Will you take me hunting? I won't complain. I'll carry the game."

"Be delighted to take you. Remember, it will be rough walking and muddy sometimes."

"I don't care about the mud." Charles said.

A good, well-behaved child, he appeared open and outgoing in the British tradition.

I did take Charles hunting. On that day it rained, the fields were muddy. His shoes were not suitable for walking in the muddy fields. However, he carried the game as promised. My GI shoes were excellent for hunting and walking over rough terrain. I carried Charles through the worst muddy spots.

"Charles, is this mud too much for you?" I asked. "You have low-cut shoes with knee-length socks and have stepped in mud over your shoes."

"No, but it's hard to walk. I'll wash my shoes when we get home. I want to be out with you," Charles said.

My visits were timed to Charles's return from school. We hunted together, then returned with the game as Ruth arrived from work. Ruth and I also became friends. Her mother liked me and encouraged me to return.

One night, while I was in the house at Yew Tree Farm, some planes were taking off for a night mission. B-24s came over with all engines revved up to 2,700 revolutions per minute—full power. The noise inside the house made conversation difficult.

"How can you stand it?" I asked. "On our daylight missions a minimum of forty-eight planes take off. All this noise would drive me mad."

"We are accustomed to the noise and don't want to complain because we like living here," Mr. Wilson replied. "You probably haven't noticed, but housing is hard to find. We are content to wait out the war in this house."

William Wilson was a major in the British Army. At Dunkirk, an Englishman in a sailboat took him and a dozen other soldiers off the beach. On the way back across the English Channel, he was strafed by an ME109. His right leg was badly damaged by gunfire.

Most of the time William was away on some kind of secret duty for the British Army.

My contact with the family continued. As often as possible, I found myself at Yew Tree Farm. One day I came by early to find Ruth working, William away on temporary duty for a week, and Charles was not yet home from school.

I knocked, and Sara opened the door. She appeared very glad to see me. She threw her arms around me and started kissing my face and lips. A little taken aback at the warmth of her greeting, I wondered why I had never really considered this attractive woman as a sex partner. Now in the dim light of her spotless house, I took another look. She was conservatively dressed with an English woolen skirt and thin shirt blouse, which emphasized her feminine charms. Her hair was done up on the top of her head in a twist like my grandmother's. The similarity stopped with the hair. The rest of her was totally desirable. Her skin was smooth, and her teeth were irregular but white.

Sara was unzipping my fly as she led me into the bedroom. She said, "Hurry, we don't have much time. Charles will be home from school shortly."

Vicariously she transmitted her excitement to me. Her face was flushed. The color improved her looks. She unbuttoned my shirt and then unbuckled my belt. She turned and asked me to unbutton her blouse. While I was doing this, she slipped her hand through my fly to take note of my progress. I bent over, took off my shirt and slipped off my pants. Sara still had on her slip and bra. I pulled her to me and felt the warmth and softness of her body against mine.

She fell backward on the bed and pulled me over her. The springs groaned as we landed. I rolled over, kicked off my shoes, held her close and ran my hand between her legs. She responded with a little up-and-down motion.

Scarcely aware of the creaking of the springs or the possibility that someone might walk in, I surrendered myself to the situation. Caught up in the passion of the moment, my twenty-year-old body forgot all caution, all learned responses and anything that would distract from what we were doing.

This lady was athletic and matched my efforts. I could feel her body against mine and appreciated the whiteness and softness of her skin and the smell of her body.

Then it was over, and I rested my weight on her body and placed my lips over hers. She shoved me aside, jumped up and put on her skirt and blouse. At that moment, her son, Charles, rang the bell to get in. With my clothes in my hand, I rushed to the bathroom. Dressed in my pants and shirt and sitting on the water closet, I was putting on my shoes when Charles walked in.

"What are you doing with your shoes off?" Charles asked.

"That is a good question," I said, "There was a small stone in both shoes, and I had to go to the bathroom anyway."

"What have you been doing to get rocks in your shoes?" He asked.

"Crossing some very rough ground." I responded.

He accepted my explanation.

"Are you ready to go hunting?" I asked.

Charles's face lit up. "Yes, yes, yes," he said with enthusiasm.

"Your mother has a snack for you. Eat your snack, and we'll go."

Charles rushed out to the kitchen. I arranged my clothes in order and joined them.

I noticed that only the bottom button of Sara's blouse was fastened and said, "Sara, you must have dressed in a hurry this morning. Allow me to button your blouse."

Now I knew when to visit. I always came to see the entire family, but the mother was of special interest. There were other occasions with Sara. I did continue my visits with Ruth to divert attention.

One afternoon, Ruth was to be late, so I offered to meet her at Tivietshal Station. I rode my bicycle over to Yew Tree Farm and picked up Ruth's bicycle. While riding my bike, I held hers with my left hand and led it along as I rode. This maneuver required a certain amount of dexterity. The technique was well mastered by the time I reached Tivietshal Station. The clock in the station showed 6:40. She was not due until 7:00. I was twenty minutes early. Having a glass of ale at the pub across the street seemed a good way to kill the time.

The ale went down quickly. I came out on time to learn that the train had come and gone. It was not yet dark. I looked in the direction of Yew Tree Farm. A girl was walking up the road. Two soldiers in a jeep were following her. Some GI was trying to pick up my girl.

Mounting my bike and leading Ruth's was difficult before the drink, but after the ale it was almost impossible. What I had learned about leading a bike, I forgot in the desire to come to the aid of my friend. The ale caused me to crash not once but twice; gradually I regained my skill for the task.

By concentrating and pedaling hard, I caught up with Ruth. I didn't have a pass to be off the base. I was dressed in fatigues with no indication of rank and somewhat angry already; my anger worked for me. I chewed out the military police like a professional.

"How dare you try to pick up an underage English girl!" I said.

The MPs were young and awed at my command of Air Corps talent for "chewing ass." They saluted and with no more than a "Yes, sir," turned around and drove off.

Riding separate bicycles offers little opportunity for intimacy. We pedaled back to Yew Tree Farm, holding hands in the moonlight. Sara waited on the porch for us, and as we rode up an audible sigh of relief escaped her lips.

Near the base was an old gothic-style house with the appearance of a castle. A moat around the house filled with water complimented the pointed, stone, gothic windows. One of the summer homes of Queen Victoria, the house appeared rundown and badly in need of repairs, and there was no indication that anyone lived there. The grounds were overgrown. Bushes and trees had fallen into the moat. Wood fencing had rotted away. The place looked sinister and foreboding. The large oaks cast deep shadows. Old English ghosts lurked everywhere.

One day on a hunt, a rabbit ran across the yard. Following him with the sight on the barrel of the shotgun, I caught up, led the running rabbit and pulled the trigger. The rabbit had placed himself between the house and me. The shot hit the rabbit but ricocheted from the ground and broke a small window near the entrance to the house.

The noise caused two old ladies to cautiously poke their heads out of the door. I walked over, apologized and agreed to pay for the window.

The old lady with glasses said, "It is not a matter of paying. No one can get glass."

"I'll measure the window," I said, "and bring a piece of glass from the base and install it."

"That would be wonderful," Idell said. "We're house-sitting. We are retired schoolteachers and that piece of glass will keep out the cold this winter."

"Please accept these rabbits I killed on your place," I said.

"Thank you. We love rabbit. Marsh hens live in the water of

our old moat and are better tasting than chicken. You may shoot some of those, also. They are a delicacy and are easy to clean."

The marsh hens were about the size of a large pigeon with black feathers and a beak an inch and a half long. These birds not only flew but also could swim underwater like a duck. Their feet were webbed.

Grace, the taller of the two elderly women told me, "The skin on the marsh hen is toxic. They have to be skinned before they're cooked."

When disturbed, the birds flew up four feet high and dived into the water. A hunter had to shoot quickly, or the bird would be lost. I became good at this sport. The old ladies had all the marsh hens they wanted.

One day I was hunting with Ron from another crew. Ron was on one side of a ditch on which the small trees and bushes had grown up, and I on the other. The growth prevented visual contact with Ron. A pheasant came up under my feet and flew in the direction of my hunting buddy. Surprised, I waited only a second before pulling the trigger. The bird came down in an explosion of feathers. I called my friend. Ron didn't answer. Another pheasant flew up and scared me half to death. The pheasant I shot was dead. Expecting to find a dead GI, I ran through the bushes in the ditch to the other side. I looked around for my friend and found him up the ditch to my left, obviously a slower walker.

I took the pheasant back to the base and gave it to the ordnance officer, who had it cooked in a local restaurant. He reported the bird delicious.

The English hang their pheasant by the tail feathers without refrigeration. When the tail feathers are pulled out by the weight of the bird, it is ready to cook. The enzymes work to make the meat tender. The bird also may have an odor before the drop occurs.

We flew five more missions in the next two weeks. Our flight crew had a day off. With passes to be off the base, Daughtry and I caught the train from the village near our base to Norwich. Most of the day we spent looking at thirteenth-century castles. Late in the afternoon, we were tired and hungry.

"Excuse me, sir. Could you direct us to the best place to eat in town?" I asked of an Englishman we met in the street.

"That I could, mate. Go up to the main road and take a right. It's a gothic-looking building. Looks like an old castle, it does. I want to tell ya, it will cost ya."

"That's okay. We've saved our money, and we are ready for a good meal."

Generally the British do not have a reputation for fine foods. Daughtry and I suspected that somewhere on this big island the food would be excellent. Today we would discover the truth and expose the myth.

We made the five-minute walk and found the restaurant in an old castle-like building with a very formal dining room of gothic architecture. The walls were dark stone with window trim and tracery of limestone. The ceiling was vaulted and dark. The gray stone floor appeared uneven. Walls away from the windows contained perpendicular projections into the main dining room to form alcoves. It was late in the afternoon and the blackout curtains were open. The dim light through the arched windows created an air of mystery in this room decorated with antiques. The table covers were worn. The antique furniture fit and looked as though designed for this ancient building.

There were perhaps ten other people in a room designed to seat seventy-five. The maître d' showed us to a table and a white-gloved waiter in a well-worn tux took our order.

We were pleased to discover pheasant on the menu. First we ordered a soup. Served hot in a wide, shallow bowl from a pheasant stock with barley and other unknown ingredients, it was mouthwatering and good. It warmed our insides and brightened our outlook for the future.

"My mom could cook damn good soups," I said. "Her soups were hearty and delicious but nothing like this. My food is seasoned with herbs and spices so that the flavor whacks my taste buds. I could eat a ton of this."

"Tastes like Campbell's to me," Daughtry said.

Next came the entree, precut pheasant served with a sauce, white yeast bread muffins, new potatoes, and brussel sprouts. The delicious pheasant came deboned. The lighthearted sauce with a hint of raspberry provided drama and distinction.

"This meal is a treat beyond my expectations," I said. "My taste buds salute our capable chef. The brussel sprouts are steamed and tender but not overly done. The food is more than delicious. It makes me feel good about myself and the world."

"You mean it's better than a Krystal hamburger?" Daughtry asked.

"Yeah."

Even though my stomach said, "Go, go, go!" I slowed my eating to allow my taste buds to enjoy the culinary artistry, and the succulent goodness. Caught up in the magic of the meal, I forgot about Daughtry. He had finished his dinner and was sitting across the table, looking at me.

He said, "Are you going to take all night to eat that bird?"

"Daughtry," I said. "I have always associated a wonderful meal with all the rights and freedom of democracy. Tonight, I am very much aware of that freedom. Fighting the Germans for another meal like this would be only a small inconvenience."

"I'll eat Krystal hamburgers for the rest of my life if the Eighth Air Force will let me go home," Daughtry said.

I met an English girl in a local pub and learned that if I helped her with her rent, there would be other privileges available.

CHAPTER FOURTEEN

We met in a pub near Tivietshal after my return from a long mission. She was five feet two, blonde and frail looking with sharp facial features. Without her milk-white skin, golden blonde hair and blue eyes, she would have been a washout. Her name was Nora.

She looked into my eyes and said with a sob in her voice, "My mother and father were killed in the German bombing of Coventry."

Sadness clouded her face and made her appear like a disturbed child. Her anguish was real when she told me the story of the bombing and finding her parents dead. I almost cried with her.

With tears in her eyes she said, "My sister and I were buried by the German bombs for eight hours under the debris that killed our parents. The stone house was blown over us. Sometimes I think I will die just thinking about that night. The memory is difficult to shake."

"You have a reason to be sad," I said.

The low level of light in the pub and the drab decor did nothing to lift her spirit. The rough-sawn dark wood soaked up the light from the electric lamp and the coke fire. The rain outside ran down the glass window and spread the gloom.

"I have gotten over the death of my family. My reason for being sad now is another matter."

"What could make you so unhappy?"

"I have been living with a U.S. Air Corps captain," she said with a sad expression on her face. "He's being shipped out. He's been paying my rent, and now there isn't enough money from my job for the rent and board."

"That's rough," I said with sympathy. "How much is your rent?"

"Four pounds a month," she said as she looked up with tears in her eyes.

Quickly I calculated that to be twenty bucks in U.S. dollars.

"You want someone to pay your rent?" I asked. "How about me?"

She said with a frown, "I don't know you."

"How well did you know the captain?" I asked.

"I met him in this same pub. He was very nice to me, but he is now being shipped out."

"I am one of Uncle Sam's finest. It's possible that you might like me. Do you want to give it a try?"

"Perhaps just until I become financially able to pay my board," she said and smiled.

"Here is twenty bucks. Shall we set a time for tomorrow night to consummate the arrangement?"

"Yes. That would be fine. I look forward to seeing you here tomorrow around seven."

Today, things had not gone too well. I too had experienced a bad time and was drinking more than I should, rather than face the grim reality of our combat losses.

On a mission that day, we lost the Keiser crew from our barracks, the second crew lost to combat since our arrival in England. These guys were our buddies. Now they were gone. I saw their plane explode in a ball of fire from a direct hit by an eighty-eight-millimeter shell. They were flying in the box formation below and in back of our plane. No parachutes were observed.

Our crew had walked off the base without leave. The group commander had assured us that no crew would be required to fly two missions back to back.

Daughtry, Jackson and I staggered back to the base and plopped in bed at 2:00 A.M. At 3:00 A.M., they shook us awake for another mission. Trapped, there was no way to admit we had been AWOL, without being court-martialed. We had no choice but to go. I was delighted the pilot and navigator were in good health and had not been a part of the party.

We three airmen mastered the usual routine of breakfast, dressing, and briefing and were ready at the hardstand. To my surprise, I felt alert. The hint of danger, the thought of losing my life sharpened my senses.

We flew a nine-hour mission to Ludwigshafen to bomb a chemical complex in southern Germany. Fighters covered us part of the way, spitfires over the channel to the landfall on the Dutch coast, and P-38s for the next 250 miles which was only a part of the long land leg in. We dropped the bombs on a chemical plant and returned to our base. The group was hit by three fighters at one time and five later. The attacks were not aggressive. They seemed only to want the 445th Bomb Group to know they were there. The fighters made passes at the formation from a distance. The few flak holes in our plane did not matter. I did not see the two planes in the group go down. We did have plenty of flak before and after the target. The group following the 445th took more losses. I couldn't tell if their losses were from fighters or flak. I counted seven planes from the group behind us as they rolled over and dived straight down.

We landed, were debriefed, had chow and were dead tired. Bloom, Crimes and I headed for the Rose and Crown Pub. Tonight I would consummate my arrangement with the English girl with the milk white skin and beautiful blue eyes.

In the pub, the boys met Nora and some of her friends. Nora seemed genuinely glad to see me and excited at the prospect of a new affair.

"I am glad to see you lover boy. Did you have a rough day? You do look a little tired."

Everyone had a pint and talked of the day's mission in general terms. Soon it was 10:00 P.M.

"Are you guys ready to go?" Ron said. "I am so bushed that I can't see straight."

Crimes admitted, "I'm in the same shape." As they walked to the door together, Ron said, "Jones, are you coming?"

"I'll go with Nora and join you later," I said.

"They might schedule another raid tomorrow," Ron said. "Wouldn't want you to miss anything. Seriously, make sure you get your butt back tonight. We want you along if we have a mission scheduled."

"Come on, good looking," Nora said. "It's time for you and me to go."

We walked about five blocks to her room. She had an outside door and a tiny fireplace with a small coke fire burning. She said, "Make yourself comfortable, and I will do the same."

I took off my flight jacket and dropped it over a chair. I threw my flight cap on top, sat in the easy chair in front of the fire and slipped off my shoes.

Nora's place was comfortable. The double bed, two easy chairs, a dresser and table made up the furniture in the room. To the right of the entrance door, another door opened into a full bath. The windows were equipped with blackout draperies.

Nora punched up the fire and added a little coke. The fire now burned brightly. I lay back and soaked up the heat.

Nora changed into a nightgown in the darkened room back of me. She came over and got in my lap in front of the fire. The gown was made of soft cotton and followed the contours of her slim, childlike body. Her small, firm breasts shaped the gown to the satisfaction of the most demanding.

My interest perked up as she pressed her lips against mine, felt me and unzipped my fly.

That was the last thing I remembered before I dropped off to sleep. The two days of flying, the ale, and the warm fire were too much. There would be other nights. Nora woke me and suggested I return to the base.

We continued to fly, and the Germans were making a determined effort to break the spirit of the Army Air Corps. Our losses were mounting. Old friends in the flight crews disappeared from the scene. Back from a mission, we discovered we had lost another crew from our barracks. A light drizzle fell. The weather, the tension of the mission and the bone tiredness combined to beat down my spirit and added to my irritation. I needed a drink, but the pub and Nora were off base, and I did not feel up to the long walk

Daughtry said, "It sure is bad luck for a new crew to move into our barracks. We have lost more people out of our hut than any other crew." That knowledge colored our thinking and made us wonder if we would be next.

I needed Nora to cheer me up and breathe some of her life into my body. I looked forward to seeing her. Walking up to the weather-beaten facade of the Rose and Crown, I gripped the wrought, iron, ancient pull and opened the door. The lights were low. Looking around for Nora was not easy. The bar was crowded, but the booths along the wall were empty. My gaze locked on the corner booth. A couple seated there were kissing in a very passionate manner. I took a second look around the room, then took a second look at the couple in the corner. They appeared familiar. Yes, that was Nora! I quickly walked across the room, grabbed the GI by the front of his jacket and yanked him to his feet. In the dim light, I recognized Crimes from my own crew.

"What the hell are you doing with my girl?" I yelled.

I pulled my right hand back to hit him in the face.

"Hell, I didn't know she was yours," he said. "She appeared very available."

He sensed my aggressive mood and didn't want to be involved. We were both off the base without a pass.

He gave me a dirty look and said, "If you will turn me loose, I'll get the hell out of here."

When my grip was relaxed, Crimes grabbed his cap, went by the bar, paid his tab and left.

If Crimes keeps rubbing me the wrong way, one day soon there will be a fight, I thought. It hurt to know that Crimes had been kissing my girl. The women Crimes usually attracted were of a lower class than I thought Nora to be. This disappointed me.

I directed my full attention to Nora. She cowered in the corner of the booth. She knew better and really didn't care but did want to avoid the consequences of her behavior.

"Some girlfriend. I turn my back and you are smooching some other guy," I said in a strong voice.

"You haven't been around much lately. I thought you had forgotten me. I'm glad you're back. Come, love, give me a kiss," Nora begged.

"You expect me to kiss the lips that everybody is kissing? No, thanks! We should get something straight. If you are going to be my girl, you have to act like it. Associating with a tramp is not my idea of a relationship. I'm mad as hell about finding you this way—in the arms of another man. God damn it. I'm not going to accept this type of behavior."

The people at the bar turned their heads in our direction. They were waiting for me to bop this frail slip of a girl.

She said, "I love you when you get angry. You must have some feeling for me. I like that. It won't happen again. Now that you're here, I'm not bored anymore. Come sit down and tell me what you have been doing."

"I'm surprised you're interested," I said. "How many other guys do you have on a string? I came to be cheered up and have a good time. What do I find? You kissing the big jerk on my crew."

Lighthearted Nora dedicated herself to making the person she associated with feel good. I soon forgot my anger.

"You sure made Crimes feel good," I said. "When I came in, you also seemed to be enjoying yourself. Let's forget it. Our relationship is not a firm commitment. We are not married."

"You're right," she said. "We're not married." Later she would regret her statement and her actions. The changing needs of the 8th Air Force would be a shock for her. I felt that our relationship was coming apart. Perhaps that was not bad. I needed to think about my future and prove my dad wrong.

I learned a lot about the British while visiting with my uncle in London.

CHAPTER
FIFTEEN

Our crew had been in England for three months. We asked for and received a three-day pass to London. I was excited about the trip because before joining the Air Corps, my travels had been no farther away from home than Georgia, Alabama, and Florida. London contained an overpowering aura of history. History in the making had always been my second love after architecture. Just thinking of walking in Piccadilly Circus and London's other historical sites gave me goose bumps.

Ron, Daughtry and I walked to Tivietshal and caught the train to London. The Red Cross at the base arranged our accommodations. The old hotel had removed the furniture and installed several double-deck bunks per room, army style, to house six or eight people. We were delighted with the accommodations.

"Daughtry, what can we see next?" I asked. "Today we saw all the things a person should see in London, such as St. Paul's Cathedral, Trafalgar Square, Piccadilly Circus, Buckingham Palace and the Changing of the Guards. Westminster Abbey, London Bridge, and the Themes River did not escape our tired eyes."

"Next I would like to see some British girls. It's now late in the afternoon; let's have a drink in the bar up ahead." Daughtry said.

We had our drink in a bar crowded to overflowing. "The prices charged for Scotch are outrageous," I said. "I'll buy a bottle."

Our drink of Johnny Walker Red Label with water on the side went down easily. I had already learned to like the taste of Scotch. Ron and Daughtry also had Scotch.

We found a black market salesman, and I made a purchase of a fifth of Johnny Walker Red for thirty dollars.

"That is six times the prewar price but less than one-third the bar price," Ron said.

"Just think how much you could have saved if you had bought the booze four years ago."

"Four years ago, I never even thought of drinking," I said. "Shall we return to the hotel and meet my uncle Joe? It's about six, the time of our meeting."

Uncle Joe and I had been corresponding, and we had agreed to meet that evening at the Red Cross hotel. The army had stationed Uncle Joe near London as part of the invasion force.

Uncle Joe had been a heavy-crawler tractor driver as a civilian. Later, he started his own company and became a grading contractor. Then he was drafted. The army sent him to school in Virginia and assigned him to a group to do maintenance on heavy equipment, including tanks.

He was six feet one and weighed 190 pounds. At twenty-eight he was in excellent shape, with big, powerful hands and forearms. His slow way of acting and speaking reinforced the concept that he was a nice guy. His friendly smile and regular facial features made him popular with the British women.

Most people have their own ways of solving shortages. On my grandfather's farm in Alabama during the thirties, Uncle Joe made his own drinking liquor. At nine years of age, I spent the summers with my grandparents and Uncle Joe and loved it. There was plenty to do on the big farm, and my help was needed.

Ron Wills, my first cousin, who was also spending the summer there said, "I am wasting my young life doing farm work."

"Ron," I said, "in another week we will have the entire crop laid by, and we can play ball and go fishing."

"Yeah. Why can't we go today?"

My grandfather wanted us to spend our time in a more productive manner. At his request, we chopped cotton, hoed corn, cleaned ditch banks, drove the mules to the cutting harrow, operated the planter and planted soybeans. We had plenty to do, even though our effort made a small dent in the amount of work that needed to be done. We also had some free time and tried to make the most of our time off.

My brother, Mick, was there also. We were interested in everything—fishing, baseball, exploring the turtle rock on top of the mountain and a tree house we planned to build in the woods.

My grandmother said, "One boy is almost a boy, two boys are half a boy, and three boys are no boys at all."

We made an effort to prove grandmother right.

Later Uncle Joe took his whiskey, making know-how to the army with him. In the maintenance outfit after the invasion of France, the army assigned a six-by-six truck to Uncle Joe. A fifty-five-gallon drum of fermenting raisins or dried fruit became a permanent part of essential tools necessary for his job, which were in the truck at all times. The mixture was converted into drinking liquor at an opportune moment.

"Anything that ferments can be made into alcohol," he said.

He also set up his still, which had been fabricated at army expense, on the bed of his truck. He distilled a product of questionable character, about seventy-percent alcohol. Seventy-percent alcohol is 140-proof and powerful stuff. My uncle traded some of his product for raw material. He would then repeat the process.

Uncle Joe, my mother's brother, made life interesting during the summers I spent on my grandfather's farm. He also made London a more interesting place for me. Seeing someone from home raised my spirits. To see my favorite uncle made it a bonus. This visit shall remain in my memory as a big night for both of us.

Ron Bloom and Ed Daughtry were delighted to meet Uncle

Joe and his friend, Jim Rivers, a boy from the bayou country in Mississippi. Together we opened the bottle of Scotch I had obtained at great expense. The five of us drank straight whiskey and polished off the bottle before we left the hotel.

Uncle Joe explained, "If we drink the whiskey here, we won't have to carry the bottle."

"Who can argue with such well-put logic?" I asked. "We also have some thirsty friends out there, and since we don't have enough to share, here in the hotel is the place to drink.

"Hey, this is not a weekend night, but the bars are packed," I said.

"Yes," Uncle Joe said. "They're like this all the time."

The five of us wandered in and out of several bars. Again, we found our black market friend, and I bought another fifth of Scotch.

By this time, it was around 10:00 P.M. The Germans chose that time and that night to bomb London. When the air raid alarm sounded, the British girls ran to the nearest shelter. My buddies and I stood in the middle of the street, risking death to see the action. British anti-aircraft guns opened up on the German aircraft. They were one-half mile away, but the noise was deafening. We were standing on a typical London Street, and two-and three-story buildings lined up at the back edge of a ten-foot sidewalk. I could see the bright explosions of the anti-aircraft shells as they exploded in the partly cloudy sky. I also heard the shrapnel falling back to earth near me. It was as though a dozen freight trains were bearing down on us with the whistle wide open. The air raid siren added to the clamor. To speak in a normal voice and be heard was impossible. What an inconvenience for a guy having fun!

When the Germans dropped their bombs (the ones with the whistles on the fins), I could feel the city shake with the explosions and hear the debris falling and the sirens from fire trucks and ambulances. The emergency vehicles rushed to put out the fires and pick up casualties. The moment burned itself into my memory, and the excitement pressed into my consciousness. This was the ultimate horror. Those philosophical thoughts lasted about five seconds; then my feet shifted into gear.

We ran to the subway that was deep underground. On the platform inside were double-decker bunks stacked against the wall. "What possible reason would anyone have to use this public area as a bedroom?" I asked.

"Some people sleep here every night," Uncle Joe said. "The Krouts have bombed the hell out of London. It's early tonight, some beds are already occupied. The lights always stay on. People sleep here from exhaustion."

"The German planes are gone," Uncle Joe said.

The shooting stopped, and the air raid siren stopped. People came out of the shelters back to the bars and took up where they had left off. Another raid tonight was unlikely, the British night fighters had already scrambled.

"Your friend Daughtry can't seem to hold his liquor," Jim Rivers said. "After those drinks in the room his movements have become slower and more exaggerated."

"Yeah. A thimble of Scotch gives him a high. He's a cheap drunk," I said.

As we moved from bar to bar, we saw bombed-out buildings and rubble in the streets. These areas were marked with red kerosene lanterns. Daughtry took a red one from a pile of debris and walked down the street, singing and swinging the lantern. I retrieved the lantern and put it back in place, but I couldn't stop his singing. The straight Scotch in the hotel room had been too much for Daughtry.

"Look at London now after all the German bombing. It is still vibrant and wide awake," Uncle Joe said. "The British are tough people. The bombing and the shortages have not broken their spirit. They are real troopers in the battle for Britain."

They also liked to have fun. Soon, the bars again were full of Englishmen and Americans living it up. The Americans and the British made a good team.

Aside from a few isolated incidents, the Americans were well treated by the British. I became very fond of some of the Brits.

The pubs were packed three deep around the bar, and the tables were packed in so tightly that the person near you had to stand to let you out.

I met an Irish girl named June in one of the pubs. She was a nurse in a hospital in the suburbs of London. Her hair was down to her shoulders and turned up at the ends. A few freckles on each side of her turned-up nose gave her a mischievous appearance. Over drinks, she told me about herself. She made the best of a bad situation and looked good doing it. She showed concern for the bombing casualties which would likely show up at her hospital.

"I was engaged," she said. "My fiancé and I decided to wait until he came back from North Africa. He didn't come back. The Germans killed him in the battle of El Alemein."

"Too bad," I said. "It must have been rough on you."

She had to catch the last train at 12:00 A.M. from Charring Cross-Station. I walked with her to the train. We arrived early, stood in a doorway and kissed. I pulled her close and felt her hand fondling my crotch.

"Hey! We can't do anything here," I said.

She said, "It's here or nowhere. We don't have much time."

She took off her panties and put them in her bag, then raised her right leg for me to hold with my left arm. Standing in the dark doorway, we were making out with people walking by twenty to thirty feet away, taking no notice.

The position was a bit uncomfortable, but as we made progress, position became less important. When I kissed her good-bye, June promised to meet me the next night at the pub where we originally met. She didn't show. I felt badly about not being able to see her again. She was pretty and good company.

When our three-day pass expired, my uncle Joe had a few more days on his pass and took the train with us back to our base. My crew showed him around the air base and told him how we made our contribution to the war effort.

The next day our crew was scheduled for the first daylight raid ever to be flown over Berlin, the most dangerous target in Germany. The losses were expected to be high.

Uncle Joe left that night for his outfit. He wrote home about the raid and said, "I never expect to see John again."

This upset the entire family. In my next letter home, I assured my kin I would do my best to stay alive.

Because of bad weather, the 8th AF canceled the Berlin mission. Shortly thereafter, and several missions later, the Air Corps scheduled our crew to be shipped to North Africa, and we never flew over Berlin. Perhaps with this kind of luck, we might survive the war.

A mission across the channel to Calais was not the milk run we thought it would be.

CHAPTER
SIXTEEN

It was my seventh mission. It took all the courage I could muster to get out of bed, get dressed and get myself to the plane with the other members of the crew. Takeoff was at 7:00 A.M. The day before, from twenty-two thousand feet, the group had searched for our target through the clouds near Calais, France. The formation flew over some uncharted flak guns. The plane returned to the base with sixteen holes in the fuselage.

The crew arrived at today's briefing, and our target was just across the English Channel in France. We expected the mission to be a milk run, somewhat like the day before with no fighters and very little flak if we kept on course.

The previous day the target had been obscured by clouds, so we bombed an alternate. Even though we took a lot of flak, everyone in our squadron returned and seemed delighted to go after the original target the next day.

Later we learned we were bombing a buzz bomb installation. Buzz bombs were jets with wings with an explosive charge in the nose. These bombs were responsible for unbelievable destruction in London. The jet-propelled buzz bombs or the V-1 flew so fast they were almost impossible to shoot down; however, they were not accurate. No one knew where they would fall. The bombs were aimed at London and usually fell somewhere there were people. This uncertainty raised the tension and the demand that these sites be eliminated.

The day before, the crew had drawn flak as they made their

landfall on the French coast, and P-38 fighters covered us all the way to the target and back. The group expected the same treatment as yesterday. Since crew members were to be shipped home after twenty-five missions, we were eager to make any mission we considered easy. We expected this flight to be as easy as the one yesterday. However, this mission was to make all others seem like a walk to the corner drugstore.

The day started badly and got worse. My job on the airplane as chief engineer required the crew chief and I to run up the engines on a preflight procedure. Our inspection revealed the automatic speed control for the propeller on engine number three was defective. A decision would have to be made as to whether or not the crew should fly this mission. That decision was the prerogative of the first pilot. The prop governor could not be repaired before takeoff.

Daughtry said, "That prop is not that much of a problem. Our crew should make this mission. I am ready to go. How about you?"

"If the prop has a small defect now, how would it affect us if we have other difficulties?" I answered.

The crew chief ran up the engines again. Everything was in order except the prop. I would have to make a recommendation to the pilot.

My confidence for the trip was shot when I stepped out from the hatch on top of the wing, twelve feet off the ground to check the safety wire on the gas caps. Although the temperature was above freezing, the humidity in the air combined with the swift passage of air over the wing to form ice. The rapid movement of air over the wing during the engine run-up caused evaporation of the condensate already on the wing and dropped the temperature below freezing and caused the remaining moisture to freeze.

The light was poor. When I reached down to check the safety on the gas cap, my feet hit the ice on the wing and my legs popped straight out. Before I could say, "Oh, shit," I was sliding down the trailing edge of the wing, like a roller coaster gone wild.

My body seemed to be in slow motion. I saw the jeep parked below. There was a flagstaff alongside the windshield. I visualized my body impaled on the staff. Then I stopped abruptly, draped over the back seat of the driver's side of the jeep. With the small amount of dignity the situation allowed, I gathered my wits, sucked air back into my lungs and completed my inspection.

"Next time, Jones," Daughtry said, "if you have to fly, go by plane."

At 7:15 A.M., the crew saw the flare signal to start the engines. Should we go or not? The decision had to be made quickly. The preflight procedure revealed number three engine prop mechanism was out of control. The governor inside the hub of the Hamilton hydromatic propeller designed to maintain a constant selected rpm was inoperative. To slow the engine I pressed the feathering button primarily used to turn the variable propeller blades so as to take a bigger bite out of the air and thus reduce the revolutions per minute.

"Lieutenant Brecovitch, we have a malfunction of the prop on engine number three." I said. "We can control it with the feathering button. Everything else is okay. Since it's a short mission, I recommend we go."

"Thank you, Sergeant, for the recommendation. I'll make my preflight test, and if the plane is okay except for the prop, we'll go."

Lt. Brecovitch decided the mission was a possibility if the crew exercised care. We were always careful. What could happen to the crew on a milk run like yesterday?

The copilot, Murphy, said to me, "Let's go. I can control the engine speed with the feathering button. Tell the crew to rest easy. Lieutenant Murphy will not allow the engine to run away."

The plane roared down the runway with its eight thousand pounds of bombs. The copilot pulled up the landing gear and the flaps. The pilot found our niche in the group formation. The group then headed for the channel crossing.

The group commander did not realize how important the Germans considered our target. Upset with yesterday's raid, the enemy was very eager to protect the buzz bomb launching sites.

Overnight they had moved some mobile flak guns into the area for the turkey shoot they knew was coming.

The 445th Bomb Group flew in at sixteen thousand feet. The sky turned black with the explosions of the shells. We were hit as we made our landfall on the French coast.

The exploding shells shook the aircraft and caused the plane to move around. The formation loosened up. Shrapnel peppered the metal skin, and the plane bounced around. The explosions occurred one after the other. The gunner on the ground knew our altitude, and our sixteen-thousand-foot altitude made us a good target.

Ed Daughtry, flying in the waist gun position, saw the fire first and jammed down the intercom button, "Waist gunner to pilot! Waist gunner to pilot! Number one engine is on fire!"

"You lunatic!" I shouted over the intercom. However, my voice was not transmitted. If a station's button was pressed, no one else could talk on the intercom until it was released.

I also saw the fire. It was not number one but number four, the engine on the opposite side of the plane. Daughtry had confused the location of number one.

Normally good natured, easygoing, and not excitable, Daughtry lost his cool when he saw the engine burning. Confused and excited, he wanted to tell everyone about the fire.

Flying over enemy territory is very stressful. Seeing an engine on fire adds to that stress. However, observing a situation gone wrong due to stupidity, and not being able to do anything to correct the wrong reduced me to the straightjacket crowd.

While the fire continued to burn, I looked down from my turret at the radio operator. But the radio operator had already cut the gasoline to number one. The pilot cut the mags or magneto that fired the cylinders and feathered number one. With number four burning and number three on runaway status, only number two engine was healthy. The plane dropped out of formation. I looked up to see the group pulling away. The plane lost altitude fast. The pilot closed the cowl flaps on number one engine and operated the CO_2 extinguisher. I was in a state of panic. I could see everything going wrong but could do nothing to change the situation.

Finally, Daughtry exhausted his little speech on the intercom and removed his finger from the button.

On the intercom immediately, I spoke in a calm voice because the safety of the crew depended on what I said and the way I said it.

"Top turret to pilot. Number four engine is on fire, not number one. The smoke is white and looks like an oil fire."

"Pilot to crew. We will reverse the procedure. If we can't put out the fire, prepare to bail out. Do not leave the plane until I tell you. If the fire gets worse let us know. Correct John?"

"Roger," I said.

The flak continued fast and furious and followed us. The lower the plane dropped, the more likely we were to receive a direct hit.

The pilot didn't waste any time with a reversal of the shutdown. The copilot closed down number four and restarted number one. With hand signals and the intercom, I made sure the radio operator on the flight deck cut the gasoline to number four engine and turned it on for number one. Number four engine continued to burn for a while after the CO_2 had been applied, but soon went out.

"Top turret to pilot. Fire out. No fire. No smoke," I said.

"Roger," Brecovitch said.

The plane lost four thousand feet before our descent could be stabilized. Our position was back and below the group. The pilot continued to follow the course to the target, made the turn on the initial point and the bombardier dropped the bombs on the target.

Lt. Brecovitch came on the intercom. "Pilot to top turret. Do we have enough gasoline to make the trip back?"

"Top turret to pilot. I'll check and let you know."

Did the plane carry enough gasoline to make it back to our base? An airplane burns more gasoline with three engines running than with four. I checked the fuel level and monitored the fuel consumption for fifteen minutes and decided gasoline would not be a problem.

Our group pulled out of sight. Because of the fighters in France, we sweated the trip back to our base. With the other 999 airplanes flying that day over that part of England, getting on the ground would not be easy. Would we have fog? Could we land with three engines? Would good navigating and pilot procedure save us? As we came closer to the base, we saw the fog moving in.

"I'm glad we we're not thirty minutes later," the pilot said. "Now that we've found Arden Tower, we can home in and land safely through open patches of fog."

After landing, we were debriefed, dressed out in our fatigues, had dinner and went in to rest for the next one.

"Hey, Daughtry. Hold up four fingers," Crimes asked. "Now one. Tell me the difference."

"Up your ass," Daughtry said.

That night in the barracks, we had something to talk about. Daughtry was very sensitive about his mistake. He felt so badly about mixing up number one and number four engines it took all the fun out of kidding him.

We were lucky this time and were able to overcome the problems. Would our good luck hold out until we finished our tour of duty?

Nora, the English girl, had a big surprise for me.

CHAPTER SEVENTEEN

Whenever possible, I continued to see Nora. Our routine was born out of convenience and a love of sex. We met at the pub, had something to drink and eat and retired early to her room. The relationship did have ups and downs, but we both looked forward to being together.

Nora developed an attachment for me and I for her. She pulled herself together and got a better job with a government agency. Her new lifestyle raised her self-image. She lost her despondency and perked up and seemed to have more interest in living. I was still paying her rent and delighted to see her take more interest in her life. However, she did drink more than she had earlier. Concerned, I wondered if she would become an alcoholic. Sometimes stress can create a dependency.

I knew British girls seemed to drink more than they should. They had an unusual ability to hold their ale. They could down four or five ten-percent-alcohol beer pints in one evening and never go to the ladies' room. One night, while I was walking Nora and another girl home in the blackout, they excused themselves and disappeared into a dark little side street. A minute later, I heard the sound of water hitting the cobblestones. I stood there in the dark for ages before the noise stopped. The moon reflected off a wide silver stream as it flowed out of the alley into the gutter.

"Nora, what did you girls do up that alley?" I asked, "Turn on a fire hydrant?"

"Don't be silly," Nora replied. "No, I avoided an explosion."

As Nora's girlfriend walked up, Nora said, "John, you have met Polly, but I haven't told you much about her."

"And why not? Hello, Polly."

Polly was very English. She had light gray eyes, blonde, shoulder-length hair and a pleasant face which had lost some of the blush of her teen years. She looked at me in the poor light and smiled, exposing irregular but white teeth.

"Polly lives nearby, and we visit a lot," Nora continued. "Polly is looking for an arrangement with an Air Corps man, the same as we have. Do you know anyone?"

"Not at the moment," I said. "Give me a couple of days. There must be someone. How about me?"

"You big lug. You're mine!" Nora replied. "Polly will have to get her own man."

"I'll ask around," I said, "and let you know."

Sitting around in a pub and drinking ale or beer was not my idea of a pleasant evening, but a way to sidestep the tension of the moment. The club atmosphere of the pub relaxed me. The drinking Brits sat around the open fire in a homelike situation, drank their ale, laughed and talked. Most GIs were accepted by these locals.

Playing darts with the English could be fun. An obligation for the loser to buy drinks was a standard. The pubs had cold beer in the winter and hot beer in the summer. The ingenious British had a way of making the cold beer hot but no way of making hot beer cold. In the winter, the kegs were kept outside. The beer was brought in and served cold. In the winter, the warm beer became more desirable to drink. It warmed your insides and gave the drinker a rosy glow. Heating the beer could be done with a poker with a round ball on the end, the size of a large marble. A poker placed in the fire soon became red hot. The ashes were knocked off and the poker placed in the beer. The taste of warm alcohol made one forget the fog, rain, and combat.

Hot beer is just as devastating as hot sake. In a very short time, the drink could have the consumer walking in circles. To come in out of a cold drizzle, slightly wet, and chilled to the bone increased the pleasure of hot beer. It helped everyone to tolerate the English weather.

As the flying schedule picked up and there was less and less time for Nora, I began to hear about her dating other boys. I never had any strong claim for all of her attention, but I didn't want her to go to bed with someone else.

Because we lost the Whitfield crew to flak on the last mission, our crew members walked around with sad expressions. We could do nothing but accept the loss. They were the fourth crew lost from our barracks in less than five months. Daughtry saw them go down and reported no chutes. They were flying the tail end Charlie position in the group at the end of the formation.

"It's plain unlucky to live in our barracks. Everyone gets killed," I told Nora.

"What's so unlucky? You're still around," she said. "Now don't get yourself killed. It would ruin our relationship."

In the three months of our arrangement, Nora and I had some good times together. We told jokes and laughed a lot. She knew and liked the entire crew. The crew appreciated her good company. Because of the unsettled nature of the times, no one made plans. Abruptly, orders were cut. Our crew was transferred to North Africa; later to Italy. After receiving the orders, my instructions were to contact no one and remain on the base.

I had to see Nora to say good-bye. She was at the pub talking to another GI when we arrived. We asked for a table to ourselves, and I told her about our transfer.

"You can't go, love. I am pregnant," she said. "I've been waiting until I was sure. Now I'm sure."

She seemed reluctant to talk about her condition and blushed with some agitation as she talked.

My mouth dropped open. Preoccupied with the dangers associated with combat, I thought she was taking care of the birth control. She knew how to shock. It is easy to get sidetracked in life. Because of the uncertainty of the future, my main struggle was to stay alive.

"You haven't been practicing birth control?" I asked. "You've become careless. Did your drinking cause you to be careless?"

"It's your responsibility as much as mine. Our female parts are the same as women in other countries."

She cried a little and asked, "When can we get married?"

"Married? We have an arrangement. Besides, we don't love each other that much," I said.

"You told me you loved me."

"I love to be with you and that's true. I just can't marry you."

Her temper flared. She looked at me, and the hostility showed in those blue eyes. They became hard, and her voice took on an edge.

"It's your bloody baby, and you bloody will marry me. I'll go to your base commander."

"Don't do anything rash. Think it over and meet me here tomorrow night."

Other Englishmen at the pub hinted that Nora had taken other soldiers to her room. At least they left the pub together. Several people told me they had seen her with other men. How could I prove the baby mine or prove that it wasn't?

Upon my return to our hut, the crew was playing poker. I retold Nora's story. Bob Jackson seemed sympathetic. Older and more mature, he looked out for the younger members of the crew. Bob felt a strong identity with crew members. "I don't want to see you ruin your life," he said. "Why worry? We'll go with you tomorrow night and tell Nora if she goes to the colonel, we'll also say we all had a little of the same stuff."

Daughtry and Jackson went with me the next night.

"Nora, I don't believe the baby is mine but have no way to prove it is or it isn't. You asked for this relationship which I paid for. The problem of the baby is yours. If you go to the base commander, Daughtry and Jackson will say you also made love to them."

Nora cried again. I felt awful. The strategy worked. Nora said, "I won't contact the colonel."

We said our good-byes. I gave Nora all the money in my wallet, some two hundred dollars. I kissed her good-bye and walked out of her life forever.

Our transfer to the 376th Bomb Group and our trip down was spiked with adventure.

CHAPTER EIGHTEEN

Our flight to North Africa on March 12, 1944, was in an ATC C-54, a large four-engine cargo aircraft. We were on our way to join the 376 Bomb Group in Italy.

"We are being transferred out because we've lost so many crews out of our barracks," Bob said. "The group commander wants to keep the secret that flying over Germany may be hazardous to your health. Shit, we know that. We also know what happened to those crews who didn't return to our barracks. They want to start over on the count for our hut."

The 376 and the 98 Bomb Groups also had their troubles. They had been almost wiped out by the low-level bombing raid over Ploesti, Romania.

The two groups had been over the target, just as delayed action bombs were exploding from earlier drops. Since the raid was at low level, the Air Corps not only bombed the oil fields but also bombed their own bombers. The raid damaged the oil fields but did not put them out of operation.

The 376 Bomb Group needed experienced bomber crews. We were experienced.

Our C-54 landed at Casablanca. Next day we were off for Oran and later Algiers where we spent some time. The crew made plans to see the city.

We were disappointed to learn that in Casablanca, a number of Moslem women still wore a veil and a hood according to the ancient custom of Purdah. The girls were kept hidden from the local men and visiting American soldiers.

Moslems lived in the Casbah, the oldest part of the city.

These sections surrounded what had been old Arab forts. The narrow streets of the Casbahs are crowded with open shops. Vendors sold rugs, jewelry and other products made locally.

In this area most of the houses were made of brick and stucco, the most readily available construction materials. Sun-dried brick are easy to maintain where the rainfall is low. Flies and other insects were prevented from breeding because of the dry heat. There were enough insects to go around, but not as bad as other parts of Africa where the rainfall was higher.

Many of the houses were built with small windows to keep out the heat. In the desert, the nomads lived in tents around water holes. The tents were heavy and made of thick camel hair which acted as insulation against the heat.

The next stop was Algiers. The crew landed, left a guard on the plane and went into the city by jeep. Sleeping accommodations had been arranged for transit crews in an old hotel in the city. We checked in and rushed out to see the city. The weather was beautiful. There was not a cloud in the sky, and the temperature was comfortable.

The city of Algiers is laid out around a bay, shaped like a horseshoe with the open end to the sea. The terrain sloped up from the water and was steep enough, so the streets and the houses stacked on that slope around the bay all have a view of the water and the ships. The bay is deep, well protected and ideal for anchoring boats. The gleaming white houses above the blue water presented a postcard picture. If Humphrey Bogart and Ingrid Bergman would only step onto the *Casablanca* set, the picture would be complete. Perhaps somewhere in this romantic city another Ingrid could be found.

"Let's go out and make our impact on this part of the world," Daughtry said as he flexed his small upper-arm muscle. "We should let those Arabs know we have been here."

"We can go out and let the women know we are here," I said. "Other invaders killed off the men and enslaved the women. Is that what you have in mind?"

"Count me out for the murder of anyone. Right now my concern is for the well-being of the women," Daughtry responded.

We walked into a sidewalk bar and sat down. The tables were on the sidewalk with an umbrella in the center. The inside saloon had some tables near the bar. Just to sit and watch the people walk by became recreation. There wasn't much to drink except muscatel. I ordered some and found the taste to be mild and sweet with a sour aftertaste.

After the first sip I said, "Hell, a guy could drink a gallon of this."

"If you drink a gallon of that stuff, we will have to carry you back to the hotel," Bob said. "Have you noticed the local women don't hang around bars? The ones available are in brothels. The ones not available are in private homes and beyond reach. I don't see any in this bar."

The wine was served in a liter bottle with the top cut off below the neck and the rim fire polished. A wicker handle fastened to the side formed a mug. The mug held almost a quart.

After one of those, drunk down like water, the world took on a rosy glow. Well into my second drink, I noticed my friends were gone. Some friends! Real friends are those who, when you have made a fool of yourself, don't feel the damage is permanent.

A solo conquest of this ancient city was not what I originally had in mind. However, even without my crew, I felt the gates would fall before my onslaught. I girded up my loins, or at least hooked up my trousers, and headed in the direction of where I thought the action would be.

Exploring a strange city is always an adventure. Exploring a strange and undisciplined city during a war and slightly drunk is foolhardy. I had been taught to be more careful. The late hour and the dark streets should have made me cautious but didn't. The streets were narrow and dirty. The shops were closed. I had difficulty finding my way. However I kept walking, hoping the neighborhood would improve. It got worse.

"My God," I thought. "I'm in the Casbah, a lawless part of the city."

Here the Arabs kill for a pair of shoes. There were stories

about American soldiers who disappeared in the native quarters of Algiers and were never found. Could this happen to me? Beneath the glow of confidence brought on by the wine, a small quiet voice told me to be careful.

The Casbah, originally built by slaves, had no planning for utilities or streets. The slaves built as they chose. If a slave wanted to build in the middle of a street, the city fathers did not object. There were no sewers. Filth thrown in the street was washed down the hill to the bay and out into the ocean.

No code determined how much land a builder could cover. However, each hovel had access to some kind of path or alley.

I walked a street paved with cobblestones and lined on each side with two-story houses without a break. The second floor stuck out past the first, so as to provide a covered walkway below and shade in the daytime. At night very little light penetrated to the first-floor level, providing an ideal place for murder and other fun and games.

The so-called street was about twelve feet wide with some sidewalk. The second floor of the houses extended so that no more than ten feet of open sky remained above the street. Everything was drab and foreboding. The evening air smelled strongly of decaying food and sewerage.

A door opened, and light spilled into the alley. A young girl in a veil beckoned to me with her hand. Her motions were slow and exaggerated. She acted strangely, as if she were floating. She wore a partial veil, and her diaphanous clothing gave her the look of a girl from *The Arabian Nights*, and she wasn't bad looking either. My spirit of adventure and the wine caused me to want to explore the situation.

I walked up to the door. Her dress was not a dress but a costume made of strips of cloth tightly fastened at the ankle and wrists. She wore a spot on her cheek and an Arabic symbol over the center of her forehead, which was supported by a thread from each side of her head. The allure of the woman and the ambiance of the place gave me goose pimples. In the bad light, this young woman looked very desirable, my type of female.

I stepped inside to view a scene from *The Arabian Nights.* Three girls were lying on mats on the floor, taking turns sucking on a tube attached to a very ornate water pipe about two feet tall.

Between twenty and twenty-five, the girl had a well-shaped face with regular features. Her dark skin, hair and eyes indicated she was Arabic. It startled me to note that she had an intelligent face, and she smiled as if she liked her profession.

The young woman ushered me in, took one look at me and realized I did not speak French or Arabic.

She said, "Monsieur, a woman?"

By this time, the heat, excitement and the exercise of walking had sobered me somewhat. Out of my element and in dangerous territory, I looked around, bowed, backed out and walked quickly down the street.

There was little time to think what a fool I'd been. I acknowledged my mistake. Now was the time to summon my natural intelligence and find a way out of this stinking Casbah.

Inside my shirt I carried a hunting knife made from a power hacksaw blade with some clear Plexiglas for a handle. Determined to make it very unprofitable for anyone to jump me, I opened my shirt and let my fingers close around the handle.

Relieved to be out of the room, I began walking fast down the dark alley. My toe caught something and caused me to fall headlong into the filth of the alley. Turning around to search the cause of the stumble, I felt a human leg attached to a human being. The human had his back to the wall. His feet were out in the alley. I suspected he must have been a beggar. He showed no signs of life in the dim light.

I stood up, wiped the filth from my hands on my trousers and again started out. A splash of liquid to my left indicated someone had dumped a chamber pot into the street from a second floor. The liquid missed me, but the stench was awful.

The presence of danger cleared my head. This was not a place of human habitation; this was hell. My paramount thought was to free myself of this foreboding place. All my senses were directed toward survival. No obvious way out appeared.

I wanted to kick myself in the seat of my pants for being so stupid as to get involved in such a difficult situation; however, another part of me seemed glad for the adventure. If I had not imbibed, I would not have the adventure to remember.

Two Arabs were following me. I was walking at a fast pace they had to run to keep up. Never had my life been in such peril except in the heat of combat.

Looking up and using the slit of light above as a guide, I broke into a slow jog. A masonry wall appeared from nowhere and arranged itself in my flight path. My nose was flattened and my progress impeded. What would Dad say now?

Dirty and with a bleeding nose, I knew my prospects were dim. Slowing to a walk, I wiped the blood from my nose with my handkerchief. The alley opened up onto a square with a single streetlight. Thankful to be in the light, I looked for someone to give me directions. The two men following me walked over to the left side of the open space but continued to watch me. Other people were walking around in the square. They looked preoccupied and in a rush to reach their homes.

When I was one-third of the way across the square, a boy of ten ran up to me and said, "Hey, Joe. Want a girl? Very pretty. My sister."

My spirits soared. The kid's words had a heavy accent and were difficult to understand. When their meaning became clear, I laughed out loud.

At this one time in my life, sex took a secondary role. I pulled out a five-dollar bill and said, "This is yours if you get me back to my hotel."

"Sure, Joe," he said.

In less than ten minutes, we arrived at my hotel. I gave the kid five dollars, and he darted away in search of his next customer.

The wine must have been toxic. It is possible that poison had been served in the wine. Sick and tired I tried to sleep. When I closed my eyes, the room spun around. Opening my eyes caused a shock; the spinning stopped quickly. Regurgitating several times

emptied my stomach, and I drank water not to have the dry
heaves.

To sleep with the room turning seemed as impossible as
sleeping with my eyes open. After a long night without sleep,
my head felt the size of a watermelon. Two weeks and several
days passed before my health returned.

Two days later, our crew took off for Bari, Italy.

Arriving at the city of Bari, we looked out at the calm waters
of the harbor, the limited access from the sea, and the buildings
lining the waterfront. Back of the waterfront was a stone dock
with paved walks backed up by trees. The construction and design
of the masonry houses and the dock gave order to the scene.
Later this order would be changed to rubble. Thirty American
Liberty Ships loaded with five-hundred-pound bombs would be
docked in the harbor, and one of these ships would take a direct
hit from a lone German plane. Everything close by was blown to
smithereens.

Finding transportation to the 376 Bomb Group was difficult.
After a day of waiting, our crew boarded a B-25. The pilot took
off. Pulling up too fast, the pilot almost stalled on takeoff. The
plane yawed a bit but overcame the bad piloting. The worst part
of the flight occurred when we reached our base, San Pancrazio.
The pilot tried to fly into a landing without flaps. We hit the
ground fast, like a ton of bricks. Shook up, we crawled out. The
pilot, a second lieutenant of about twenty, said, "How did you
like the flight? First time I have ever been in a B-25. I'm a fighter
pilot."

"Gee, thanks," I said. "It's nice to have that information. You
could have told us earlier before we boarded."

We were home. We had reached our future field of operations.
The base was made up of English desert tents and spaced between
the olive trees along the side of a hill. We stared in disbelief. The
scene appeared so unattractive and primitive I looked forward to
finishing my missions and returning stateside.

We were startled to find that in Great Britain we only had to
fly twenty-five missions. In Italy, the number changed to fifty.

The difference supposedly was justified because the flights were shorter and easier. We found this to be wrong. Our crew made flights into Austria and Romania that were long, difficult and dangerous. They did give us double credit for our missions out of Great Britain.

CHAPTER NINETEEN

They located our base at San Pancrazio, a small town near Lechi in the southern part of Italy. The ideal climate suited us most of the time, sometimes it rained. However the base registered several notches lower in accommodations related to comfort than the base in England. Tents alongside an airstrip gave it a camped-out look. I tried hard to remember that our sacrifices and discomfort were for the war effort. Later, after I experienced the inconvenience of a badly laid-out base, I liked it even less.

General Sherman, the Yankee general in the American Civil War, said, "War is hell." And so it seems. I didn't look around for picnic tables or dancing girls, but the first trip to the latrine in an open field lowered my expectations for the other facilities.

A friend said, "If you go to Italy, don't miss it. It's just wonderful."

If I left now, I wouldn't miss it.

Our new outfit in Italy, the 376 Bomb Group, and her sister group, the 98, were combat seasoned. The 376 had come up from Benghazi, Libya and North Africa, where they bombed targets around the Mediterranean. However, the tremendous losses at Ploesti had decimated their numbers and lowered morale. We were part of the transfusion expected to perk up the outfit. The transfer also solved another problem. Now the 445th could start a new count on the crews shot down out of our barracks.

The 376 also bombed for the invasion of Sicily and Anzio and other parts of southern Italy when southern Italy was under control of the Germans.

Looking down the runway, my mouth flew open. It was too short, no more than three thousand feet in the full length. Each takeoff would build tension for the flight. When fully loaded, our bombers needed extra room for takeoff. Many times our plane bounced off the ground as we ran out of runway and became airborne.

Daughtry said, "This base is crap. The only permanent buildings are the parachute packing room and the Officer's Club." Everything else was housed in tents. "Wouldn't that just frost you?"

"The tents are not so bad," I said. "They are English desert tents with an extra top which stops leaks and makes the area inside cooler in the summer." A wood base six inches off the ground was constructed under the tent to keep us out of the mud. We did have army cots and blankets. The tents were not comfortable, but these were better accommodations than the infantry.

Three men were assigned to a tent. To take the chill out of the air, in each tent, a five-gallon can dripped oil through a copper tube into another five-gallon can with a stove-pipe vent at the top and a hole near the bottom. The dripping oil fell into a concave nose cover for the fuse from a five-hundred-pound bomb. As the oil burned, the pipe supplying the oil became hot and improved the efficiency of the stove. Unless the tent occupant regulated the oil supply, the stove became hotter and hotter. Several tents were lost to fire. The heaters burned used oil from the airplane engines.

"It is difficult to read in bed," Ron said. "Our tent has a sixty-watt electric bulb. The power from those wires laid across the ground to an emergency generator lowered the output to the bulb. Surely the air force could do better."

"You think that's bad," I said, "my bed is so hard I have to get up during the night to get some rest."

Located between two rolling hills covered with olive trees, our landing strip dominated the low-level ground in the small valley. Low hills looked down on a single asphalt strip bordered on one side with "hardstands," or paved asphalt spaces for parking airplanes.

"Did you see those two men sawing those stone blocks with a cross-cut saw?" Daughtry asked. "That seems a little strange to me. We use the same saw to cut wood in the U.S."

"The limestone blocks are sawed by hand after they are quarried because at that time the stone is soft," I said. "Later the stone hardens when exposed to the carbon dioxide in the air for a few weeks."

"The weather here is nice," Crimes said. "Vendors have sub-tropical fruit for sale in the village markets nearby."

"The weather should be beautiful. We are halfway down on the boot and except for the high humidity, the weather is like middle Florida," Crimes said as he flopped down on his bunk.

"There is very little rain, but who cares?" Ron said, looking up from his bunk. "Any is enough to make one wish for something more permanent than an English desert tent."

"Everything is cold in this hotel room but the ice water," I said.

"Why do you complain? You have a room and a bath." Ron said.

"Yeah. The bath is a mile away," Crimes said.

"Crimes, that's not as bad as having to share the tent with you and Ron," I said. "This tent is making me stoop shouldered. It is not high enough for anyone to stand erect except in the center.

"If I lose my military bearing I will blame it on the British. Hopefully, our stay in this paradise will be short lived. Finishing this tour of duty is my main concern," I continued.

The bomb group of approximately fifty airplanes and seven hundred men was divided into four squadrons. There was only one set of showers, located a one-mile walk away at the headquarters squadron. This same situation occurred in England. Water for our squadron was trucked into our bivouac area in five-hundred-gallon trailers.

Using just one helmet filled with water, I could keep clean if

I bathed in the right sequence. My face and teeth had the first priority.

"Have you had to go yet?" Crimes asked. "The toilets are two fifty-five-gallon drums placed on top of each other and buried in the ground with a wood top and a toilet seat. They arranged seven of them in a row for your convenience. The five sheets of toilet paper a day rationed us doesn't guarantee a clean wipe, and there are no Sears Roebuck catalogs."

"The planners have thoughtfully placed the toilets outside in a field," Daughtry said. "To keep them sanitary, they burn them out daily with used oil. You can smell the procedure now. The burning stinks up the area for miles around and smells worse than what they are burning."

"The air force planner, in his infinite wisdom, selected the site to have access to a female audience. I am impressed with the location," I said. "The open latrines are placed along an old trail the village women used on their way to work in the olive groves."

"When the first ten or fifteen women walked by, I wanted to crawl into the damn thing," Daughtry said. "Despite having been in the air force for almost two years with the damage to my sense of modesty, I am never comfortable sitting on the potty with a female audience."

"During a rain, a visit to the potty is tricky," I said. "Wearing only my hat, my shoes and a raincoat, I walked into the field and sat on one of the stools provided. This experience will do absolutely nothing to elevate your self-image. However when the trips become frequent as a result of eating the Air Corps menu, it is a time saver."

"Jones, are you saying in your less-than-cultured voice that you have had the GIs?" Ron asked.

"Well, yes," I admitted.

Some of the flights out of Italy were ten hours or more as the 376 Bomb Group penetrated deeper into southern Europe. Not as many German fighter planes were around; however, that risk was balanced by the concentration of flak guns around cities like Ploesti, Romania. Ploesti was protected with more than three hundred flak guns concentrated around the oil fields. Three hundred flak guns in one small area is frightening. To sit still in a slow-flying B-24 while it moved the crew through a sky filled with exploding shells took a set of cast iron nerves.

"Flying through a sky black with bursting flak scares the shit out of me and makes me want to take up basket weaving on the ground," Daughtry said from his seat on the flight deck. "Even after the shooting stops, it's hard to stop the shakes. I take some to bed with me. If you hear me scream during the night you'll know the Germans scored a hit."

"You're just trying to impress me," I said as Daughtry and I walked to the shower. "It's scary to see a burst of flak one hundred yards back of the plane, a second burst at fifty yards, and a third burst at twenty-five yards. The next burst you don't see. You feel the shrapnel rake the plane like buckshot fired against a tin roof."

"Some didn't bounce; I picked up a double handful of shrapnel inside the plane, would you believe that? Shrapnel blew its way through the skin on one side of the aircraft but didn't make it out the other side. We are lucky it didn't hit a vital part of the plane or a vital part of a crew member."

"You are right about luck," I said. "I lost the plastic cover on the top turret. That thing keeps the cold air out and cuts down on the noise. So far I've lost three domes to falling and exploding flak. Without that dome, the icy cold slipstream freezes my butt and reduces my efficiency. Not having it makes me want to leave the turret and curl up on the flight deck. Without the cover the wind howls, somewhat like a cat whose tail had been caught under a truck tire."

On our twenty-sixth mission, the navigator, Roy Watson, pressed the intercom button and said, "I've been hit!"

After leaving the target area, I went down to determine the extent of his injuries. He couldn't have been hurt badly if he could remain calm.

"See that red spot on my neck?" he said as he pointed to the back of his neck and then to the hole in the side of the airplane. I looked down on the flight deck and saw the piece of shrapnel that made the mark. "The skin's not broken," I said. "You'll live." Picking up the piece of flak, I said, "You should keep this. I hope this is as close as you ever come to a Purple Heart."

"Let me make you a hero," Logan said. "I can make a little cut on your neck, and you can apply for a Purple Heart. How about it, lard ass?"

"Go piss upwind," Roy mumbled.

Usually, if a hit was bad enough to kill someone, the plane exploded or went out of control. In that event, no one came back.

On the morning of March 28, 1944, the crews took off in twenty-second intervals to minimize time in the air for getting into formation. At the end of the runway, one plane turned left, and the next one turned right to avoid the prop wash of the preceding plane. This process always frightened me because some prop wash always occurred and caused a wing to drop.

For maximum lift, the wing must be level by level. If one wing goes down, some lift is lost, but if too much aileron is applied to correct or to level the plane, the wing looses even more lift. With the short runway the crew always sweated takeoff, the most dangerous part of flying, because on takeoff the engines and all the systems were making a maximum effort. Our planes were always fully loaded with eight thousand pounds of bombs and 2,300 gallons of high-test gasoline.

The pilot taxied the plane around and took our place in line for takeoff. Fourth in line, we waited. Our generators malfunctioned. The pilot pulled out of line while I made some adjustments.

Before I could repair the generators, the last plane in our group had taken off. The crew watched as the plane left the runway and tried to pull up. The left wing was down. The pilot applied too much aileron which slowed the flying speed and stalled out the wing. The plane made it a quarter mile out of the flight path and then struck the ground. The low wing hit first and spun the aircraft into the ground.

The planes were loaded with Composition B bombs, an explosive so unstable when dropped they exploded without a fuse. The people in our aircraft saw the plane hit. One moment it was a plane, the next moment it was a bright ball of fire. From two miles away we felt our plane lurch as the shock wave hit us.

Flight crews do not welcome an event of this kind before a mission. We were already late. As soon as the smoke cleared, Brecovitch pushed the throttle forward. The plane roared down the runway. The pilot kept testing for flying speed by lifting the nose. I looked out, and the cowl flaps around the engines were open. It was the copilot's responsibility to close the flaps. I hit all four switches on the pilot's aisle stand, and the flaps closed. At that time we were at the end of the runway. The plane bounced three times on the earth but stayed airborne. The pilot kept her in the air. I looked down, and the sweat was popping out on the back of the pilot's hand. I also felt sweat forming and running down the side of my face, inside my flight helmet.

German equipment and the train yards in the Poe Valley in northern Italy were scheduled as targets for the day. We found our place in the formation and climbed to twenty-three thousand feet.

Just before we reached the target, the flak came up thick and fast. We lost the lead aircraft in our formation. I saw two other planes from our formation go down behind us.

We flew through black clouds of smoke made by the bursting shells. They spewed shrapnel in all directions. Our plane shuddered when the bursts were near. We heard the shrapnel as it peppered the plane. The Germans had moved some mobile flak around the target. They were making the 376 pay dearly for the damage the group intended. Ominous and threatening, bursting shells darkened the sky. Bright flashes could be seen through the haze before the black smoke formed after an explosion.

We were sitting ducks at twenty-three thousand feet, flying

150 miles per hour. If there had been something to do, it would have been easier. On the ground a soldier can dig a foxhole and fire back at the enemy. Our only enemy at the moment was the flak guns twenty-three thousand feet below. So we sat, waited and sweated.

The plane ahead dropped its bombs. I felt the plane rise as our bombs were dropped. Other planes in the formation did not drop theirs. We had dropped early, but why? I would find out later.

We continued with the formation. Over the target, the other planes in the group dropped their bombs. From below, thick black smoke billowed up, almost obscuring the red flashes of the exploding ammo trains. The pilot turned off the bomb run, followed the formation and headed for home.

I received a call on the intercom from the radio operator. "We have a hit. The bomb bay doors won't close."

My job was to close the doors, if that were possible.

Still at twenty thousand feet, I hooked on a "walk around" oxygen bottle and checked the pilot's aisle stand. A red handle with a cable attached through the aisle stand was in place. If the pilot pulled the cable halfway up, the bomb bay doors opened. If he pulls the cable out the entire length, the bombs were salvoed. In that event, a cam under the flight deck had to be reset. The bomb bay doors could be closed in the normal way after resetting the cam. Closing normally required pulling a selector valve on the starboard side of the flight deck at the bulkhead separating the bomb bay from the flight deck.

I searched for damage to the aircraft and found none. In the meantime, large quantities of gasoline were required to fly the plane because of the drag of the open doors. With the present consumption rate, the plane might not be able to make it back to the base. There was no Sinclair station on the return trip with a free windshield wash.

The pilot's instructions were, "Get those damn doors closed."

The backup system could do the job.

The doors could be cranked down manually. This procedure

required someone to walk out on the catwalk from flight deck to bomb racks in the front bomb bay. That designated person was I. The crew expected me to go out on that one-foot-wide plank without a parachute, and with nothing below me but twenty thousand feet of fresh air. "Could I do it?" I asked myself.

In high school, I had discovered my fear of heights while painting the roof of a dormitory. I had walked over to the edge and looked down over my toes and found it difficult to move back. To move would cause me to tilt forward. For a brief second, my body seemed out of control.

The radio operator asked, "Can you do it?"

"I fell down a set of steps one time. That was okay. I wanted to get down anyway."

As I looked from the flight deck through the open bomb bay doors at the ground twenty thousand feet below, the panic from high school returned. The bomb rack in the bomb bay was only five feet from the number six bulkhead and the flight deck, but that five feet looked the length of a football field. The memory of the high school experience wrecked my self-confidence. Could I do it, I asked again. Not to do it would always undermine my confidence for any critical demand in the future. I made the decision to do it now.

My actions were restricted by the electrically heated suit under my flight clothes and made it impossible to wear a chest chute on my harness. The helmet, oxygen mask and walk-around bottle further restricted my activity.

The twelve-inch-wide catwalk ran the length of both forward and rear bomb bays. My job was to walk out, insert a handle, now flat against the bomb rack and crank down the bomb bay doors on one side.

That seemed easy enough. I stepped out on the catwalk and held onto the bulkhead at the flight deck. I could touch the forward bomb rack. The slipstream caught my walk-around bottle, and it disappeared into space. My body tilted back and forth for a second. My foot slipped, but I held on. Gradually, my body got used to the lack of oxygen.

The oxygen mask was no good without the bottle. I unbuckled it and dropped it in the slipstream below. Moving the crank into the operational position was easy. The crank handle now was out between the bomb racks. Slowly, I began to turn the crank. The doors on one side of the bomb bay came down slowly. Turning around to crank the other side, I was off balance. The engaged crank was protruding out in the space between the bomb racks. The navigator, who had been holding the selector valve for the doors in the down position, turned it loose. The valve went back to the natural position. The pressure I had built up in the hydraulic accumulator on one side of the diaphragm exerted pressure on the other side of the hydraulic piston. That piston now moved and again opened the doors. The movement of the door caused the crank handle, which was still engaged, to turn. In turning, it struck me on the upper part of my body, knocking me loose from the bomb rack. I grabbed at the sharp metal of the rack. The sharp edges cut my hands. My fingers became sticky and slippery with blood. My feet dropped in the slipstream below. Slowly and painfully I pulled myself back up between the racks, avoiding the crank above. The oxygen-starved air at twenty thousand feet caused me to have a dizzy spell. The exertion had not helped. I locked my arms around one bomb rack and breathed easier. All my faculties would be needed to get me back on the flight deck.

The bomb bay doors were again open all the way. My reaction was not a fear of falling but of anger, anger directed at the navigator who had not followed my instructions. He had let go of the selector handle before it was safe to do so. All my choice words of condemnation tumbled out. "You goddamn shit for brains cock sucker. You couldn't stick your finger up your ass with both hands." First, it was garbled, but as my mind cleared, my words became fluent and biting. Mad as hell, I yelled, "You no good, SOB. You have no right to be in the service if you can't take instructions." The navigator understood the stress and danger he had caused me and took my verbal abuse without comment.

With the radio operator's help, I made my way back into the flight deck. Now I knew the source of the trouble. The cable on the pilot aisle stand had been pulled and stuffed back in the slot. Our bombs had been salvoed. No one told me. I went below the flight deck, reset the cam and closed the bomb bay doors in the normal fashion. There had been no combat damage to the hydraulic system.

That night, back at the base, the crew celebrated the fact that I had been pulled back from the jaws of death. My knees still felt rubbery, and my hands hurt like hell, but I remained in one piece.

The radio operator said, "If stupidity doesn't kill you, anyone has a good chance of surviving this war. The best time to miss a train is at a crossing. You did that, and we are proud of you."

As usual, we talked and laughed about this experience. Laughing helped. The hour became late, and we hit the sack. Then a thought occurred to me. "My God! I've got to fly again tomorrow."

On our thirty-seventh raid, made on March 29, 1944, to Bolzano, Italy, we were developing as an experienced crew and proud of our record. We tried to do everything right, but sometimes that was not possible. At the initial point, we turned on the bomb run and tried to open the bomb bay doors. Today, they would not open. With the flak coming up thick and fighters harassing the group in back of us, I could not leave the top turret for maintenance. Over the target, the bombardier dropped the bombs through the doors. The doors swung out, were caught by the slipstream and fluttered their way to the ground. Because of the loss of the bomb bay doors, our flight from the target back to our base was drafty but uneventful. The distance was shorter than the March 28 flight, so fuel was not a problem.

When something exciting occurs on any plane, everyone on the base finds out and has something smart to say. Our crew was the butt of a number of jokes. "How do you let a bird out of the cage? Drop the bottom out."

"Yeah, I know," I said. "I'm giving you the bird."

James White, a gunner in another squadron, said, "Don't

you know what that little handle on the starboard side of the flight deck is for? Bet someone in northern Italy is using those bomb bay doors as a tent."

The crew continued to fly and chalk up missions. Experience does not make the exposure to combat easier. The continued exposure numbed the senses and caused the person exposed to be jumpy. However, our crew made the combat missions over enemy territory with an increasing degree of professionalism.

In a combat situation, action is fast. My eyes were alert at picking up specks on the horizon, a possible fighter plane. Sometimes I would watch a speck for several minutes before it revealed its true identity as a spot on the Plexiglas dome.

Even with our constant searching of the sky, the fighter planes always surprised me. They came from nowhere out of the sun or clouds and were near the plane before they could be targeted. However, they made just as good a target going as they did coming, except straight down.

On April 2, 1944, the raid to Steyr, Austria, was a trip to remember. Fighters hit our formation one and one-half hours before the target and two hours after the target. The Germans threw everything they had into the battle. I recognized JU-88s, ME109s and ME210s. The tail gunner ran out of ammo and borrowed some from the waist gunner. On that trip, the tail gunner scored a confirmed hit. The pilots flying the German planes appeared to be less well trained than those we had encountered over Germany. The pilots had the ability to destroy our formations but appeared to lack the aggressiveness and daring to come in close enough even though they were firing twenty-millimeter cannons against our fifty-caliber machine guns.

I shot three hundred rounds out of my guns but did not score. The star of the crew was Crimes. He got a JU-88, a twin-engine fighter bomber.

We continued to chalk up missions, but we were restless and sometimes on edge because of the tension of combat. However, flying out of Italy was not as dangerous as England. We'd been lucky. Would that luck hold until we finished our tour of duty?

Now that we'd flown most of our missions, I thought an all-out fight with Crimes might not be necessary. No such luck, Crimes made that decision for me.

CHAPTER TWENTY

I always tried to avoid a fight. Confrontation did not suit me. In some cases, however, there is no way out, and fighting becomes the natural thing to do. Sooner or later Crimes will pick a fight with me, I thought. I won't welcome the occasion.

Older than other members of the crew, Crimes had involved himself in many things including life as a trick rider in a rodeo and work as an orderly in an asylum for the insane. He participated in procedures that brutalized the inmates and told many sordid stories of his work in the asylum. The stories did not endear him to me, or any other member of the crew.

"A standard procedure is used to get inmates in the asylum ready to meet with a visitor." Crimes said as he, Ron and I sat on our bunks in our tent, talking. "Bathe them. Dress them. Help them put on makeup. Then lead them into the visiting area. Some inmates did not want to visit. We put a bar of soap in a sock and knocked the hell out of the inmate. They received punishment until they did as they were told. Sometimes an inmate came out with a bruised face. If a member of the family commented, we had a standard story the inmate must have fallen."

"Do you expect me to believe that, Crimes?" I asked.

"Jones, you wouldn't believe anyone. Hell, I even had sex with a sixteen-year-old mongoloid at the asylum, and she loved that good sex. She didn't look good, but her deformed body really knew how to lift me up."

"Crimes, I can't believe that," Ron said in a cynical tone. "It must have been impossible for you to have your way with a female inmate? It just doesn't make sense."

Crimes explained as he sat up in his bunk and looked directly at me, "The inmates were locked in their rooms at night. The hospital was not well supervised. On my rounds, I would stop by her room. The girl would be ready and waiting. She loved sex. Hell, she fell in love with me," Crimes said. "If she saw me when she was out of her room, she ran to me and pressed her body against mine. I didn't want everyone to know I had sex with her. She didn't know how to keep a secret. When my boss found out, he fired me."

"He found you with her in her room?" I asked.

"Yeah."

Crimes seemed not of the best character, but because he was a member of the crew I tolerated him. No close friendship existed between him and any other members of the crew. However the hostility built up between us would soon explode into a real fight and further change our relationship.

Handguns were issued to each crew member. One day I decided to go out and practice shooting my forty-five. The army forty-five is not accurate, but it does have firepower and could easily knock a man down at fifty feet. To be good with this gun requires practice.

"I'll go with you." Crimes said.

"Remember, Crimes," I said, "The more friends you outshoot, the fewer friends you will have."

We strapped on our guns and walked out to the firing range together. Our target was a round metal lid from a K-ration cheese portion, three inches in diameter. To make it more visible, I placed it on a stick and fired from forty feet. After three shots each, we both put a hole in the lid, knocking it off the stick. My next three rounds again put a hole in the tin.

Crimes fired three rounds and the lid fell. He said, "We are even, two to two."

I saw the bullet hit the stick and not the lid. I laughed and said, "You dumb ass, you hit the stick."

"No, I didn't hit the stick. Look for the hole in the lid."

"Only three holes in the tin, two are mine and one is yours."

"My shot went through one of the other holes," Crimes replied.

I laughed out loud at that one. The laugh hurt Crimes and made him angry.

He said, "Jones, you think you're Jesus Christ. I can shoot better than you any day."

Again, I laughed. Crimes had a better score at skeet than I, but at this time I wasn't about to admit it.

"Jones, you're a son-of-a-bitch liar," he said and walked off.

Until now, it had been fun and games. I enjoyed pulling Crimes's leg. When I reached out and caught him by the shoulder to pull him around, I planned to tell him I did not intend to hurt his feelings. After all, Crimes was a fellow crew member and deserved some consideration.

Crimes vicious attack caught me totally unprepared. He turned around and came across with a strong right that caught me full in the mouth. The force of the blow snapped my head back. I ducked his next right. With my body low, I charged Crimes. The force and weight of my charge took Crimes to the ground with me on top. I hit him on the jaw on his way down. While on top, I continued to pound Crimes's face with my fist. I was angry and didn't count the blows. My continued punishment could kill him. His face bled all over. I let him up.

Crimes appeared groggy and stood for a minute without saying anything. We were both breathing hard. Crimes lunged at me with his hands out. I stepped aside, knocked his arms down with my left and caught him on the side of the head with a hard right. He went down and rolled over on his back.

Crimes bled all over his face. His fair and thin skin broke with each blow and bled. He lay on the ground, looked up at me and placed his hand on his gun. Matching his move, I did the same. For another moment, we looked at each other.

After what seemed an eternity, I extended my hand and said, "Crimes, let me help you up."

Crimes extended his hand, and I pulled him up.

Back in the tent area the other airmen saw us coming. They also saw the blood on Crimes's face and my busted lip.

"Did you fellows run into some of those Italian women?" one asked.

"You should have seen that bunch," I said. "We were lucky to get out alive."

Crimes never made trouble for me anymore. He appeared friendly but cool. For the sake of the crew, I always tried to have a normal relationship with Crimes. Our jobs called for teamwork.

The Air Corps checked our records and found that we had not had a vacation. We were later pulled out of service and shipped to the Isle of Capri for ten days.

CHAPTER TWENTY-ONE

The crew continued to fly out of San Pancrazio. When we had flown forty missions, the Air Corps sent down an order that our crew must attend a rest camp on the Isle of Capri. The date was April 6, 1944. A vacation! Wow! An opportunity to take it easy and not worry about combat. Going home dominated our list of wants, but if they would not send us home, a vacation wasn't all bad.

"People go on vacation to forget things," I said. "When you get there and open up your B-4 bag, you will know what you forgot."

"Let's forget about the rest camp, finish the fifty missions and be shipped to the good old U.S.A.," Daughtry said. "Too bad we don't have that option. The air force has decreed that we get some rest."

"It's not where we want to go," I said. "However, it is at government expense."

The prospect of a vacation and the unspoken promise of adventure sparked my attention. Something exciting other than combat could happen in our lives.

We packed our vacation clothes, GI issue khaki pants and shirts and took off for Naples in southern Italy. We flew over Vesuvius, the volcano that had buried the city of Pompeii. We could see the lava and the ash bubbling in the large cone-shaped opening. It has been active earlier that year.

We landed and took a boat to the Isle of Capri just as the sun was setting. The sun highlighted the brown rock and the rugged character of the island. In the semidarkness with the wind blowing,

the island looked inhospitable. All eyes were looking for girls as
the boat pulled up to the stone dock. There was none. The mayor
of Capri wasn't there to greet us and had failed to produce the
dancing girls.

"Because the mayor wasn't here, I plan to restrict my stay
here to ten days." Daughtry said. "I'm disappointed the band and
the hero welcome committee did not make it."

"I could be happy without the dancing girls if the locals let
me get some rest," Ron said.

"That is probably the only thing you will get on this rocky
island," Crimes assured him.

Capri is located in the Bay of Naples. Visitors to the island
arrived by boat. An incline train, called the Funicular, takes
passengers from the port up to Capri, 488 feet above sea level
where the hotel is located. Frequently we took the fun ride.
Because of the sea breeze and cool temperature, Capri was a
popular vacation spot for all Europe before the war. The
Roman emperors, Augustus and Tiberius, built splendid palaces
there. Wine, fruit and olive oil were the cash crops. We were
billeted for ten days in a Red Cross hotel in the largest city on
the island, Capri. Grateful for the free time, we could swim,
lie in the sun, look at the Italian girls, or explore the island.
The area experienced an April that was too cold to swim or
lie in the sun for any extended period, so we looked for
something else to do.

I chose to explore the island. Ed Daughtry and Ron Bloom
came with me. We took a boat and a guide and made a visit to
the island's grottos, the most famous of which is the Blue Grotto,
a cave cut out of rock by the action of the seawater. The entrance
is only about six feet wide and five feet high, but the cave inside
is 150 feet across and thirty feet high. The sunlight reflected off
a twenty-foot sandy bottom outside into the Blue Grotto and
up through the blue water and created different hues of blue on
the cave ceiling. The highest part of the ceiling of the cave is light
blue and gradually darkens where the ceiling meets the water.
The view inside is awe inspiring and inspirational. Touched by

the beauty of the spot, I wanted to feel it, experience the magic of the color and let the water heal my tired body.

A way to project oneself into the magic of the moment was facilitated by something from my past. Before joining the Army Air Corps, I had read all of the books written by Richard Haliburton. He had swum in the reflecting pool of the Taj Mahal in India, climbed the Matterhorn and generally led an exciting life. At least I could swim in the Blue Grotto.

Slipping out of my clothes, I dropped over the side into the water. The water was 70°F, but the air was colder. I frolicked for a while, swimming around and under the boat. In the light blue water the bottom was clearly visible. My skin took on the color of silver. It was great to be alive. The Italian boat handler decided that all Americans were crazy. Why would anyone in his right mind swim in water that cold?

After having been in the water for fifteen minutes, my skin turned the color of the grotto. Another boat came into the grotto with an American Red Cross nurse aboard. I scampered to the far side of the boat and pulled myself aboard.

Pulling my clothes on over my wet skin was not smart, but I refused to allow the Red Cross nurse an unrestricted view of my nude body. I was proud of those three hairs on my chest, but they were not ready for a public viewing. The nurse would probably not be impressed anyway.

The guide rowed us out through the opening to the outside into a light breeze. The wind evaporated the water from my wet clothes and made the principles of refrigeration easy to understand. Cooled by the process of evaporation, I suffered from a mild case of hypothermia. My teeth were chattering and my body shivering. Only when we came ashore and began our walk over the mountain to Anacapri did I regain normal body temperature.

We saw the ruins of the homes of Augustus and Tiberius. The soil was volcanic and very rich. However, the grade was steep and there were outcroppings of solid stone.

On the third day of our vacation, we took a boat to Naples and made a visit to the ancient city of Pompeii.

On August 24, A.D. 79, the volcano, Vesuvius, erupted and covered Pompeii with ash. Pompeii remained buried for years. Now most of the excavation has been accomplished, and the ash hauled away. The wood in the buildings decayed, but the masonry walls, plaster, and tile survived the ages. The homes of the wealthy were very elaborate with baths, fountains, and inside courtyards. Courtyards were surrounded by stone walls with metal gates for security. Lead pipe brought water from the aqueduct to the city fountains and the homes of the wealthy. Wine merchants in the city sold wine from burned clay vats sunk in masonry counters to sidewalk customers through large windows. The first walk-up windows.

Brothels were a part of the city culture and contained beds built up of stone, covered with straw and a fabric.

We viewed with interest the security problems of this ancient city. Iron gates protected major facilities. It was late in the afternoon when we returned to Capri. There were other forms of recreation on the island. The few good-looking girls were much sought after. I did make contact with one. She was pretty, about five feet three with blonde hair. She had a square look but was nicely padded with attractive skin; a Venus de Milo with arms, nice, round, and well shaped. The distance from her wrist to her elbow was much shorter than arms on most Anglo-Saxon girls. This short forearm did nothing to distract from her youth and good looks. She was eighteen and the daughter of the good Catholic mayor of Capri. He would not let her out of his sight when I was around. Her name was Sofia. She liked having me there. Her dad didn't run me off, either, but he wouldn't allow me to take her to a nightclub.

The mayor's home was modest. The walls were stone block, stacked on each other, plastered on both sides and painted. The floor in the house was ceramic tile with a patterned glaze coat. Most of the walls were painted white. Everything was plain except some bright-colored tile around the front entrance door. The dark finish on the furniture obscured the grain of the wood. The chairs in the living room were wicker with fabric-covered cushions.

The Italians used their natural resources to the best advantage. Limestone sawn out of a quarry and allowed to harden made their building blocks. Ground-up volcanic stone produced Portland cement. Glass was made from the sand on the beaches. Coal and iron came from northern Italy.

Southern Italy is very poor. The people were just able to sustain themselves from the land. They were gentle and easygoing, as the Spanish say, "Muy simpatico." The southern Italians were somewhat like people in the southern part of the United States. They did not look like them, but they seemed to have some of the same qualities.

Two American destroyers pulled into the harbor at Capri. The Germans still controlled Rome. These destroyers had been shelling the coast of northern Italy. The names of these ships were the *Hughes* and the *Hillary P. Jones.*

The *Hughes* was 350 feet long and loaded with high explosive shells, torpedoes and depth charges. It gave me the creeps just thinking what would happen if an enemy shell landed in the right spot on this ship.

At night, festive Italians came out for their customary visit to the bars and restaurants. The evening visits seemed very civilized and unrushed.

The crew visited several bars, the most popular boasted a very buxom singer who could belt out opera like Renata Tebaldi. We watched with pleasure, sipped a little wine and observed the rise and fall of opera as it burst forth from that ample bosom.

There were a few prostitutes on Capri and a very few young pretty girls. I read and rested enough to restore my health and improve my outlook on life and fulfilled the purpose of the trip.

The mayor's daughter found a navy lieutenant, whom she liked better, and she stopped letting me drop by.

My good fortune had run out with the girl. Perhaps my good luck would continue in the arena of combat.

Our last mission would be scheduled soon. Would we make it?

CHAPTER TWENTY-TWO

Daughtry looked at me, pushed his hair back with his right hand and shifted his weight from his right foot to his left. Then he scratched his left armpit with his right hand. His sharp pointed face was concerned when he said, "I've been counting the days and the missions. Jones, do you realize that tomorrow, May 24, 1944, will be our last mission before being sent home for rest and rehabilitation? I am sweating this last mission more than the first one. To be shot down at any time is bad. To be shot down on the last mission is a crock-of shit. It couldn't happen to us, could it? I hope our good training and good luck will continue to get us through. Been afraid of flying combat since our first mission and now, this last one is the worst. Couldn't sleep last night just thinking about it."

"You and me both," I said. "However, you are not the only one who has been counting missions. Everyone on the crew is fully aware this is our last."

"Our target is Weiener Neustadt, Austria." Ron said as we climbed into the plane for takeoff. "Why couldn't they have given us an easier and shorter mission for our last one?"

"The air force doesn't want to see you get soft," Crimes said.

At 5:45 A.M. the group took off, climbing to 20,500 feet with eight thousand pounds of bombs. The temperature was—24ºC. The weather was fair and windy.

An hour from the target, fighters jumped the 376 Bomb Group. The seven fighters made single passes at the group formation and then concentrated on the 450th, the next group back of the 376. I saw nine planes from that group go down to fighters. I could see the flashes of their twenty-millimeter tracers as they raked the 450th formation but could not identify the fighter aircraft type. The 376 Bomb Group lost one plane over the target to flak. The plane received a direct hit. There were no chutes. The plane flipped over to the left and dropped straight down.

After we left the target, Daughtry came to the flight deck and helped me down from the top turret.

"The 376 Bomb Group was lucky," I said. "For some unknown reason, the German fly boys wanted to wipe out the 450th. If they had made the same decision about the 376th, the odds of our returning would have been different, assuming of course that they would have done as well with the 376th as they did with the 450th. Those odds for our survival were greatly increased when the fighter ignored us. Flak and mechanical difficulties are bad enough."

"Yeah! Thank God for the 450th," Daughtry said.

While we contemplated our chances of survival, the engines droned on and returned us to our base. Having completed my tour of duty made me happy. A tremendous feeling of self-worth lifted me out of the ordinary. After having made it this far, I wondered if I would survive the trip home—a flight to Naples and a long boat trip across the U-boat-infested Atlantic to the U.S.A. The Germans continued to sink ships. After a few hours of endless speculation of the possibilities, I said, what the hell! What will be, will be. Wonder what my dad will say when he finds I have flown fifty combat missions?

"This is the happiest I've been for some time," Daughtry said as he jumped up and down on the hardstand outside the plane. "We have returned from this last mission unscathed, unhurt and ready for the trip home. I'm gonna take that drink of whiskey the Army Air Corps doles out after a mission."

The Air Corps had a policy of giving each crew member a double shot of whiskey after each mission. Prior to this mission, I had not asked for this largesse but tonight seemed a night for celebrating. Taking the air force up on the offer, I tossed down the double shot. That drink was the start of a downhill decline in my usual good health.

The radio operator, Bob, and I had been saving two bottles of Gibson's rye whiskey for this occasion. When I reached Bob's tent, he was well into one of the bottles. The flap on his tent was thrown back, and he was resting on his bunk, drinking the straight stuff.

"Come in and have yoself a drink," Bob said.

"Pour some of that liquor in my canteen cup," I insisted. "Plan to do some drinking. I'm gonna splash in a little branch water out of this trailer tank outside."

"Don't want to dilute this rye nectar with anything. It will ruin the taste," Bob said.

"Hell, it's ruined my taste already. That first sip of the raw alcohol is strong enough to remove house paint. I want to keep the lining in my stomach."

Several members of the crew came in and joined us.

"I've never felt so good about anything," I said with a satisfied smile. "To know I have finished fifty combat missions without a scratch is a tremendous relief."

"Think I will have another drink," Bob said as he sat up in his bunk and reached for the bottle.

"In my rush to celebrate, I had forgotten to eat." I said, "I don't feel so good. My stomach wants to turn inside out."

"That's a bad mistake, Jones. You can take hardships but not success. This is success," the radio operator said. "My body couldn't stand the success either. Tell me, do you feel like a hero?"

"To tell you the truth, I feel sick," I said. "Know what I'm doing, but the hell of it is I can't do anything."

Having a fine old time and whooping it up was my plan for the evening. Soon I felt the need to throw up. There was nothing in my stomach to move out. I was a victim of the dry heaves. For one who has never experienced this malady, the patient is not afraid he will die. The pain is so great he is afraid he won't.

I contemplated a long evening exchanging war experiences and enjoying the fellowship of my crew. It didn't happen. The raw alcohol worked on my tender sensibilities with mind-deadening intensity. The drinking left me sick and distracted. My cast-iron constitution and general good health worked in my behalf. I survived.

Next day, my body was in a weak condition and needed a transfusion of the good life. Three letters arrived from Mandy, providing buoyancy for my spirit. The letters were written as only Mandy can write. She soothed my frayed nerves with her logic and concern. Perhaps I would see her back in the States.

Daughtry came by our tent and said, "Gentlemen, you are not gonna believe it, but the air force does not think we are heroes. While our crew is waiting for transportation to Naples, the point of debarkation, the base commander put the entire crew on guard duty. One man will be assigned to guard each aircraft on the ground. This is boring. The nights will be long and cold. I plan to protest to my congressman."

"If that will speed up our departure I will do it with style," I said as I sat up on my bunk.

Some boys slept in the aircraft they were guarding and were caught sleeping on guard duty. They were reduced in rank and threatened with a court-martial. I chose a toolbox to lean against away from the aircraft and the hardstand. One night a jeep came up to the aircraft. The officer of the day assumed I was on the inside. He yelled with the jeep engine running, and he didn't hear me as I walked up behind him. I dropped the clip from my forty-five about an inch and caught it with my little finger under the butt. Then I charged the gun quickly and placed the muzzle against the neck of the officer in the jeep. Then I asked for the password. The young lieutenant appeared shook up he couldn't remember his own name.

"Raise your hands and step out of the jeep," I said with authority. "Lie face down on the ground."

By this time the lieutenant had recovered his composure and remembered the password. I let him up and holstered my forty-five. The lieutenant did not report me. To admit he had forgotten the password would have been embarrassing. By this action, I did not ingratiate myself to the lieutenant. On future trips the lieutenant was careful how he approached the aircraft I guarded.

Orders finally came through. Our crew flew to Naples, a staging area for the Air Corps and the army. Some army units were arriving and moving up into northern Italy to fight the Huns. The Germans still held Rome.

While we were waiting for transportation, we were restricted to the base in Naples. The day was June 6, 1944. By radio we learned the Allies under Eisenhower had landed on the French coast. The crew members were overjoyed. The odds for survival had now moved in our favor. We knew the war would end soon, and we would not have to fly another fifty missions.

Finally, we were loaded aboard liberty ships in the Naples harbor. None of my crew was assigned to my boat. The boat sailed out into the Mediterranean through the Straits of Macina by Sicily. The going was slow. When the boat passed Gibraltar, it joined a convoy of more than a hundred ships. As far as the eye could see, there were ships lined up three abreast about a mile apart each way. Destroyers were charging up and down each side at about three times the speed of the convoy. There was no enemy action. The trip quickly became boring. It took a month to cross. Exercising and reading were my only recreation. Time hung on like the seven-year itch. Our slow boat, the liberty ship, earned my low regard.

Almost a hundred GIs were aboard our ship. All the men had access to food, a bunk and toilet facilities.

The sleeping quarters were located below in this slow, flat-bottom iron tank. Bunks were four high, thirty inches apart vertically and placed parallel to the ship's length. Rows between the bunks were four feet.

"Our bunks are fashioned with a metal pipe frame covered with a canvas bottom," Ralph Bell from Dalton, Georgia said. "These bunks have no rail to keep a sleeping occupant in the bunk when the ship rolls."

"You are very observant, Ralph," I said. "These swells or waves were from the port side and caused the flat bottom to rock sideways about fifteen degrees on each side of center. This wave action makes it difficult to stay in the bunk." Many GIs were seasick. Some regurgitation occurred, and in the close quarters the smell of puke seemed overpowering. I spent most of the thirty days on deck and enjoyed the nice weather.

"Damn! Wish there was some way to speed up these flat-bottom junkyards," Ralph said as we walked around the deck for exercise.

Ralph screwed up his face into a look of mystery and motioned for me to come closer with his index finger.

I walked over and asked, "What's up?"

"Guess who we have aboard."

"Betty Grable?" I asked with a broad smile as we sat on some ship's gear on the forward deck.

"We have the GI aboard who was slapped by General Patton."

"Really?"

"That's him on the bow by himself."

"He's an ugly bastard.

"Why did Patton slap him?" I asked.

"He was in a hospital with wounded soldiers, and he had not been hurt. He is a psycho case.

"Some conversation occurred between him and Patton. He screamed, and Patton slapped him. That's all I know."

"If the press gets this, it will be in every paper in the U.S.A," I said.

The toilets were toilet seats over a metal trough. Water constantly circulated through the trough. One day a troublemaker lit a piece of paper and dropped it in the trough. As it passed under the rear ends of the sitting customers it singed hair down the line. The injured parties were ready to beat the perpetrator to a pulp. They were not sure who did it but walked around with their pants at half-mast.

The fresh air and the sea raised my spirit. We settled into a pattern of powdered eggs and grits for breakfast and chicken à la king for dinner. We were fed only two meals a day with a snack for lunch. The food and the trip were boring.

The most interesting occurrence on the boat was a continuous poker game. Anyone wishing to lose his money could do so in short order. Many boys did. One GI won most of the money. A rumor placed his winnings in excess of three hundred thousand dollars. That possibility existed but not likely because soldiers were not paid very much before leaving Italy.

"The winner is a professional gambler who has been drafted," Ralph said. "He takes advantage of the GIs who know nothing about gambling. The soldier who won the money hired two big guys as bodyguards. The gambler keeps the money on his person at all times in several money belts. It is rumored he bathed very little."

"That professional gambler will not win any of my money," I said to Ralph as we walked the deck for exercise. "I plan to keep it in my pocket."

Back in the 376 Bomb Group, I played poker with friends. The games were friendly, with a maximum bet of twenty-five cents. Even with those restrictions, I lost fifty-two dollars one night. Earlier, my winnings averaged twenty to thirty dollars a night. The loss, however, made me decide not to gamble anymore on the way home, and that decision allowed me to arrive in the U.S.A. with cash.

An army band played as we made our way into New York Harbor. In the distance we could see the Statue of Liberty. The captain took his time with the docking process. Tugboats pushed the flat-bottom tub into the slip, and the hawsers were made fast. We were home.

The arrival was very emotional for me. I thanked God for a country such as the United States where people live in freedom. At times in the past, I had bitched about having to do some of the things the Army Air Corps required. I fought for that freedom, the freedom to complain, and proud I could do it.

Some lines from Walter Scott's poem, "Love of Country," raced through my mind:

> Breathes there the man with soul so dead
> Who never to himself has said
> This is my own native land.

We were loaded into six-by-six trucks and taken to a base in New Jersey. Next day, we were paid and given thirty-day furloughs. I caught a bus to the nearest train station and purchased a ticket to Atlanta.

Mom and Dad met me at the terminal station in Atlanta. I was delighted to be home and see my folks, but something had changed. I felt ill at ease with my family and a vague restlessness.

"So much has changed in this family," Mom said. "Your brothers and sisters have graduated from high school and are out making their mark in the world."

At home we sat in the living room on the sofa and talked for hours. Dad left for work with little or no conversation. I no longer hated my dad.

"Mom, the tension is still there. Why, Mom?" I asked with disappointment in my voice. "What can I do about it? I know he is uncomfortable. Both he and you go all out to make me feel wanted and have treated me royally. You look upon me as a hero. It bothers me to receive so much attention. I feel ill at ease with all the preferential treatment. It is uncomfortable to be so highly regarded. Please consider me an equal member of the family. That's good enough for me. A position I enjoyed in the past."

I looked at my mom. Her kind face was lined, and her stout torso was bent by the years of hard work to raise five children. Her most compelling attribute was her open and honest countenance. I knew she cared and would do anything for me.

"You will have to accept your dad as he is. He loves you but will never say he does. He will never change. We love you and are proud that our son made such a contribution to the war," Mom said. "We cannot treat you the same as before you went to war because now you are grown up."

The family would not allow me to act like a normal family member. They treated me like a guest. Mom continued the same as always, the sweet considerate person.

"What do you want to eat?" Mom asked. She cooked or baked special things for me, and she invited relatives and neighbors over for visits. She had a son who had returned from flying fifty combat missions and wanted her friends and family to know how proud she felt.

"Mom," I said, "the more time I spend lounging around the house with everyone else working, the more useless I feel. I want to be productive. Do you think a visit with my grandparents and my uncles and aunts would be the right thing to do? They have always been wonderful to me. Spending my thirty-day leave sitting around is a drag."

"Son, why don't you catch a bus over there," Mom said. "They will be glad to see you. Fishing and doing those things you did during childhood will make the time productive as well as entertaining." Mom continued. "The exercise, fresh air and good food will raise your spirits. By all means, go."

I caught a bus to Leesburg, Alabama and walked the six miles up the mountain to my granddad's house taking the same shortcut trail Black Hawk and I had struggled down when I was ten. The hot weather of August drained my energy as I made my way up the dusty road. What would I find when I arrived? An hour until sundown, Granny and Granddaddy would be alone in the big house. Somehow the place seemed quiet and deserted. When I walked up they were relaxing in the swing under the large red oak in the yard. The sun had dropped down behind the mountain. Tears came to Granny's eyes as she hugged me and said, "It has been three years since we have seen you. You grew up fast. Only a few months ago you were a small child.

"For me," Granny said with the glow of genuine love on her wrinkled face, "time has passed too quickly. I busy myself with work around the house during the day. Your granddad works on the farm. We remember your summer visits to the farm when you were younger. We loved having you here. Those were precious moments. You grew up so fast. Now you will go about making your own life. I want to live as long as I can to see you mature and have grandchildren. However, Mother Nature will soon move me off the stage. I have learned the play. It will be my time to go.

"Only a short time ago you were four years old, running around, chasing the rooster in the yard. Now you have grown up and involved yourself in the war with Germany. We are so proud of you," she continued with tears in her eyes.

I looked into the sweet, kind, wrinkled face of my grandmother. She was so small, and her hair was streaked with gray and pulled into a knot at the top of her head. There were spots of sun-damaged skin on her face, and the skin was drawn tightly over her high cheekbones. She wore low-heel shoes and a print dress. Her bearing was authoritative but kindly.

My grandfather was trim and wore a work shirt and pants held up by suspenders. His clean-shaven face and jet black hair indicated he was concerned about his looks. The look on his face also indicated he had a lot more living to do. He was a builder and a farmer and loved the things he did.

"We love you, John," Granny said with a catch in her voice as she spoke from her seat beside my grandfather in the swing. "You have no idea how lonesome it is here by ourselves. Your uncles and aunts have all married and have their own families. Because of the gas shortage, we are stuck here on this four-hundred-acre farm. It is difficult for Papa to get help. Carse Williams is still here and helps. We do need more."

"Over the years both of you took an interest in everything I did. Now that you are older, I want to spend more time with you and share your lives," I said. "After surviving fifty combat missions over Germany, I am also filling the void in my life created by the war effort."

"Many family members and friends have moved away from the Leesburg community. They were attracted by good-paying, war-related jobs," Granny said. "I will be glad when the war is over, so they will return."

Granny was seventy-three, but she made a dinner that was special: fried chicken with all the trimmings. My granddad was seventy-four and asked a number of questions.

"What was it like to get shot at?" he asked.

"About the same as standing right here," I assured him. "Surely someone shot at you during your lifetime. Some irate father perhaps when you were young."

"No, not really. My life has been uneventful."

"Granddad," I said, "the war isn't over yet, but I am still trying to decide what to do with my life. The right decision made as soon as possible will give me an edge. Already more than three years have been lost because of the war. Do you have any suggestions?"

"You don't have to make up your mind today; you should know what you plan to do by the time you get your discharge. That will be soon enough. You can hit the ground running."

I would spend two wonderful weeks with my grandparents, my aunts, uncles and cousins, and I enjoyed every minute of it. It was great to be alive and know my life had been spared. It was also important to me to know that my family appreciated my war experience.

Helping Uncle Bill work on his farm gave me the feeling of a provider, a gatherer. I felt a strong desire to get the war out of my mind and get back to some kind of normal lifestyle. Uncle Joe was still in Europe. I missed him.

After dinner, we sat under this big oak tree in the yard and talked. Surprised how well informed my grandparents were even though they had no radio and only books and newspapers.

I rebuilt the chimney and fireplace on the house. The chimney had become a fire hazard and was about to fall. Granddaddy and I pulled it down, and my rockwork turned out great, and it pleased me that I could do something for my grandparents.

Under the shade of the big oak at sundown, I was enjoying a

conversation with Grandfather. "It's a real pleasure to be home. Other GIs must feel as I do upon returning home," I said. "I didn't realize what I had until the war came along.

"After I finished my fifty combat missions, I started drinking. Now I like to drink. A short drink relieves the tension, and I think that everything is okay.

"When I talk about myself, I want to assure you that I'm the same, but I'm not. I have no intention to mislead families and friends. There is some tension I can't shake. My friends and family expect me to be the same as I was before combat. However, this is not possible. Anyone experiencing combat had been affected, some more than others. A person can't be trained to be a killer, practice that profession and still be the same person."

"You are right, Son," Granddaddy said. "Any conflict or prolonged tension will have an effect. You have experienced fifty combat missions, and you look and act okay. Do you feel okay?"

"Yeah. I think it will pass. I do drink alcohol now and didn't before combat."

"Some effort will be required to remove the war mentality from your mind." He continued, "I make this judgment after observing others who have returned. They seem to be experiencing some difficulty readjusting to a normal life. Yes, John, you will have your war experience with you for some time as you struggle for some relief. It is my suggestion that you get busy with your education as quickly as possible."

"I have been thinking about the future. To make progress toward my professional goal to be an architect will not be easy. The conditioning received growing up, and the military service has had their own effects. To overcome this preconditioning will require a special effort. As you know, our family has produced a long line of teachers, preachers and farmers. Dad wanted me to be a preacher. When he insisted, I said, 'I don't want to become something I am not suited for.' He gave up the idea early."

"You have a strong will like your dad. It is right that you should make up your own mind about a career."

"Granddaddy, after flying in the Army Air Corps, my interest in airplanes and aeronautical engineering grew and expanded. I wanted to learn all about airplanes. This learning caused me to lose interest in architecture. However, I did find, to my disappointment, most of the airplanes are designed by two or three aeronautical engineers. This knowledge switched me back to architecture."

"Son, it is getting chilly out here, and it's about bedtime. Let's talk again tomorrow."

"Good thinking, Granddad."

I spent a delightful two weeks with my grandparents and then headed home.

Several days were left on my leave, so I decided to go to Perry to visit Mandy.

Would that be a mistake? I had to go and find out how well I cared for her and to find out if her letters were the only quality that caused me to regard her highly.

To facilitate a career in architecture, it was essential that my education be in a first-class architectural school. Looking ahead, I saw a mountain in my way. How could I go to school for five years. Then three additional years as an apprentice architect were required before becoming registered. At this point the task is barely begun.

Not many things impressed me. Brains and power did. While in the service I saw what training and education could do. The ability to think could make a difference between success and failure.

Not having made excellent grades in school, I realized it would be necessary for me to develop to my full potential in order to reach the goals I set for myself. The right marriage could blend my drive and persistence with a girl of superior intelligence and be helpful in keeping me on the path of learning and achievement. To have bright children would also be a plus. Together with a dedicated wife, I might be able to compete in the postwar economic boom expected to occur. One of my goals was to earn a share of the wealth generated by a booming economy. The thought of getting ahead stimulated me to anticipate the possibilities of making money for my family.

I promised myself to think about the problem later and caught a bus for Perry, Georgia to visit Mandy, a girl from school.

Why would anyone just returning from flying fifty combat missions think of marriage?

CHAPTER
TWENTY-THREE

Mandy was two years older than I and much smarter. She graduated "summa cum laude" from college and was mentioned in *Who's Who in American Colleges and Universities*. This girl was a natural student throughout college and was active in student activities. In her senior year, she was president of the college student government. A good student, she did everything right, well almost everything. She did date me.

Mandy had naturally curly black hair. Her face seemed sculptured for beauty out of good character and good health. Her five-foot-five height was perfect for her weight of 115 pounds. Nature had been generous to Mandy in the distribution of her weight. However, an attractive perky personality brought to gather and blended those physical assets into an understanding personality. Most people felt good in her presence. She had a knack of knowing what to say and do to earn affection and hold it.

Her near perfection in all things made me take a look at my natural ability. Could I accomplish things that would cause this intelligent girl to look up to me as the family provider?

Proud of this girl's achievements, I felt fortunate to be associated with such talent. Even though superior in education and brains, she did not try to make her friends feel inadequate. This talent earned my respect.

Ambitious since high school, I wanted a successful career. As an achiever, I could say, "Dad, I made it in spite of you." An all-out effort by me would require a great deal of understanding and patience from a wife willing to invest the time and effort in a marriage. Without extra effort, an architectural career would be impossible. Success for me must be accomplished by my effort with my talent. Anything short of this would not have the merit necessary to raise my spirits and keep me inspired.

The bus stopped in Perry, Georgia on the Courthouse Square. Mandy and her father were there as I stepped out of the bus. Mandy walked over and kissed me on the cheek. Not much of a welcome for a guy who has ridden a bus all the way from Atlanta to see her. Perhaps she was shy because of her dad's presence.

I shook Mr. Hamilton's offered hand. Just under six feet, Mandy's father had a rugged look and a strong body. The roughness of his hands and the firm handshake assured me he was what he appeared to be. Sun-damaged skin and thinning black hair dominated his appearance but in no way detracted from his look of concern and kindness. His khaki shirt and pants added to his look of competence. Mandy's father impressed me. Basically the same as my relatives and the people in my hometown, he seemed a modest, sober, hardworking, and patriotic American. Having experienced hardships, he knew how to deal with disasters and the heartaches of life.

"How was your trip?" he asked. "Mandy told me you have just completed fifty combat missions over Germany. My hat is off to you, Son."

"Thank you, Mr. Hamilton," I said. "You are very kind. I understand you have a farm which is very productive."

"The farm has not always been a producer. Now it's making money. We have experienced crop loss and natural disasters. That is farm life. I'm sure you understand if you grew up on a farm."

"Yes, my folks have experienced their share of crop failures."

Mandy's mother heard the car and came out to meet us. Six inches shorter than her husband, the skin on her face was wrinkled and sun damaged. Dressed in a cotton print dress with low-heel shoes she had adjusted well to farm life. Her most prominent features were her nice well-formed teeth and radiant smile.

She smiled at me and said, "Welcome to the Hamilton farm.

We are delighted you could come. We are not fancy here, but I can guarantee you some delicious home cooking."

"Thank you, Mrs. Hamilton. Having been raised on a farm, I have a strong preference for home cooking. I will love what you cook."

"Mandy's brothers are gradually taking over this six-hundred-acre farm," Mr. Hamilton said as we walked into the house and sat down in the living room. "My two boys will keep it productive and in the family. Mandy's mom and I can relax now and travel. We have earned some retirement time.

"Farm life has shaped the outlook and character of our sons as it has shaped the lives of my relatives for generations," Mr. Hamilton continued as he relaxed in a large chair. "If you lived on a farm, you know what I mean.

"Mandy's mother and I are looking forward to being grandparents. We want all our children married and established in a worthwhile job or profession. As we get older, we also understand the importance of grandchildren and will be glad to have a few."

"I understand Mandy has been working as a librarian and has chosen to continue her education in a medical school in Macon to become a medical doctor," I said. "I'm flattered she seemed to like me. At least she must be aware of my potential. However, potential is nothing until it is developed. I want to be an architect but becoming an architect is a very difficult task."

"Don't worry about it, Son. You will make it. Just work and study hard," Mr. Hamilton said.

Mandy's family proved a source of interest to me. Going over the family tree, it appeared there were no close mentally retarded relatives. My questions were polite and discreet. I learned and became impressed. Her family had good bloodlines and genes and maintained order and purpose in their lives. Perhaps I needed this.

Mandy walked back into the living room and said, "I've placed your bag in the guestroom. John, you may want to freshen up before lunch."

On leaving Atlanta for Perry, I had no intentions of marrying anyone, but after seeing Mandy again with her family, I was convinced it was the thing to do. Because of the tension of combat, my mind functioned less well. My schedule for achievement had bogged down. I needed to get started. With my family life settled, I could concentrate on my education. The next day Mandy and I walked in the woods and enjoyed the summer weather of middle Georgia. I talked of my plans for the future. There I asked Mandy to marry me. She didn't hesitate.

She said, "Yes. Let's do it now, this week."

Somewhat surprised by the enthusiasm of her acceptance and the quickness with which she wanted the consummation of the vows, I was pleased and held her close.

"Okay," I said. "Are you sure you don't want more time to prepare for a wedding? We need to notify your folks and mine."

"I know what I want," Mandy said with a smile as she looked around at the pine tree forest.

The next day, the pastor of the local Baptist Church—the church Mandy's family attended—married us. Only a few of her friends and immediate family members were present. I didn't notify my family, and they didn't attend. We would surprise them with the news later.

After the wedding, her non-alcoholic family hosted a small reception of tea and cookies. Later Mandy and I registered at a local hotel for our wedding night.

I felt bad about not giving notice to my folks, but this was wartime. I was sure they would forgive me. We planned to stop one night in Atlanta and visit my family. My mom would recognize the good qualities of my bride and love her. The remainder of my family would not be impressed. For the honeymoon, we would ride a bus back to Harvard, Nebraska. The Air Corps stationed me there and reserved a small two-bedroom apartment for me on the base.

My past experience as a girl chaser did not prepare me for the events that occurred on my wedding night. Mandy surprised me as no other girl had.

My early conditioning led me to believe that "good" girls do not like sex and are always modest, even a little prudish. I believed that Mandy would go into the bathroom and return to the room in a black nightgown. She would never want me to see her nude body and would insist the lights be out before making love. That evening caused me to believe that the librarian-style exterior housed the inclinations of a professional.

I carried Mandy across the threshold and kissed her warmly, then set her down.

Abruptly she said, "Let's make love before we go out to dinner."

A little shocking but not objectionable, as the same idea had occurred to me. My prudish background had prevented me from making the suggestion.

The recent events of the last few days and today left me somewhat tired. I took off my air force jacket and flopped down on the bed.

Mandy looked at me, a long searching look, and smiled. She put her clothes in place and arranged her toilet articles in the bathroom and on the dresser. All the while, I lay on the bed and looked at her. She was conscious of my gaze and would occasionally look up and flash her personality-plus smile.

When she had taken care of her clothes, she bolted the outside door, stood directly in front of me with a pleasing smile, took off one shoe and let it drop. She then took off the other shoe. All the while she was returning my interested, searching gaze. This gorgeous girl looked directly into my eyes and soul from about ten feet away.

She then raised her dress and unfastened her stockings, rolled them down and took them off. I could see her panties and a lot of white leg with her dress still raised. She undid her garter belt and let it fall on the floor.

Now she struggled to undo the buttons on the back of her dress. She unfastened them down past her waist, still returning my gaze and smiling.

Pulling her dress forward, she shook the sleeves off her arms, lowered the dress and stepped out. Then she laid the dress on the dresser.

Standing before me in her slip, the outline of her fully developed breasts appeared through the slip and bra. Mother Nature had been generous. Picking the slip up by the hem, she crossed her arms, pulled it over her head and laid it on top of her dress.

Hypnotized by her actions, I felt no desire to move or to speak. Then she reached behind her and found the catch on the bra, and it dropped to the floor, revealing a perfect pair of tits. To myself, I thought, John, you are a very fortunate man. Perfection like this is very rare. She was a pleasure to see. I contemplated touching those red-bud nipples, and the thought aroused deep primitive feelings in my loin. The panties came last and slithered down her legs.

Her librarian identity disappeared to be replaced by a magical feminine mystique. She beckoned with the promise of immortality, endless pleasure and good; the seduction of universal man by the infinite woman. Transfixed by the magic of the moment, I could not take my mind or eyes off this gorgeous hunk of feminine pulchritude.

She walked over and laid her soft body on top of mine. Then gently she got up, took off my shoes, then my pants, shirt, and underwear, all the time I looked into her eyes, and she smiled. We didn't speak. The spoken word would have shattered the magic of the moment. There was no language, words or phrases to express the intensity of the mood. Passion and purpose combined to satisfy the order of creation. We were both ready for the consummation. We spoke to each other with our bodies giving and receiving as the Maker intended.

Mandy was a virgin as evidenced by the dark red drops of blood on the sheets. She did her part with great joy and enthusiasm. Was it possible that she had learned without doing? Who cared! This was a night to remember. The time passed quickly. At dawn I fell asleep with the feeling of utmost satisfaction.

We had forgotten about dinner.

The next day, we caught the bus to Atlanta and visited with my folks. Mandy made a hit with my family. Mom was delighted that I had married someone so pretty and intelligent. Next day my dad took us to the station. We decided a train to Nebraska would be more comfortable than a bus.

Mandy got a job on the base at the PX. I occupied my time training other GIs in the maintenance of B-29s. The base commander appointed me hangar chief in a sub-depot hangar, then sent me to school on B-29s for three months schooling at the Boeing Renton Plant in Seattle, Washington. The Air Corps ordered, and I obeyed. Mandy felt that she should have gone with me. The separation became the beginning of a misunderstanding that would continue to trouble our relationship.

"I don't want you to leave," Mandy said. "I've tried to be understanding. Your trip is for the war effort. Everyone should make sacrifices for their country, but I can't give you up." With tears in her eyes she said, "Don't go."

"Mandy, I have been ordered to go. The Air Corps didn't ask."

Our minds were not as compatible as our bodies. As the misunderstanding spread, I questioned why our relationship came apart even though we loved each other. The tension of combat continued to dominate my thinking and sometimes made me irritable.

Without the matrix of mental compatibility, the relationship became difficult to hold together. My immaturity and preconceived notions of what our lives should be strongly undercut the relationship. It was now August.

After returning from Seattle, I continued to be sent out of town on special assignments. I reluctantly left my young bride and disappeared for ten days at a time. The demand of the war effort received priority number one. A soldier does not question the call.

In December, I had just returned from an assignment out of

town to Harvard, Nebraska, and the hour was late. There was no phone in the apartment, and I was unable to get in touch with Mandy. My arrival home at 1:00 A.M. was not a real treat for anyone. I looked forward to surprising my bride and the warm welcome I knew would be waiting. Nothing could change this belief, I thought.

As I walked through the dry snow on this cold night, my arctic galoshes crunched through the lightly packed snow. In the strong wind the snow fell sideways.

The wind produced a static electricity that stretched my nerves and made me feel irritable. Tired, cold, hungry and somewhat put out, I felt ready to do battle with anyone who got in my way. The long walk from the hangar to the apartment added to the tension. Transportation at 1:00 A.M. did not exist, and the walk was long through the driving snow.

Reaching the locked apartment, I knocked, but no one answered. I remembered turning the knob hard to the left and pushing would open the door. The routine worked.

After turning on the light in the kitchen, I took off my heavy coat and arctic galoshes, then my cap and dress coat. From the refrigerator, I took out a bottle of milk and poured a glass, then walked through the living room to the bedroom. I just wanted to get into a warm bed near my warm woman and relax.

Two bedrooms opened out into the living area. I walked to our bedroom and looked in. Totally unprepared for the scene before me, I stood immobilized, unable to move or act. A man occupied the bed with my wife. He shared the bed with her and held her close. In the dim light, his interest was possessive. Her head was snuggled up close to his, and the embrace seemed passionate even in sleep.

Quietly closing the door, I stepped back into the living room, walked over to the couch and sat down. My mind raced wildly, and my heart pounded. I couldn't think. My emotions were out of control. Never would I have suspected Mandy capable of such a thing as infidelity. She had surprised me before on our wedding night and at other times. This surprise was too much.

Already on the edge because of the weather and fatigue, the blood rushed to my head and fueled my anger. Another time, I would have walked out of the apartment and Mandy's life forever, but not tonight. I would have revenge. My army service forty-five automatic was strapped under my armpit. I took the gun out and looked at it. It was not my nature to kill or hurt anyone, but the situation demanded revenge. My ego was crushed, and I couldn't bear to think about it. How could my bride of such a short time forget her wedding vows? What a tramp, how long has this been going on? I felt miserable.

Fatigue numbed my mind. Why not let them kill themselves? I would break the light bulbs in the living room, turn on the radiant gas heater and not light it. The room would fill with gas. When Mandy turned on the light, it would blow both of them to hell!

Where would I go? The base commander knew the time of my return. It would be absolutely necessary for me to leave the apartment.

While planning the murder of my wife and her lover, I heard a plaintive voice calling, "John, John," from the other bedroom. The woman in the arms of that man in my bedroom couldn't be my wife.

Walking into the second bedroom, I buried my head on Mandy's bosom and wept, large tears rolling down my cheeks when I realized what I thought could not have been a reality.

Mandy said, "I'm so glad you're home. I missed you so. Why are you crying? You must have had a bad day. Come to bed, my darling."

The fatigue, tension and anxiety were too much for my ruffled nerves. A wave of relief swept over me. The fear and hatred were immediately forgotten in the warm embrace of an understanding wife. Fatigue generated by long hours on duty melted away.

Intelligent enough to understand my thinking, Mandy with her beautiful body let me know that I was the one and only man in her life. With a smile on my face, I fell into a deep sleep.

Mandy had allowed another couple to use the other bedroom because she knew them, and they had no place to go. She wasn't expecting me back, so she let them use our bedroom.

Later, in a thoughtful mood, I asked myself, "Why had I even thought about killing anyone? Was the violence that dominated my thinking a result of my strong dislike for my father?"

My eight-to-five job turned into a seven to seven, and still there wasn't enough time for me to catch up.

CHAPTER
TWENTY-FOUR

My nine-to-five job became an interesting learning experience. The satisfaction of knowing that my contribution helped the war effort raised my spirits. However, the job proved to be more than nine to five. I worked from seven to eight most days, and the air force didn't pay overtime.

At an intimate moment in our apartment, I had good feelings about being with Mandy. I watched her face light up when I said, "Mandy, I love being with you. When I was in Europe flying combat, I dreamed about this. It seemed so impossible. Now here we are together.

"Honey, after those fifty combat missions without injury and being with you here in the U.S.A. is great. You understand how I feel and how being with you builds my self-confidence. Your good looks and good nature are treasures to have around."

"Thank you," Mandy said. "It's also a pleasure to be Mrs. Jones."

"The invasion of Normandy has been made, but the war in Europe has not yet been won. The best effort the United States can muster is still required. Japan has suffered some losses but is still a functioning and dangerous enemy. I am trying to say, 'The war is not yet over.' However, it is comforting to be safe here with a woman who loves me. These extra hours I work are a small inconvenience to pay for this pleasure."

"What you say is true, and I love you for it," Mandy said. "The Air Corps should relieve you of some of your responsibilities. You work too hard.

"We should be able to have more time to ourselves. As of

now, you are almost an absentee husband. You flew fifty combat missions. Doesn't that count for something?"

"Yes, but we can't stop until we have won the war. Because of my maintenance and combat experience, they made me hangar chief in a sub-depot hangar," I said. "Our job is to keep the B-29s flying and facilitate the training of the crews that will be shipped to the South Pacific to take the war to the Japanese. The people who do the maintenance and work under my supervision are people who have returned from combat or young GIs with no real training. This makes my job at the hangar more difficult."

"Please make sure we win the war before we end up in a divorce," Mandy said.

"I could never give you up," I said.

The Air Corps relaxed its discipline for returned combat veterans. The vets knew it. Some veterans felt they had made their contribution and getting productive work out of these combat-wise boys was sometimes difficult. They had learned the system and were experts at goofing-off.

The GIs with experience were not just goof-offs. They were outstanding goof-offs. One day I received two four-star goof-offs. Their names were Prim and Quirl. They came to work straight from the stockade.

They were locked up for having some "good-old-boy" fun. They created a disturbance in the Cornhusker Hotel in the downtown area of Hastings, Nebraska. A bellboy shortchanged them on the purchase of a bottle of illegal liquor. They were holding his feet with his head and shoulders draped down into the elevator shaft from the top floor.

The bellboy had a healthy pair of lungs and let everyone near know of his peril. People gathered—not just those registered at the hotel, but those from blocks away. They hastened to the site to witness six military police arresting two drunken airmen. Hastings is a small town.

To avoid a public display of GI misbehavior, the Air Corps

asked its men to maintain a low profile. They had been trained not to create law-and-order problems for the local constables. Prim and Quirl were drunk. Those rules and regulations were ignored and forgotten.

MPs came to drag them off to the base. They were not yet ready to leave and registered their refusal. "We aren't going," Prim said. "It will take more than six MPs to take me." It did take six MPs to get them into a wagon and get them to the stockade. Now they were my responsibility.

I walked into the sub-depot hangar latrine. From back of a modesty panel, I heard one ask the other, "Where's that SOB Jones?"

The other responded, "I don't know, but I saw the SOB at the other end of the hangar a few minutes ago."

I walked around the partition and said, "Here is that SOB Jones."

They looked up in surprise.

"You are smoking in a restricted area and goofing off. Your ass is mine," I said.

My rough talk did little to faze them.

"Take these rags and wipe up the oil on the hangar floor. The noncom in charge of your detail told me he couldn't get you two to do anything in the other hangars. We haven't won the war yet," I said. "We need your help. Now get off your asses and get busy, or I'll call the stockade and have them pick you up again."

"Don't do that," Prim said. "We'll clean up the oil on the floor. We're good mechanics and were tech sergeants before we were busted."

"The air force really needs you. They are making a tremendous effort in the B-29 program, and skilled mechanics are scarce."

Two nine-cylinder Wright Cyclone engines were mounted back to back on a common drive shaft to make the powerful engines required for the B-29. Chrysler built the B-29 engines, and now the company workers were on strike. In short supply, these engines were critical to the entire B-29 training program. We at sub-depot hangar were put on notice to do anything to keep the B-29s flying. An order came down to change all eighteen cylinders on an engine if necessary. That type of maintenance required manpower, manpower not available even when the sub-depot GIs worked overtime.

How to improve efficiency and keep the flyboys in the air challenged us to be more efficient. One morning several maintenance crews were working in other hangars. The productive people were already assigned duties. We had stretched our talent thin. I put Prim in charge of one detail and Quirl in charge of another on planes in other hangars. To check their progress, if any, I made a surprise visit, and both crews were working. The people working the hardest were Prim and Quirl. Individual responsibility became the key to productivity of these two goof-offs. With their increase in productivity they also improved their self-esteem.

One day, one of the Air Corps truck drivers was speeding down the parking ramp in a six-by-six truck and ran under a low B-29 wing. The truck hit the nacelle supporting the outboard engine on the right side.

To replace the nacelle, the maintenance crew had to disconnect all electrical, power connections and remove the bolts from four sheer plates. Each plate required four one-half-inch chrome steel bolts of different lengths. They were color coded as to the length required for each hole in the sheer plates. Channel nuts behind the sheer plates received the bolts and fastened the nacelle in place.

We hoisted the new nacelle into place with the sheer plates matching up. I gave the bolts to a corporal to fit into the holes. He fitted the long bolts in the short holes. When he couldn't tighten them down, he twisted out the channel nuts. Refastening the channel nuts required three times the effort of the original installation. The corporal was colorblind.

The air force used inexperienced people to maintain their

complicated aircraft. Sometimes the system failed. Most of the time, however, it worked. The air force divided aircraft care into first, second, third and fourth echelon maintenance. Instrument repair and rebuilding components were fourth echelon. This work required shop conditions. Routine maintenance by a crew chief on the airplane on the hardstand such as changing the oil or slight engine adjustments was first echelon. "Remove, replace and adjust" involved second and third echelon, our assignment at the sub-depot.

The long hours caused additional friction between Mandy and me. With more time together we might have made it. The outlook for making a life together looked bleak, and also the long hours at a boring job, she decided to go back to her home and file for an uncontested divorce. It was now late January and cold.

But I didn't run her off. Perhaps by making an impossible situation, one she could not accept, really did cause her to leave. Life would not be easy without her. She gave purpose to my existence. She made her decision and left when I was out of town.

I still felt strongly about Mandy and went out of my way to avoid other women. Getting involved with someone else while still married worked against my nature. Perhaps my job and the overtime created a no-win situation. Maybe I should have asked for more time off. But that opportunity passed, and Mandy had made her choice. I felt sad, gave up the apartment and moved back into the barracks because of the work required. With Mandy gone, I suddenly had time on my hands, and the work bored me. To keep my mind active, I decided to enroll in two night courses at Hastings College, one in writing and one in typing.

Taking the courses helped with my loneliness, however the time continued to drag by as the courses wound down. When the air force asked me to go to Jamaica to be in charge of engine build-up on B-29s, I agreed to go. I had become one of the 2nd

Air Force's most experienced people. It would be a relief to get away from the things that reminded me of Mandy.

Air Transport Command flew me to Miami. While waiting for transportation to Jamaica, Major Cottingham approached me to serve in a gypsy task force, transporting supplies to B-29 crews training in the Caribbean. The major made a good case for his outfit. I would be flying in a C-47 as well as acting as line chief in charge of the maintenance on the three aircrafts. The C-47 was the military version of the DC-3, a two-engine cargo plane. My previous experience had been the maintenance of the R-1830 Pratt and Whitney engines which were also on the C-47.

The major's need and clout were great enough to have me taken off the order for Jamaica and assigned to his task force. Next day, I flew to Cuba, an island of adventure.

I wondered what Cuba was like? Was prostitution really the second-largest industry after sugarcane?

CHAPTER TWENTY-FIVE

"Major Cottingham, what's our job?" I asked, seated in his Havana Airport office.

"About the same as Air Transport Command. We will be more responsive and specialized in hauling cargo. Our task force will fly out of here—Batista Field at San Antonio de Luis Banos, Cuba, near Havana. On a typical trip, the C-47 crew will fly to Miami, pick up some airplane parts, fly them to Borinquen Field in Puerto Rico, then fly back to Cuba to spend the night. Your job will be to fly, of course, and supervise the maintenance of the other two C-47 aircraft assigned to us."

"We'll be hauling supplies and airplane parts to the 2nd Air Force B-29 crews training for over-water flights in the Caribbean?" I asked.

"Yes, and soon these training crews would be shipped to Okinawa or somewhere in the South Pacific to take the war to the Japanese," the major continued. "All of our thirty-five members of the task force have specialized skills combined to make up a functioning branch of the Air Corps. Pilots, maintenance people, and cargo handlers will do a good job and keep the B-29 crews supplied."

Articulate and athletic with a slender build, the major was clean shaven with good skin and a ready smile. He was thirty-five years old, and his education and experience facilitated his ability to lead our outfit.

The Air Corps engineers had been to Batista Field in Cuba and constructed it as per their standards for airstrips, administration buildings and barracks. If it were not for the warm weather and the tropical vegetation, the base would have been like any air base in the United States.

The 2nd Air Corps people in Harvard, Nebraska also needed trained people and kept asking for my return. A TWX arrived: "Return Jones to his base in Harvard, Nebraska." Major Cottingham sent a TWX reply: "No transportation available."

Flying in the Caribbean was educational. Every day we learned something new about the area. The weather was fair and warm, and only occasionally did we fly through a storm. We stopped at different bases, got passes and went into town. The girls were like the weather, fair and warm, and the rum appeared plentiful. The flying hours were easy to make. I enjoyed my tour in Cuba but drank the rum with too much gusto.

Occasionally, the crews took passengers back to Miami. On one trip we took Eddie Rickenbacker from Puerto Rico to Miami. He was an impressive man; however, the good-looking blonde traveling with him was also impressive. She had a sparkling personality. While Eddie dozed, she and I talked about the effect of the war on the U.S.A. and what to expect after the war. Optimistic about the future, she passed on her enthusiasm to me. I was not sure about her relationship with Eddie and asked around. No one else knew. They did seem to have an attachment for each other.

Sometimes our trips were long. Occasionally we stopped on the way back for lunch at the chief petty officer's mess at Guantanamo. The buildings there were permanent and well ordered. Guantanamo had the best food in the area. The chef had established a reputation with the navy as well as the other services. It has been said, with some truth, the navy serves the best food of any military service, and I found it easy to believe after having a lunch cooked by this talented chef. The menu contained smothered steak with mashed potatoes and fresh green beans. For dessert, he served apple pie with a scoop of ice cream. The chef took fresh vegetables and meat and cooked them with tender loving care. The flavor still lingers.

"Major Cottingham, our gypsy task force has been in operation for two months," I said. "We need more equipment and are maintaining three C-47s out of a small toolbox and flying at the same time. We desperately need a work stand for access to the engines."

"Borrow one from the 2nd Air Force," he said.

The process for requesting equipment was long and detailed. We did not have time to order equipment or go through the necessary channels, so we stole the minimum equipment needed from other outfits.

The midnight requisition of a piece of equipment required a jeep and two determined GIs. My friend drove up the ramp to where the B-29 crews parked their planes. Locating the right stand out of a group of five, I lifted one end of the stand and held on. The stand rolled on the wheels on the other end. We drove back to our area, dragging the stand. Our group became a successful unit and kept the planes flying. We earned a reputation for getting things done with very little equipment and personnel.

Major Cottingham, our commanding officer, suggested that because the group had done so well, the entire task force would be allowed a day off to go to the beach one Sunday.

We took a six-by-six truck and decided on Tarara Beach, located on the other side of Havana from our base. We were twenty miles away from Havana, and Tarara was ten miles east of Havana on the north side of Cuba.

Fifteen of the group piled into the six-by-six and headed for the beach. The group didn't carry food or drink. Each person planned to buy his own food and drink there.

When we departed, everyone was clean and well dressed. The two Waves we picked up in Havana also were neat and well groomed. These navy women were officers dressed in their summer uniforms of gray seersucker. They were friendly with people in the task force and wanted to come along.

On the trip to the beach, nothing eventful happened. I sat at the very back of the truck and watched the beautiful Cuban landscape. The coconut palms, the sugar cane fields, and the small villages were nice to look at. Because of the ease of growing food, no one went hungry.

The truck passed through several small villages. Each contained a square with a well or water source. Women came to the square to pick up water for household use and drinking.

The village natives were friendly and waved to us as we drove through the villages. The boys waved back. The day was pleasant, and a small breeze made it appear cool.

Upon our arrival, the group climbed out and took stock. A gorgeous beach lined with palm trees stretched out in a long, white arc. The beach edge was sparkling clean. I soaked up the heavenly scene and burned it in my memory. Hemingway loved Cuba; now I knew why.

Just off the beach a simple, boxlike, weather-beaten building stood with an open space through the middle of the long side and doors at each end. It was approximately thirty feet wide and fifty feet long with access over two big steps up to the wood floor. On one side, a bar sold drinks and sandwiches. Tables and chairs at that end accommodated the customers. The other end housed a gift shop. Local handmade items were on sale-items one would buy on vacation or at a beach. There were no local customers because it was Sunday.

Most of the fellows and the two Waves seated themselves in the bar and ordered drinks. At 10:00 A.M., the temperature became warmer. A refreshing rum drink after the hour-long ride proved most agreeable. I finished my rum and Coke and walked outside. Several people were on the beach, among them a pretty girl of not more than seventeen.

Walking over to this Cuban beauty, I used my few words of Spanish to ingratiate myself.

"I live nearby," she said. "My father told me not to talk to soldiers. With you, I make exception," she said in her broken English. "My name is Maria. What's yours?"

"My mother calls me John. Tell me about yourself. What do you do? How many people do you have in your family? What does your daddy do? Is the weather like this all the time?"

Laughing, she replied, "Yes, weather always beautiful. My dad is local constable; put people in jail. We peaceful people. No one in jail." She said, "You see little house through trees near beach? Where I live. I scream loud, my dad come. What will do when he come, not sure."

I didn't want to find out either. She was pleasant company and held my interest.

"I go University of Havana," she said. "Major is health services. Nursing a good job. Take care of sick people. Give me great pleasure."

"Take care of me, I sick," I said, mimicking her English.

"You kidding. You berry healthy."

Five feet four inches, her body was formed in soft, attractive curves. Her eyes and hair were dark. She had a straightforward manner and looked directly into my eyes when she spoke. Her swimsuit left little to the imagination. Over the swimsuit she wore a sheer cotton blouse which clung to her upper body and dramatized her femininity. Her most impressive attribute was her simple, wholesome, unhurried dignity; a part of her personality.

She said, "Let's swim."

She ran out into the surf and plunged into the water. Right behind her, I hit the water and came up swimming. She was about ten yards ahead, and I made my best effort to catch up. This girl swam fast. The distance between us lengthened. At 150 yards out, I looked back at the beach and decided this was far enough. Looking down I checked the depth of the water and judged it to be over twenty feet deep.

She looked around to see that I had stopped and yelled, "Come on."

"This is far enough for me," I yelled. Swimming back to shallow water, I touched down, and again I yelled, "Come on back."

She yelled, "Chicken."

Standing in water up to my neck, I saw eight or ten barracudas swimming between the Cuban beauty and me. Four to five feet long, they swam in a slow, sinister, effortless way. I didn't want to put myself on their menu for lunch.

With some urgency in my voice, I yelled, "Maria, come in quickly. There are barracudas."

Her musical voice came across the water, "Ha! Ha! You no fool me. You want get me in not-so-deep water."

Only fifty yards from shore, I had a chance to survive an attack by these vicious fish. She was two hundred yards out in deep water. An attack there would be more likely and successful. How could I make her understand the urgency of the situation?

I dropped below the surface and came up flailing the water and yelling, "Help! Help!" Several times I went under and came up the same way. In less than a minute she was near to help if she could.

She said, "You silly. You not attacked by barracudas."

"My acting brought you in," I replied. "It served a purpose."

She laughed, "I also saw the barracudas. They brought me in."

This beauty totally absorbed my interest with her good looks and gentle nature. We swam together and played in the water along the beach and had lunch in the weather-beaten building. She refused my offer of a rum and Coke. "You're sure you don't want one?" I asked. There was no way to disarm this girl.

After lunch, I suggested a walk up the beach, so we could be alone. She refused and said, "This is the nicest part of the beach. Didn't you come here to swim? Why do you want to be alone with me?"

"To kiss your rosebud lips and hold you close," I said.

"You not do that here or anywhere. We stay here," she laughed.

The lazy day passed swiftly. Soon it was 4:00 P.M. and time to return to the base. This Cuban beauty did favor me with a good-bye kiss. I could tell she liked the kiss. She gave me her name and address, with a promise of a date supervised by her dad.

Looking around for my friends, I found them bunched together in the bar, talking loudly. Everyone appeared drunk, including the Waves. The group had not put a foot in the water.

The adventurous ones did go down to look at the beach after lunch, but they brought a drink with them.

The clean, crisp look of the morning had become a red-faced wilted look. Everyone managed to get into the truck. I talked to the truck driver and decided that he might be sober enough to drive and realized my mistake when the driver quickly got the truck in high gear and drove as fast as the road would permit. The truck bounced down the road at thirty miles per hour and was dangerously fast on an unpaved road filled with potholes.

I took a seat on the left side at the very back. The six by six had wood sides around the truck bed except for the back, which remained open with a canvas strap stretched across. On each side the wood seats could be fastened up against the sides when hauling cargo and let down for seating when hauling troops.

No one appeared to be in charge of this picnic. I tried to get the boys to settle down and sit on the benches. Most of the picnickers were standing in the middle of the truck, talking loudly and gesturing enthusiastically. Four people were sitting on the top of the three-foot sides with their feet on the seat. Only the two Waves and their dates and I were sitting on the seats.

While I watched the action in the truck, the driver took a wrong turn and became lost. When the truck stopped to check directions, everyone jumped out. Those who wanted to go to the bathroom did so in the Village Square. Two relieved themselves in the fountain just below where the drinking water is caught. With the help of one of the lieutenants, courting one of the Waves, I got the drunks aboard and, hopefully, started the driver in the right direction.

Someone started an argument. The standing GIs began to shove each other around. Shoving would not have been dangerous if the truck were not speeding down a road full of potholes and bouncing up and down like a bucking bronco. The ride became extremely hazardous.

My friend, Snyder, stood in the rear of the truck and wasn't involved in the argument. A boy smaller in size moved over to him, looked him in the face with a drunken scowl, placed both hands on his chest and pushed. The truck hit a big bump at the same time. Snyder went out of the truck over the canvas strap. I grabbed his belt as he went over, and he grabbed the canvas strap with his left hand. His feet hit the ground and dragged on the rough road. The lieutenant up front saw what was happening and beat the top of the cab for the driver to stop. A sober person would have stopped gradually. The driver locked all wheels. The truck came to a bouncing, sudden stop. All those who were standing surged forward in one big pile.

The rear window of the truck measured about eight inches high and sixteen inches wide and was covered with a mesh wire screen around a one-fourth-inch steel bar frame. This frame came loose at the top, hinged out at the bottom and lay horizontal across the wood siding that made up the sides and ends of the bed. This frame projected about six inches into the truck cargo area.

The small guy who had shoved Snyder over the back now stood in front, facing the back. When the surge came, it caught him with his back on the metal frame of the window guard.

As the group plowed into him, he screamed loud and clear, then slumped unconscious to the floor of the truck. The others picked themselves up and looked at their fallen comrade.

Now that the truck had stopped, I pulled Snyder aboard and took a look at the boy who was hurt. Unconscious but still breathing, he appeared in bad shape.

Now on the outskirts of Havana, we asked directions to a hospital and took the injured boy to the emergency room. A vertebra was cracked and pushed out of place. The boy would spend some time in traction. Greatly relieved that he would be all right, we left him at the hospital to be picked up later by an ambulance from the base.

Happy to arrive back at the base, I decided never to attend another unit outing. Major Cottingham agreed and never allowed another picnic.

Things in Cuba were so distracting to the military, that our commander would not allow us into town until we had spent six weeks on the base.

CHAPTER
TWENTY-SIX

Our group had been in Cuba six weeks before we were allowed into Havana on leave. The fabulous stories about the girls and the famous Tropicana nightclub had sharpened our desire to see the real thing.

The great day came, and with a soft south wind. My friend, Snyder, and I went into town and hailed a taxi to take us to the Tropicana. The club had old-world Spanish-style decor, white plaster, marble and dark wood—the look of old wealth. The prices were also sky high. We decided to look for something more in keeping with Air Corps pay.

Our taxi driver then took us to a taxi dance where anyone could buy tickets and ask any girl not busy to dance. We loved the low cost of twenty-five cents per dance. All the girls were nice looking and danced well. Soon we became bored with dancing and wanted to do it all, to experience the real flavor of Havana.

The taxi driver took us to a brothel. I had never been in a brothel except for the show in Mexico. There the brothel had destroyed our interest in sex. Tonight would be different. We were in Havana, and it was our night to howl. For six weeks we had listened to the stories about Havana, and now we looked forward to the trip into town.

Prostitution was Cuba's largest cash crop, after sugar cane. We were about to check out the statistics, perhaps even a Cuban girl.

Our taxi driver made his way through the busy streets to a brothel. Located in an ancient hotel in the old part of Havana, it looked as if it had been there since Columbus. The aged hotel lobby had a high ceiling and was ornate and stately, clean and rich in architectural style. The well-kept classical staircases, windows and columns added to the ambiance. The marble and plastered walls seemed to make the air cool. Music with a Cuban beat was played on a piano in the background.

The girls walked out for our observation. They were gorgeous and young with lovely brown skin and white teeth. Supposedly they came from poor families. If this were true, it was difficult to tell by looking. They were well dressed and sedate. Our taxi driver told us the house madam taught them how to walk, act and apply makeup. Their hair and clothes were part of the mystique. They wore cocktail dresses with a lace shawl. A professional applied makeup for the hair and face. The over-painted look of stateside prostitutes was avoided. The girls were schooled to look innocent, wholesome, and as fresh and clean as the members of a Sunday school class.

"Snyder, have you noticed these ladies of the night have not exposed their charms by removing clothing. No one has to guess that they are physically endowed. The sex appeal is there, promising and provocative," I said. "If a client wants only a short time with a girl, he spends it here at the hotel. If he wants to keep a girl all night, he can register for a room at the Rex Hotel across the street and take her there."

"I'm taking the Rex Hotel option," Snyder said as he smiled and looked in the direction of the girls. "My pass is for thirty-six hours, and I don't want to waste any part of it."

"You've made the right choice. I'm with you," I said. We paid our money and moved to make our selection.

With a red face, I looked the girls over and became conscious of their fresh, dewy skin and dark, appraising eyes. Without being too obvious, they also looked at Snyder and me. The procedure was somewhat embarrassing. They appeared as interested in us as we were in them. Walking over, I said, "My name is John." One of the girls stepped forward and said, "I'm Mimi."

Mimi had caught my eye. Five feet four with an impeccable

complexion, her age was sixteen or seventeen at the most. A look of intelligence indicated that her nature could be mischievous. I was now twenty-one and a veteran of fifty combat missions, but I still didn't know much about girls.

"To be able to have that good-looking girl in my bed for the night gives me goose pimples," I said as we leaned against the bar. "Lady Luck has never been so kind. In England, North Africa and Italy, the women were different. They were sexy but not as soft and feminine as these gorgeous creatures."

"They are good looking and sexy," Snyder said and made his selection of Maria.

I walked over to Mimi and asked, "How about a drink?"

She smiled and said, "Sure. You want girl for short time or all night?"

"All night."

She smiled and seemed delighted. With our dates we walked over to the bar and had a drink. A three-piece band began to play. We asked the girls to dance, and both girls danced well.

The stories we heard on the base had been believable and an understatement of the actual conditions. This place appeared to be a little piece of heaven. A shiver passed through my body in contemplation of the things to come. We walked across the street and to the rooms assigned to us in the Rex Hotel. Snyder's room was down the hall from mine.

The rooms were clean, the bed linen spotless. Some of the sons of the best Cuban families had also occupied these rooms.

My sexual appetite was stimulated by the selection procedure. The promise of having sex with this good-looking girl excited me. My inclination was to rush into intimate contact and go for broke until I could go no more. Mimi spoke some English and would not be rushed. She ordered drinks for her and me from room service, sat down and looked into my eyes.

"What your name?" she asked as she looked up through her long lashes from her seat across the table.

"My name is John," I told her as I took the other chair.

She said the name slowly, "Juan. Juan."

The softness of her Spanish word for John was pleasing, a silky sound. She drank her rum slowly and looked at me with those liquid brown eyes. The shy quality of her gaze was provocative. Everything about her aroused me sexually. In the quiet area of our room, I had an opportunity to look her over more closely. Her teeth and complexion were perfect. She was not dumb, and she looked at me in a way that was surprising. "I know what I'm doing, and I like what I'm doing," she seemed to be saying. Shy about taking off her clothes, she would not remove anything until I cut the overhead light.

"What do you take me for—a bad girl?" she asked in a soft sexy voice.

Eager to get things underway, I cut off all the lights. Some light from the street lamp outside came in through our open second-floor window. A soft breeze from the Caribbean Sea moved the white draperies and cooled the room.

I helped Mimi off with her dress and her slip. She stood before me in panties and bra. The panties had a v-cut up each side, were loose, cut straight across the bottom and decorated with lace. The dim light softened her features. A Greek goddess— a damn good-looking woman, she carried with her the great promise of the universal affirmation of life. She stood by, willing and ready to consummate all my unrealized fantasies with guaranteed satisfaction. If someone had asked at that moment the most powerful desire of my life, it would have been this brown-skinned girl.

I felt Mimi's breasts. They were conical, very firm, with ample cantilever. They were not oversized but large enough and well shaped. Her tummy was flat, her flesh firm yet somehow soft and yielding.

Never having been in bed with a prostitute before, I really didn't know how to act. When we first entered the room, I slapped her on the butt and said, "Let's get on with it." She stopped me cold. I decided to play her game and let her be the aggressor. She was subtle and knew her trade. She kissed me on the neck and chest and teased me with the tips of her fingers. With the whole night ahead of her, she was in no hurry. The care and patience of her attention created the impression that she really liked me, and what she did. She appeared not to be motivated by money. Something genuine appeared in her caring, in the way she made me feel as though I were the most important thing in her life.

Now, I caressed her body, the inner side of her thighs and between her legs. Her body was ready, and she moved with little up-and-down movements. Pulling her legs apart with my right knee, I felt the softness of her body. My lips on her breast made her shiver. The smell from her young body was healthy and provocative.

What was the rest? A procreative surge lifted the human spirit as the wonders of sex raced through the fantasies of my mind. A sea of passionate searching lifted us as we experienced the intensity of the moment.

I held her to me and matched the rhythm of her body. Passion flowed between us like a great wave with its ebb tide.

My link with immortality was clear. Through the act of sex, one can live forever. All that ever would be became possible for me as the summit approached. Nothing mattered but the brown-skinned girl beneath me. Her breathing now coming in short breaths as she anticipated the climax for both herself and me. I experienced ecstasy heaped on ecstasy as the climax approached and overwhelmed us. A passion swept us onward as the wave pushed and pulled back from the shore.

This fulfillment, this order of creation swept us along. The moon and the stars stood in infinite awe and sparkled brightly. Life flowed from man to continue and perpetuate the saga of creation—woman received it with the secret formula of creation locked in her loins.

Mimi must have felt the same thrill. She bit hard into my shoulder; no hurt or pain, only passion. The body could not stand forever on Mount Everest. We both lay tired and relaxed, locked in each other's arms. She held my hand, stroked my hair and looked into my eyes.

She smiled and said, "You are something."

I was flattered to be held in high esteem by someone so young and good looking and surprised that my feelings for this prostitute were so intense.

The room did not have a private bath. I walked down the hall to a bathroom with a towel around my waist. On the way, I remembered Snyder and wondered how he fared and knocked on the door.

A feminine voice said, "Come in."

Opening the door, I saw Snyder's date in the bed, nude.

I asked about Snyder and sat down on the bed. In a friendly gesture, I caressed her thigh under the sheet.

At that moment, Mimi opened the door and looked in. A tremendous look of hurt came over her face. She fled back down the hall to our room.

Snyder returned shortly, and we had a drink together and then, with only a towel around my body, I walked back down the hall to my room.

Mimi had her clothes on and had touched up her makeup. She was crying.

"I leave," Mimi said, sadly.

Mimi was not prepared for the seamy side of my personality when drinking. Everything would have been fine if I had refused the last drink. Unfortunately, the GI mentality overcame me.

"Mimi, you can't leave! You are mine for tonight."

"I not good enough for you. You make passes at Snyder's girl. You think me no good," she said as if her heart would break.

"That's not true."

My candy-store appetite dismayed her. I tried to rebuild the relationship. She had been hurt and wanted nothing further to do with me. She started out the door.

In a voice made sharp by too much rum, I said, "Take off that dress."

She answered with hurt in her voice, "No" and went into a long explanation in Spanish that I think included the following: "You are an unfaithful SOB. I thought you felt something for me. You don't care for anyone. Juan, you can go to hell!"

I reached out, took the shoulder strap of her dress with my hand and gave it a yank. The dress split down the side. She slowly took off the dress and folded it carefully. She removed the remainder of her clothes and got back into bed. She lay there still and angry. I felt terrible.

The rum and the events of the evening had been too much. I lay down beside Mimi and almost immediately went to sleep.

At 10:00 A.M., Snyder shook me awake. Mimi had gone.

My head ached when I remembered the events of the evening and how I had treated Mimi.

"Let's have some breakfast and see the rest of Havana," Snyder said. "My girl is still with me."

"Mimi left angry," I said. "I must find her and apologize."

Snyder's girl, Maria, said, "I know where she lives."

We called our friendly taxi driver. He took us to Mimi's house on the outskirts of Havana. I got out of the taxi and walked toward the poor farmhouse near a cane field. Mimi heard the car and saw me coming. She ran out and threw her arms around me.

I looked into those liquid brown eyes and said, "Mimi, I'm sorry. I want to buy you a new dress. First some breakfast, then the dress."

She said, "Sure, Juan, you wait here un momento. I be right back."

She picked up some things in her house and ran back to me. We walked hand in hand back to the taxi.

The four of us went to one of those wonderful Cuban restaurants on the main square in old Havana. The wood in the bar and the tables were dark. The white tile floor was accented with a few black tiles and met the white plastered wall with a heavy dark base. From our chairs we could see people passing on the sidewalk through a series of folding doors which had been pulled back to make one long opening. We ordered chicken with rice. The baked chicken, the rice, colored brown with saffron, came with bits of vegetables for a delightful meal and cured my upset stomach and my headache. After the army food for six weeks without a break, the Cuban restaurant was dining at its best.

We looked for a dress for Mimi. She took us to a moderately priced dress shop. The four of us, and the taxi driver, picked out a fantastic dress for Mimi. We decided to buy a matching pair of shoes, then another dress. When we left the dress shop, Mimi was radiant and well dressed, and my pockets were empty. Time arrived for Snyder and me to return to the base. We said our good-byes and left.

"Thank you, Juan," she said. By the look and the hug I knew she meant it.

Next week, I received a pass and came into Havana. I didn't tell Mimi I planned to come. She found me in my hotel about midnight and slipped into my bed. She wouldn't take any money. Sex with Mimi filled me with ecstasy all over again. A kind of magic occurred in our lovemaking, producing the pleasures of sex with an additional bonus of satisfaction and self-esteem.

Next week, passes were issued again, and I headed straight for the brothel. Mimi had a date. I was disappointed. I passed the time with Snyder by going to a taxi dance. Afraid of offending Mimi by having sex with another girl, I waited.

One of the girls put her head on my shoulder and left a lipstick stain on my uniform shirt, not obvious to me. Again Mimi found me back at the hotel. She also found the lipstick. Looking at the stain, she raised hell in Spanish. Taking my shirt, she went to the bathroom, washed out the stain and returned my shirt, soaking wet. This girl felt too much. I had not bought her. She owned me. She was poor and exploited by the people who managed her but liked and trusted me and gave to me without reservation her one asset, her young and beautiful body.

My greatest downhill slide was the Cuban rum.

CHAPTER
TWENTY-SEVEN

Major Cottingham finally lost his battle to keep me in his outfit. Those TWXs saying, "No transportation available," did not serve their purpose any longer.

Major Cottingham received a TWX saying, "Have Jones ready on Wednesday. We are sending a B-24 down to pick him up."

The day came too soon, and it was beautiful. When the plane arrived, I climbed aboard. The semi-vacation in the sunny Caribbean was over. Now I had to get back to work.

Back in Harvard, Nebraska the sub-depot hangar people continued to maintain the trainer B-29s. The combat crews were almost ready for missions over Japan.

Experienced people were still needed. No longer hangar chief, I found work in maintenance and inspections. It took long hours to do what had to be done. However, the service crews derived a certain satisfaction from doing a rather complicated job well. Most of the service people connected with the maintenance program were conscientious. The GIs worked the long hours with the usual amount of griping.

In this maintenance program for the B-29s, I met a staff sergeant named Hogan.

Later at the NCO Club he said, "They assigned me to the 450th Bomb Group in Italy. My last mission occurred on May 24, 1944, to Weiener Neustadt, Austria."

"No kidding. That was also my last mission. What did you do to make the Germans mad at you?" I asked as we made ourselves comfortable at a table in the bar. "On that raid the

Jerry fighter pilots made one pass at our Bomb Group and then concentrated on the 450th."

"When the 450th arrived in the theater, the group commander bragged that he planned to clear the sky of Huns," Hogan said with a troubled look as he remembered. "The first mission was a disaster. The 450th lost more than fifty percent of its planes. The group commander kept trying to make good on his promise. The Germans kept trying to make him look bad."

Everyone knew the losses in the 450th were abnormally high, but no one told me why until Hogan came along. "Now I understand why the Germans left us alone," I said. "That day was also my last combat mission and could have been a lot rougher if the Germans had concentrated on us. You guys took the punishment for us. Thanks."

Twenty-three-year-old Hogan looked like a bald monk with a fringe of hair on the sides and back of his head. Of normal build and five feet nine, he was one of the worst-dressed people in the Air Corps. When you loaned him clothes, he would pack your shirt with his other dirty clothes in a dirty clothes bag to rot.

One day in the PX, I ran across Hogan talking to the local Catholic priest. The priest asked Hogan why he didn't come to mass.

"But, Father, I do in spirit anyway," he said.

The priest looked at him and said, "You are the type who comes to church three times in your life: When you are hatched, when you are matched and when you are detached. According to my calculation, you have only been once."

Hogan had kissed the Blarney stone and kept a piece of it in his pocket. He was unsuited for Air Corps maintenance work, but he could sit for hours and entertain anyone with humorous stories or his unusual experiences. A great baseball fan, Hogan could remember games played five years earlier and who hit a home run or struck out. As long as he had an audience and a glass of whiskey, he was tireless. The hour was never late. He was at your disposal.

Because of his drinking, Hogan's health was not good. He would wake up with the shakes and couldn't stop. He had to have a drink. As entertaining as he was when sober, he was pitiful when the DTs took control of his body.

Perhaps the Air Corps had ruined his life. It had taken him away from his family and friends, an environment he knew well and respected, and placed him in an outfit with other men his age to fight a war. The Air Corps also exposed him to the stress of combat that triggered excessive drinking in some soldiers.

Reviewing the information about him, I always came to the same conclusion. Not everyone reacted as he did. In fact, no one I knew was so eager to throw away his health. Life in the service offered access to clubs and a drinking environment.

A master of GI slang, he expressed abstract ideas with a manly flair. The way he put his metaphors together with the conviction that his viewpoint was unassailable, gave him an interesting personality. Most people liked him until he borrowed something and didn't return it. My policy was never to lend him anything I would not have given him.

Perhaps because of his drinking, he had little interest in girls and called them "ginch"; however, a WAC about forty-five with bad skin and lines on her face took a shine to the twenty-three-year-old Hogan. As a staff sergeant, she trained air force women not only for the military routine but also for office work. She had been a secretary before she enlisted in the Air Corps. When the two got together the repartee came fast and thick.

Hogan said, "You are a good head."

She said, "How would you know? You couldn't get to first base on a home run."

"Hogan, we are friends," I said. "I provide you with liquor when I have it, I provide you with a clean shirt if I have one. I have covered you at work twice when you didn't make it in from town because of too much drinking. Absenteeism has become a habit with you. You depend on friends to see you through. You are working under my supervision. I can't cover for you anymore. It bothers me to break regulations."

"That's okay," Hogan said. "If I'm late again, it'll be your duty to turn me in."

I did the next day when he didn't appear. He was fined and reduced in rank. Rank seemed unimportant to Hogan, but he did miss the pay.

We continued to be friends and occasionally had drinks together at the 40 and 8 Club in Harvard, Nebraska.

Eventually V-E Day arrived on May 7, 1945. The Strategic Air Force with its one thousand plane raids, Patton with the 3rd Army Tank Divisions, the Airborne Troops and the Tactical Air Force hit everything that moved. Beaten into the ground, German cities were reduced to rubble. Their transportation system was destroyed. There was no organized society. The Germans were on their knees. They had to surrender. I thought this would occur soon, but nothing prepared me for its impact on my life.

At the completion of my fifty combat missions, I had already proved to myself that I didn't know how to celebrate. Now the end of the war in Europe arrived, and again I discovered that my earlier drunken celebrations had taught me nothing.

My friends and I planned to make V-E Day a big celebration. Bill Robinson had a car, and his girlfriend, Sue, had some gas rationing coupons she had obtained as a farmer's daughter. On that wonderful night we traveled in style, in a '39 Ford.

First, we showed up at the 40 and 8 Club and drank the remainder of my bottle behind the bar.

Liquor could not be sold in Nebraska except at private clubs. Bars could not sell whiskey by the drink, but they could sell a bottle and charge for set-ups, provided the drinker joined the club. Most soldiers did join.

It became unprofitable for me to buy a fifth and leave it at the club. Hogan would show up and drink my whiskey. Of course, if Hogan had a bottle, he would welcome me to drink from his. Hogan never had a bottle behind the bar.

At the 40 and 8 Club, one of the bartenders had previously

ordered five pounds of steak from his black market butcher. That night, however, he had an emergency in his family.

Before he left for the train station he asked, "Does anyone want to buy these steaks?"

"We have to eat anyway," I said. "Why not eat steaks? We would take them to a restaurant and have them cooked."

Hogan said, "Okay. It will be the first time I've eaten steak in months."

We had to pick up Sue as our first order of business. She had the gasoline ration coupons. A tall girl, she walked in her high heels as if she were stepping on a sponge. Her skinny legs and jet black eyes were significant features. She wore a sweater well. We properly ensconced her in the front seat beside Bill, and Hogan and I sat in the back seat. We returned to the 40 and 8 Club. I invested in a fifth of Old Granddad bourbon and some Cokes and cups. The streets were filled with people kissing other people, drinking and whooping it up. It had become like Christmas, Mardi Gras and the Fourth of July rolled into one evening. Everyone jumped with joy over the contemplation of victory. They all wanted to get back to an abundant economy and get on with their lives.

For a while, the four of us walked up and down the streets in the surging crowd, kissing girls and enjoying the highest regard soldiers ever receive. Along toward midnight, we had not eaten our steaks or anything else. All the restaurants in Harvard and Hastings were closed. People were out dancing in the streets.

We drove to Grand Island, Nebraska, about fifty miles away and found the same thing there. We looked and looked and finally found a short-order place in the railroad yards staffed with two women cooks there to serve the railroad workers who worked on a twenty-four-hour basis to keep the railroads running.

The four of us had not eaten since early morning of the day before. We were empty. Now at 2:00 A.M., with my nicest smile, I asked the two women if they would cook our steaks. V-E night truly became a soldier's night, and the women agreed. The steaks came with some French fries cooked on a greasy grill.

"Hogan, shall we wake Bill and his girlfriend?" I asked. "They're sleeping in the back seat of the car. If we can't wake them, you and I will have to eat five pounds of steak."

"Let me try," Hogan said as he walked out toward the car and returned. "I can't get them up. They both told me to go to hell and eat the steaks myself."

We also offered a share to the ladies who so graciously cooked our meat. They had just eaten breakfast and declined. Hogan and I sat down before the huge pile of meat and ate the entire five pounds of steak and some fries. The steak was average, and the cooking a disgrace. Hunger had become the overpowering motive. We put away the red meat seasoned with a little salt and pepper and Worcestershire sauce, as if we were starving.

"For our trip back to Harvard, we need a driver," Hogan said. "You are elected. I am too drunk to drive."

Not sober but the only one fully awake, I volunteered, and just on the outskirts of Harvard, the fatigue, liquor, and the tremendous steak dinner began to take its toll. A little park on my right seemed a good place to spend the remainder of the night. After parking and turning off the lights, I watched the sun come up. My eyes closed, and the sandman dusted me into a deep sleep.

Three hours later, an awful stench assaulted my olfactory nerve center. With a mind still numbed by alcohol, I tried to piece together the events of last evening so as to remember where we were.

When I could talk, I said, "Hogan, you pulled off your shoes and placed your feet on the dash. Confess! It has been at least two weeks since your last bath. We do need air, fresh air. Open the door on your side."

I opened the door and pulled myself to my feet and stood up. A casual accounting of body parts reassured me that everything remained in place. My health was indifferent, but I could function. Thirst became my primary concern, and the water in the birdbath looked fresh. I pressed my face in the water and drank some of the cool and refreshing liquid and tried not to see the bird stools on the rim. My friends in the car were also beginning to wake up. One look at Bill's girlfriend shocked me. Sue had never been pretty, but after a night of drinking and sleeping in the car, she could have played the part of the wicked witch in *Snow White*. Bill looked almost as bad.

"You kids would not win a beauty contest this morning," I said. "Hogan and I ate those steaks. We are in better shape, but our health is nothing to brag about. Breakfast would make us all feel better."

I received dirty looks from everyone.

Sue expressed a strong desire to be taken home. I was glad I did not have the responsibility to see her home and felt blessed. Her father would probably be there with a shotgun to right the wrong of keeping his little girl out all night. She was Bill's date, he deserved the punishment, and the sight of blood always upset me.

"Bill," I suggested, "you must take Sue home, and it's a drive across town. Dump Hogan and me where we can catch a bus to the base. We will meet you later at the barracks."

"A good suggestion, John. I'll stop at the bus station ahead."

Hogan and I made our way back to the base, took a shower and in two weeks were good as new. Well, almost.

The Japanese were now feeling the effect of the B-29 raids and naval power. The United States retook the pacific islands one at a time. The war slowly swung in favor of the Allies.

Without realizing what happened, I had been sucked down the rat hole of alcoholism. My drinking problem was suddenly worse. Up to this time, I had refused to consider it a problem. Because of this thinking, this bad habit took me downhill. I continued as if my conduct were normal.

With the war in Europe over, we had something to celebrate. I didn't want to miss an occasion. No one warned me how easy it was to become an alcoholic. Drinking relaxed me. Friends at the bar bought me drinks. They considered me a hero and made excuses for my excessive drinking which didn't help.

In moderation, drinking can be fun. Becoming a drunk is wasteful and degrading. No one has respect for an alcoholic. I couldn't admit it, but I had become an alcoholic. The thought that drinking was becoming a problem did cross my mind. This symptom, like many others, I had cast aside. However, the more alcohol I consumed, the more melancholy I became, the more I wanted to drink. I was not in good health, but the problem didn't seem to be bad enough to merit the all-out effort required to get things under control. I would do that later, when my drinking really got bad.

The alcohol crutch momentarily lifted my ego, but sobering up let me down hard. I required more drinking to get me out of the rat hole of depression. All the symptoms of my condition came out and made an exhibit of themselves. Someone had to drive me back to my quarters. Sometimes, I fell and forgot my bearings. My work suffered. The ugly, dark side of drinking which I hated caused me to consider making an effort in my own behalf. My personality changed from easygoing to loud and abusive. Money became difficult to get, and drinking required a sizable disposable income. I didn't have to guess what my dad would say when he found out about my drinking.

Members of my family couldn't understand what happened and studied me from a distance on my trips from the Air Corps home. I could see the hurt in their eyes. My mother had worked so hard and made personal sacrifices for all her children, but especially for me. She had counted on me to make a success of my life. My success would have been her success. She lived through and for her children.

Now, giving up those dreams she had for it and me made her sad, showed in her face. My mom had always been willing to give up her comfort and time, so her children could study and improve their minds. She created a stable, quiet home life and demanded that her children live up to the best within them.

Because she made the greatest sacrifice, she expected her children to improve themselves. Because of me, she had a right to be sad.

One of my mother's cousins had been an alcoholic. Mom knew what alcoholics were like. She knew the promises, the unstable character, the disappointment, the lying, the waste and the brutality.

At first, she didn't say anything that might hurt my feelings. After witnessing a few demonstrations of my drinking behavior, she became greatly concerned. She sat me down and talked to me in a very positive manner.

"John, you are ruining your health and your life," she said. "If you don't stop drinking, you can say good-bye to your promising future. Look what you have overcome, dyslexia and stammering. You've been the best in your class. You've within you the ability to do almost anything you want to do. If you continue to drink, all of that talent will be lost. You will be a complete disappointment to me. I have such high hopes for you and want you to succeed in your life. You know how hard I have worked to give you the opportunity before you now."

After running off my friends, I had to finance my drinking. Money became tight. I asked my family for drinking money. When they refused, I picked up an antique vase, which had been in my family for more than a hundred years and sold it for a fraction of its value. I felt so bad I cried.

One morning I awoke, looked at myself in the mirror and felt shocked at my looks. What had been a smiling face of health and character now showed an unshaven face with pockets under the eyes—a sick face, the face of an old man. At twenty-two, I had become an old man.

I looked for an easy way to straighten out my life. It could be the most difficult thing I ever attempted. Pulling myself up by my bootstraps would be a simple feat compared to getting my life under control. Sick in body and mind, I made a promise to the Lord and to myself to try. With the support of my mother, I struggled to lift myself out of the quicksand of alcoholism. My first move was to stop drinking

Almost three months had passed without alcohol; I became stronger in my resolve to do better and made great progress. The fear that I might slip haunted me. Never again did I want to feel the hopelessness of the alcoholic. With drinking no longer an immediate problem, I became aware of a different malady. My nerves were shot. The combat experience and the alcohol-damaged tissue worked together to make me a nervous wreck.

Then the day came, August 6, 1945. The United States Air Corps dumped an atom bomb on Hiroshima, Japan. The bomb blast, equal to tons of TNT, destroyed the city and killed and maimed seventy thousand civilians. The power group that controlled Japan still would not surrender, and on August 9, 1945, the air force dropped a second atom bomb on Nagasaki.

This was more than the Japanese could stand, and on August 14, 1945, they surrendered unconditionally. The United States had won the war.

CHAPTER TWENTY-EIGHT

The war was over!

I jumped up and down, yelled at the top of my voice and hugged my friends who were present at our base in Nebraska. Alone, I thanked God for the victory, and for being on our side.

Indescribable joy filled me. For more than three and a half years I had looked forward to this event. My greatest motivation had been to defeat the enemy. The war dominated my life, and now the yoke lifted. Again free to live my own life, I had become unable to walk away from the mental anguish associated with my war effort. It gripped me like a vise, plagued my days and made a nightmare out of my sleeping time.

In route to Warner Robins Air Force Base, I stopped by Tucker, Georgia. Any homecoming was a big event in my life and also for my mom. Seated in the living room we talked and exchanged information about our relatives, while the rain outside dampened our spirits.

Mom said, "You don't look good. Son, tell me what's wrong."

"Mom, I have a real problem in my life," I said. "Now that the war is over and the Air Corps is no longer demanding, I've had an opportunity to think about myself. The tension of combat is still with me. The feeling of having been too long in the fast lane hit me. My inability to sleep and relax is ruining my health. I feel old. Mom, what am I gonna do?"

"Be yourself," Mom said. "Take your time. You didn't get this way overnight. You won't be cured overnight.

"The tension of combat affected your mind, and it is now trying to throw it out." Mom said. "This hurt can show up in many ways until you are well. Personality quirks, nervousness, irritability, fear of falling, fear of failure are the many ways it can hit you."

"As yet, I haven't made an effort toward a career, and already I am afraid of failure," I said, leaning back in my chair and thinking about my problem. "Looking back to life in the service, Mom, I searched for something to raise my sagging spirit. My combat experience has been funneled through a small opening with one purpose in mind, to win the war, to become good at killing, to kill as many Germans as possible. Killing anything is foreign to my thinking. However, as a member of a group, I was part of a team that rained death and destruction on the enemy. With the enemy on the ground, I couldn't witness the distress caused by the bombs from our plane. The crew and I could only guess. It must have been terrible when our bombs hit the ground."

"You did what you had to do, Son."

"But Mom, the bombs we dropped to knock out military installations and the German war machine also fell on houses nearby and killed people. On the ground there was no one dear to me. The rain of terror we caused must have affected the children."

"You feel guilty for killing innocent people, but how about the danger to yourself. This proves you have good instincts. You don't have to feel guilty," Mom said in a voice calculated to reassure me.

"There is more, Mom. The training and the combat missions were only part of the problem." I said as I looked across the kitchen table at her. "The end of the war left me in midair. This is a landing I don't know how to make. The war uprooted my life from a quiet learning atmosphere in a boarding school for boys, to life in the armed services. The change was hard to make."

"Take it easy," Mom said. "You won't get over this quickly, but you will get over it. Remember how you overcame your dyslexia and your stammering. I have the utmost confidence that you can do anything you choose to do."

After the encouraging words from my mom, I attended a

JOHN H. CUNNINGHAM

meeting at Warner Robins, Georgia and was flown back to Harvard, Nebraska. I couldn't shake it. My feeling of insecurity worsened.

Abruptly, I realized something had to be done. My search for a solution would have to be planned and executed by me. Only I could make the decision that would ease my mind.

The burden of living with trauma was ruining my life. The evil spirit of combat would give me no peace. My fear of the dark made sleep difficult. I was haunted by memories of my sister's tragic death, which had occurred earlier. Each night another period of dread presented itself. During the day I was busy with my work. The night brought leisure and time to think. Time alone with my thoughts provided a period of hurt. Being alone caused the difficulty, and yet the trauma couldn't be shared.

My mental anguish appeared as an unsatisfied need. I needed the assurance that everything remained the same, even though some things had changed and change occurs constantly. It did not matter that the one sure thing in life is change, and the world would continue to change. Taking my own life could be a way out. I did not feel good about myself and was uncomfortable with everyone. The joy of being with people was lost.

The approval of the family I loved and who loved me became more important. My family did give me support and supplied me with hope. Their words were encouraging. These were words I needed and appreciated. Yet I felt inadequate to make a suitable response.

In the service, I had not disclosed my alcoholism or my mental health to the Air Corps. Ashamed to have it on my personal record, I wanted to solve the problem myself. I would feel better.

I continued the struggle, to roll back the war-induced conditioned responses. My mind was crowded with stimuli unrelated to my present lifestyle and became a burden to me. Perhaps a crowded mind can be eased by open space. Wide-open spaces could help.

As time passed, my mind seemed to be more at ease. I started breaking down the large problem into small units. The strain of solving all the problems at one time became manageable. To live one day at a time became a starting place. This approach allowed me to take an inventory of my assets. The results were surprising. The war had left me with no physical wounds. I had saved some money and didn't owe anyone anything. I could get started in college.

The time in service helped with my education. The skills required in the air force would make it easier to get a job. Traveling in wartime is not a vacation, but it does provide a broader outlook.

I was now physically in good shape, and my overall appearance had improved since I had stopped drinking. I had a good, basic, high school education to stimulate my thinking and felt good to know I was ready to start college. Attending church with my family had added the healing value of the Scriptures. My church affiliation became important again.

My relationship with my father continued to be a loose end I wanted to tie up. I called Dad and said, "I'm on my way home and would like to settle the hostility between us. What can we do?"

"Son, come on home, and we'll talk," Dad said.

Apprehensive about the meeting, I hoped Dad would be civil to me. However, I had to do something to build a better relationship.

I arrived on Sunday, and the day was warm without a cloud in the sky. The family had just returned from church, and I kissed my mom and said hello to my dad. They were both dressed in their Sunday best.

Dad had aged in the last three years, and his weight gain gave him a heavy look through the middle. He did not smile, but his smooth face showed concern.

Mom smiled as we talked. She wanted Dad and me to have an agreeable meeting and did her best to ease the tension. Her dark blue dress was out of style and not well fitted, and she wore a small dark hat that covered the hair on top of her head. She was the warm and caring mother.

"You look much better," Mom said with the kindness I remembered in her voice. "I'm glad to see you again."

The three of us sat down in the living room. Mom and I sat on the sofa, and Dad took the easy chair near the fireplace.

"Dad, I've caused you trouble for the last six or seven years," I said. "We have barely been speaking. I want a closer relationship with you, to get to know you better as an adult. Please accept my apology for all the times I caused you concern. Mom has always been there to help me. You were willing to help because Mom couldn't have helped if you had not given your support. I owe you both a debt which can never be paid."

My dad came to me with tears in his eyes, put his arms around me and said, "Son, I'm so glad you said the things you just said. I've been too strict with you. You are smart and aggressive. I felt I had to bend you a little to my way of thinking. Some of the tension is my fault and some is yours. Son, God's plan for young men makes them want to be their own boss and remove themselves from the restriction of their parents. Your desire for manhood came earlier than most boys and with a certain amount of orneriness. I should have recognized your desire for independence. If we could have spent more time together, you would've known me better, and I could've enjoyed seeing you develop into the young man you are today. I've never wanted anything more than to see you mature and make a success of your life.

"You still have a long way to go. Your life is in front of you. Be productive, Son. Don't give up your talents to the sin of indolence. You have so much going for you. It would be a shame to waste your time and talent."

"Thanks, Dad, for your help."

"Lunch is already prepared," Mom said. "If you two will wash your hands I'll put the food on the table and tell you about your brother and sister who are now living in Atlanta."

I felt the tension between my dad and me disappear, replaced by a genuine affection. Our understanding was one of those small things necessary to restore me as a well-functioning human.

Next day, I left to visit my uncle Joe in Centre, Alabama.

It gave me great pleasure to see Uncle Joe, the uncle who had visited me in London.

He welcomed me with a bear hug. Uncle Joe was home on furlough from the service and had moved his wife and child into one of the houses on my grandfather's farm. He married early in the war and started a family with a baby girl.

The house was somewhat rundown and needed paint. It also needed inside plumbing, central heat and a bunch of other things to make it more comfortable.

Lara, Uncle Joe's wife, said, "We will add these things when we can afford them. Now it's such a joy to be with Joe I can put up with anything."

"You came at just the right time. I need some help on the farm," Uncle Joe said.

"Uncle Joe, helping you with the farm chores will be fun," I said. "When we catch up, let's take some time off to go fishing and visit with other relatives nearby. I never mentioned to you that I had a problem with my drinking. You were considerate enough not to ask questions relating to my problems. I appreciate that."

"We all realized you had a problem and discussed what we could do to help. We knew you were strong, and with the proper family support you could straighten out your life. We decided to give you our love, attention and some leeway in making your own cure."

Those words of encouragement and the uplifting conversation put me back in a mood to continue my education.

"You've solved your own problem. You're over that now," he said. "Let's forget and take up the new life we'll make for ourselves."

The lighthearted banter of my uncle and the support of other relatives assured me that they cared. This depth of character and unspoken values were a real part of their lives. I looked past the surface conversation, and their good wishes were obvious. Love of country, the work ethic, belief in God, love of family, and pride in accomplishment were present but unspoken.

As the days and weeks passed, my outlook improved. Examining my possibilities and options, I became aware of my potential of doing something special. The doubts and nervous anxiety changed to a more calm and determined attitude.

Another loose end worked its way up from my subconscious. What should I do about my ex-wife? She was really not an ex-wife. Mandy had stopped the divorce proceedings. I wanted to know why. After the trip to my uncle's I felt confident enough to call Mandy and ask if I might come down.

I remembered her beauty, the way she moved, and the promise of our wedding night. The gods had shaped the soft and yielding creature in a delightful way. This beauty could be strong and assertive or soft and beguiling. When Mandy left me in Nebraska, I felt the loss, a loss difficult to accept. Never again would I enjoy the soft subtle nature of this fantastic woman. Never again would I experience the love I had felt for her. I wanted to see her one more time and assure myself that she had completely locked me out of her life. This became reason enough for a visit.

The many things that destroyed our chances of staying together did not exist now. Perhaps she might be aware of this. Our life together had been difficult for both of us. She waited three months for me to return from school in Seattle. Away from her family with no friends except the few we had met, she worked and waited. She gave up her medical schooling for me.

Now that the war was over, I would be available on a regular basis without the strain imposed by the war. My mental state had improved. After the trip to my uncle's, I felt the right thing to do was to call Mandy and ask if I might visit.

She said, "Yes. We would love to see you."

I didn't think anything about the "we" because I thought she was including her family.

I became apprehensive about the meeting, wondering if she would listen to me. However, I had to know from her how she felt about our future together.

Mandy met me at the Perry bus station in her dad's '39 Ford. We looked at each other across the crowded bus station. A long, searching look. The eye contact lasted more than a minute. With that look, we searched our souls with no attempt to hide the deep emotions that surfaced in the face of each. We were both too honest to play games with our emotions. The love and respect had been there all the time and needed only the reality of seeing each other to manifest itself.

The next moment, we were running toward each other with an urgency born out of great expectations. Mandy came into my arms with a combination of tears and smiles. We kissed on the lips and on the face. We could not get enough of each other. In this passionate moment, all the problems, all the hurt was forgotten and forgiven in an outflowing of love. We held hands as we moved to pick up my bag. Every eye in the bus station followed us as we walked out the door.

On the way to the car, we continued our animated conversation. Mandy said, "I have a surprise for you."

What kind of surprise could she have for me when we have not seen each other in thirteen months? I asked myself. Because of the pleasure of the moment, I dismissed the promise of surprise. Nothing could be more important than the company of this very desirable girl.

Mandy looked different. Her figure had changed. She looked more relaxed and sure of herself. A casual observation assured me she was a wholesome, desirable woman. Her hair and skin were alive with good health. Her smile was so sweet and genuine I couldn't stop looking at her.

My best judgment told me to do everything in my power to hold onto this gorgeous creature. Your future could be enriched beyond your wildest fancies.

"Tell me about the temporary duty in Cuba," Mandy said. "Did you meet any pretty señoritas? What did you do?"

"Cuba is in the past and unimportant," I replied in earnest. "Please tell me about you—what you did and how you occupied your time."

"Wait until we get home," she said. "The surprise will give you a clue."

The surprise became more intriguing, yet I refused to deal with it. My attitude was I have seen it all, experienced it all and found the "all" a little lacking, and I shut out everything except the present events, which included this wholesome creature. Surprises have no great merit with me.

We arrived at Mandy's parents' home. She blew the horn, and Mr. and Mrs. Hamilton came out to greet us. They observed Mandy and me holding hands and were pleased. Smiling as they rushed toward us, Mrs. Hamilton hugged me tightly. Mr. Hamilton aggressively sought my hand.

I kissed Mrs. Hamilton on the cheek and shook the hand Mandy's father offered. The Hamilton's Victorian home place, built at the turn of the century and recently remodeled, sparkled in the afternoon sun.

"You can look at the house later. Now may I show you the surprise?" Mandy took my hand and led me into a newly decorated nursery with blue patterned wallpaper. I looked down into a small baby crib to see a beautiful little boy sleeping with a bottle.

"Who is this little fellow?" I asked. "He looks like a perfect human being."

"This is John Jones, Jr.," Mandy said. "We named him John, after you."

"You mean this boy is mine—yours—ours? I don't know what to say! I didn't know! Why didn't you tell me? It's not fair. I didn't even know you were pregnant. How could you do this to me?"

Mandy put her hand over my mouth to still the cascade of words that spilled out. Then she put her arms around me and said, "I didn't know if you would want him."

"Want him? How could you think I wouldn't want him?"

"When we met at the bus station I didn't know what your attitude would be. After the meeting and seeing each other, I knew you would be pleased. If I had received a negative response from you, you would not have found out about John Jones, Jr."

Taking Mandy in my arms, I buried my head on her shoulder. Big tears came into my eyes as my mind struggled to deal with this emotionally charged family situation. Too emotional to speak, I was overcome with a combination of joy and shock, and it took me some time to regain my composure.

When speech was possible, I said, "You are right. It is a surprise—a wonderful surprise."

We held hands and talked into the night about our plans for the future.

Next day, I found it difficult to leave. My furlough ended, and in two days, my unit expected me back in Harvard, Nebraska. Two months remained before my discharge date. I would be required to serve the remaining time, however difficult.

Mandy's parents said their good-byes quickly and watched closely as I said good-bye to John Jr.

"I hate to leave you, little fellow," I said. "But I shall return. Bet on it."

Mandy drove me to the bus station. There were tears in her eyes as she said good-bye. "Come back as quickly as possible. John Jr. must know he has a father."

Sure about Mandy, I was willing to bet my life on this girl. I needed the understanding and love of this wonderful woman to heal my sick mind and support me as I worked to achieve. She inspired me. We could work together to build a life. My goals would be her goals and set high. Soon I would be out of the service and working full-time for my small family and for a career. My feet hardly touched the pavement as I walked to board the bus.

Back in Nebraska, the time passed slowly. The air force had lost its hold on me. My mind was already operating in civilian life back in Perry, Georgia.

The average GI wanted to separate himself from the service as quickly as possible. The military wanted this separation to be orderly and devised a system of points that favored my category of service. I had earned an air medal with six clusters, two campaign ribbons, a good conduct medal, a sharpshooter medal and had spent three and a half years in service. I had also volunteered and became one of the first to be discharged.

While in the service, my friends talked and dreamed of getting their discharge without much of a plan as to what to do when they were released. Just getting out appeared to be their main objective. My plans after being discharged were for an education and achievement. I wanted to make my life count.

For three years and six months the air force had been my life. The regimentation had dominated my thinking, my very being, but the air force's direction and discipline facilitated my contribution to the war effort. Following orders became necessary to blend my efforts with others to get the job done.

My life in the service had been a life of adventure and learning. The air force sent me to three schools, but the training remained constant. They fed, clothed, housed, looked after my health and paid me. They gave me a chance to develop, to become good at what I did.

The words of an author of another time came to mind. "Opportunity does not lie in the past. It never did. The pioneer had to learn how to be a pioneer in his day, and that is what we have to do today." I wanted to be a pioneer.

To my amazement, the feeling of tragedy and insecurity experienced upon my return from combat seemed crowded out by a broader outlook. Being exposed to the constant danger of losing my life had caused me to regard it highly. Life became important. I wanted to make it count. Time for looking back passed.

When the sergeant handed me my discharge along with my back pay, I took it without regret. With the discharge in hand, I walked out to face the future with a good feeling about what I could accomplish.

The sergeant yelled, "Hey, Jones, just one more thing."

Turning around, I walked back to meet him. He waved a letter in his hand.

"This just came in. Thought you might want it," he said.

"Thanks," I murmured as I looked at the postmark.

It was from Perry. A letter from Mandy, I thought. My hand shook as I tore open the envelope. Inside was an official copy of a birth certificate. The letter was not from Mandy.

The print stood out on the page. "You do not know me, but that doesn't matter. The information I am giving you is a matter of public record. There is no way you could have been the father of John Jones, Jr. He was born later than you have been led to believe."

Tears formed in my eyes, rolled down my cheeks and fell to the floor.

What now? I thought. I'll get accepted at Georgia Tech and move on with my life.

BVG